"I should never ***book," Janie m***

"But you did," Rafe said, "so now we'll deal with it." He smiled, trying to communicate that she wasn't alone, that he'd do his job, take care of her.

Then she gave him a glare that almost stopped him in his tracks. He was used to people being grateful, looking up to him, believing him, wanting to be taken care of, trusting him. Janie Vincent didn't trust him.

Before he was quite ready, she stood, practically tapping her foot in impatience. "Fine. Let's do it."

"You want me to stay, Janie?" her sister asked.

"No, you go on back to work. I'll find–"

"I'll make sure she gets home," Rafe asserted.

Janie's eyes narrowed. For some reason, Miss Vincent didn't appreciate his offer. And that made no sense at all.

Dear Reader,

I read a lot because I'm in love with words. I love old, used cookbooks where someone has written notes in the margin. I love diaries and letters and newspaper so that the past comes alive for me.

Besides writing for Harlequin, I'm an English professor. I read a lot there, too. I have students who, by far, write better than me. I've read about midnight border crossings (I'm in Arizona) and about midnight escapes from the Lost Boys of Africa. I've read about near-death experiences, special-needs children and about the path back to sobriety. Best of all, I've read about the dreams and goals of our future generation. I've also read a few things I wish had not wound up under my red pen. But, while the idea for *What Janie Saw* came to me one evening after a marathon grading session, I've never read a murder confession.

Like Janie, I entered teaching through the back door. But it doesn't matter how you came to the classroom–it matters what you do while you're there. Janie makes all the right moves. She cares about her students even while trying to pursue her own dream. I think, for Janie, chasing the dream, questioning the dream and then reinventing the dream is what makes her grow. See, her childhood wasn't of the soil that allowed dreams to grow. She had much to overcome.

Rafael Salazar is too busy being sheriff to have dreams. He has to save the world. His world is the small town of Scorpion Ridge, Arizona. Soon he has to save Janie, and she could become his world if he's smart enough to realize it and change.

My story is complete fiction with the world of what-ifs, flawed people and love triumphing. It's about hope and change and romance.

My editor, Adrienne Macintosh, is a master, full of ideas for cementing conflict. Harlequin Heartwarming is an awesome place to be. If you'd like to meet some of the Heartwarming authors, please visit www.heartwarmingauthors.blogspot.com. If you'd like to learn more about me, please visit www.pamelatracy.com. I love to hear from readers!

Pamela

HARLEQUIN HEARTWARMING

Pamela Tracy

What Janie Saw

Recycling programs for this product may not exist in your area.

ISBN-13: 978-0-373-36675-0

WHAT JANIE SAW

This edition published by arrangement with Harlequin Books S.A.

For questions and comments about the quality of this book, please contact us at CustomerService@Harlequin.com.

Printed in U.S.A.

PAMELA TRACY

is an award-winning author who lives with her husband (who claims to be the inspiration for most of her heroes) and son (who claims to be the interference for most of her writing time). She started writing at a very young age (a series of romances, all with David Cassidy as the hero, though sometimes Bobby Sherman would elbow in). Then, while earning a B.A. in journalism at Texas Tech University in Lubbock, Texas, she picked up writing again–this time it was a very bad science-fiction novel.

She went back to her love and was first published in 1999. Since then, Pamela has had more than twenty romance novels in print. She's a winner of the American Christian Fiction Writers Carol Award and has been a RITA ® Award finalist. Readers can find her at www.heartwarmingauthors.blogspot.com or www.pamelatracy.com.

To Rachel Pekera,
an extraordinary second grade teacher,
who stole my son's heart and taught him to
believe in himself and much more.
Thank you.

CHAPTER ONE

KILLING SOMEONE IS not nearly as simple in real life as it is on television.

"What the..." Janie Vincent sputtered. She grabbed her coffee cup, more for comfort than for the caffeine at this late hour, and ordered herself to stop reading.

But she was already hooked.

She glanced back at the art book's cover. Yup, this was Derek's book, the one he'd done as an assignment for the Intermediate Canvas class Janie was assisting in. His first two pages had stayed true to the assignment: he'd drawn thumbnail sketches of what he was working on for the class's main project. Page three was where he'd strayed. Oh, he'd included thumbnail drawings amidst his prose. But prose didn't belong in the workbook unless he was summarizing his ideas for future drawings. She seemed to be looking at a mixture of fact and fiction, original art complementing a master. Derek had drawn windy, mountainous roads with sharp curves, a dark four-door car, and a re-creation of *The Scream* by Edvard Munch.

The re-creation had more hair.

He had, however, made no indication of what medium he intended to use or final dimension. Maybe he was planning a graphic novel?

Even though it was obvious that Derek had not adhered to the assignment guidelines, she continued to read:

For one thing, murder is black-and-white and mostly soundless after the bullet fires. Maybe the sound of the report temporarily deafens you? Or maybe you go into shock?

Derek, by far, was her darkest student. What he created in class always centered on battle scenes. Occasionally, he included bleeding dragons and eerie castles in the distance.

But they didn't scare her as much as the drawings in this art book. Derek had somehow managed to make his stick figures ominous. Frowning, she stopped reading long enough to take another a sip of coffee. Her hand, clutching the cup, shook a little. Then, because anyone could be watching, she glanced around the student union to make sure no one had noticed her shocked response. She'd hate for a student to think she was this aghast over his homework.

She didn't expect to see Derek; he'd been absent a full week—since he'd turned in the art book last Wednesday.

I knew Chad and Chris planned to kill her before we even stopped the car. She knew it, too, and looked at me with pleading eyes as if realizing I was the only sane person in the car. Before that night I was sane. But from the moment I figured out he was going to kill her, and from the moment she stared at me, silently begging me to intervene, I was no longer sane. I was simply the man in the backseat. The only one close enough to her that she could make eye contact with.

If this were truly a graphic novel, then it was pretty good. Too good.

In the drawing, a lone mailbox braved the wind by a tall, dark, ragged tree. Four people occupied the vehicle. They were stick figures, but he had added minute details—a big nose on one, hair sticking straight up on another—that made Janie long for a magnifying glass. The tiny license plate even bore minute letters and numbers.

But Derek Chaney's fiction didn't really belong in an art book.

A tiny sliver of concern snaked its way up Janie's spine. Surely Derek wasn't keeping track of actual events…?

Chad was cussing and driving. Chris wasn't saying a word, just stared out the window that wouldn't roll down. And, for the first time, no one complained about the broken air conditioner. Maybe Chad was thinking about heat. He'll feel it soon enough; Hell is hot. And that's where he's going because Chad pulled the trigger. He better get used to the heat.

Derek had always been a disturbed young man. As a brand-new teaching assistant, first time in a college classroom, Janie had been ill equipped to deal with his mood swings. She'd tried to give him some stability by partnering him with other students.

But they mostly avoided him.

She'd sought help early on from Patricia Reynolds, the course's main instructor and chair of the art department.

"Derek needs this class more than anyone else," was Patricia's response. "Right now he's antisocial with a bad temper, but if he can make a connection with art, feel good about something he's created, who knows how his future might change."

Janie had nodded. There'd been a teacher in her past—Mrs. Freshia, seventh-grade English—who'd read one of Janie's personal art-book entries and taken the time to ask, "Are you all right?" And then she'd believed Janie when she'd said, "No."

Mrs. Freshia had testified in court on Janie's behalf so that she could go live with her sister, who at just eighteen years old, wanted to be her guardian.

Katie had wanted her. Janie had hoped somebody wanted Derek.

So Janie had offered him alternatives to some of his more gruesome ideas. She'd tried to be friendly, to engage him in conversation. He'd smirked, then drawn a scar down the side of one of his female warrior's face. A scar just like Janie's, maybe a bit more pronounced.

She'd long ago come to terms with her physical scar, though. He couldn't hurt her that way.

She'd lent an ear, but he hadn't wanted to talk. So she'd backed off, hoping Patricia was right. Derek hadn't been willing to talk to her, but maybe he'd been willing to draw and write.

I've never been a nature boy. I prefer the city with its bright lights, crowds and constant noise. I never want be hot again. It was so hot that night. The radio man said we'd broken a record for heat. I never want to hear the noises of nature again. I hate the eerie sound the wind makes. It's like someone's walked over your grave. It's like a loud whistle, prob-

ably to get your attention. It says, "I know what you're about to do."

Janie heard the wind outside the student union windows and shivered. If she were painting tonight's scenery and mood, she'd only use black, white and grays.

Her least favorite colors unless she was painting zebras.

In the animal world—and she was a nature artist—bright colors dominated. Tigers were orange, giraffes were yellow and camels smiled.

As a rule, she didn't watch horror movies or read scary books. Like this one…

Brittney Travis didn't scream. She didn't beg. She tried to run and stumbled. Why do girls always stumble? Then, Chad shot her in the back. It was all in black and white. The blood was even black. Funny, I expected to see red, even in the darkness.

The art book dropped from Janie's hands, and a shiver of doubt spiraled with such sincerity that she stood up, almost upending the chair she'd been sitting on.

Brittney Travis?

Janie knew the name…but from where? She wasn't sure. Couldn't remember.

Suddenly, there wasn't enough light in the student union, not enough people, and the air seemed to decrease in volume. Scanning the room, she searched for a familiar face: a teacher, a student, even a janitor would do. Two students, not hers, cuddled in a corner. They were young, innocent. She recognized one of the English adjuncts. CeeCee Harrington. She was an animated woman who would talk your ears off if given a chance. As the shadows of evening fell, people were leaving. At this time of night, people didn't linger.

Except for Katie.

Pulling out her cell phone, Janie started to call her big sister, but changed her mind. Katie was eight months pregnant and didn't need the worry. Besides, this could be nothing. Just the crazy rant of a student wanting attention.

Right?

Patricia would still be in her office. Janie was supposed to take her the art books when she finished checking them anyway.

Holding the art book pressed to her chest, Janie hustled out the main doors and headed for the building that housed the faculty offices. Patricia didn't leave until every class had ended and every light was turned out. Which was why in a hallway that housed more than a dozen faculty offices, hers was the only door open and the only beckoning light.

The cold finger of doubt tapped Janie on the

shoulder. What if she was overreacting? What if Derek was just trying to scare her because she was young and new to her job?

She needed this opportunity, needed to do well at it and get a glowing recommendation so she'd have a shot at her dream: an artist residency in Africa.

Yet tonight, her feet didn't falter; her mind didn't change.

After all, she might have just read an art book detailing a murder.

When she finally got to the professor's office, though, she wasn't sure how to begin, so she simply stood in the doorway, trying to find her voice.

There were stacks of art supplies on every surface of the room, including chairs. Textbooks were stacked in towering rows. When Janie'd come in last August for her interview, she'd had to stand and answer Patricia's questions.

Finally, she managed to clear her throat. Patricia turned around, all smiles.

While her office was a study in organized chaos, Patricia wasn't. She wore a blue pantsuit with a red blouse underneath. Her hair was short and she had a thing for red high heels, almost stilettos. An angel pin was clipped just above her heart. It was her most cherished possession. Her father had given it to her before he died. It was solid white gold with a natural diamond.

Taking one tiny step into the room, Janie handed Patricia the art book. “I just read something, written by a student, and I think you need to take a look.”

“Personal issues? Is a student in trouble?”

Janie paused. Personal issues might be one way to sum up Derek’s art book. “It’s Derek, and I’m not sure.”

Patricia frowned. “What’s in it that concerns you?”

“Does the name Brittney Travis mean anything to you?”

Patricia leaned forward, her expression so stern that Janie almost took a step back. “Why are you asking?”

“Her name’s in his art book, and it’s worrying me. He wrote and drew pictures of her murder.”

Janie didn’t quite catch the interjection Patty muttered under her breath, but she could guess what it might have been. Patty scooted her chair to the left, lifted a manila folder and took a page from it. She scanned the words before handing it to Janie.

It was a campus email alerting faculty and staff that over the winter holiday an Adobe

Hills Community College student had gone missing.

Brittney Lynn Travis.

SHERIFF RAFAEL SALAZAR didn't need another thing to do this morning. He already had a full slate. He was due at the courthouse in a little over an hour and still had three phone calls to make before he could leave. None of them involved good news. His afternoon included a long drive to Phoenix and an overdue visit to a correctional facility.

So when his phone rang, Rafe wished he could ignore it.

"Salazar!" he barked into the phone. Maybe his tone would let the caller know what an inopportune time this was.

"Morning, Rafe."

Suddenly, court dates, phone calls and the visit to the correctional facility seemed irrelevant.

Nathan Williamson was a detective and the director of the drug task force in nearby Adobe Hills, Arizona, located right outside of Tucson. Adobe Hills was not part of Laramie County, the area Rafe was in charge of. But occasionally their paths crossed, and usually the two departments worked well together.

Right now, Rafe and Nathan only had one case in common, and it was cold.

The Brittney Lynn Travis case.

She was from Rafe's town, Scorpion Ridge, but she'd gone missing from Nathan's town, Adobe Hills.

Nathan's voice sounded terse, and in the background, Rafe could hear the sounds of other people, probably cops, doing their job.

"What's going on?" Rafe asked, cop's intuition telling him this wouldn't be good news.

Nathan didn't even pause. "What do you know about Janie Vincent?"

"Why do you want…?" Rafe started to answer but stopped when the door to his office flew open.

The woman in question stood in the doorway, looking tense. At her side was her big sister, Katie Rittenhouse, eight months pregnant and with an expression that said she was ready to take on the world.

"You have to talk to him," Katie was telling Janie. "You can trust him. I promise."

Janie didn't appear convinced.

Behind them, his front-desk officer, Candy Riorden, hurried up. "I tried to tell—"

He halted Candy's admonition, dismissed her with a wave of the hand, and motioned Janie and Katie toward the chairs facing his desk. Without missing a beat, he continued, "They're here right now. But, to answer your question, Janie's from Texas. Her sister and brother-in-law run BAA, Bridget's Animal Adventure."

"I need her to come here sometime today so we can question her." Nathan didn't sound interested in Janie's connection to wildlife. "I've spent the last hour at Adobe Hills Community College, and I've got more questions than I have answers."

"Questions about what? You haven't exactly said why you want to speak with her."

Janie was looking at the door as if she were ready to bolt.

"The kind that will help me solve a case!" Nathan snapped, bringing Rafe's full attention back to the phone.

"Is it about—" Rafe started, but Nathan butted in.

"You're aware she teaches at Adobe Hills Community College?" Nathan said quietly. "Well, Miss Vincent apparently read something in a kid's art book last night, a kid by the name of Derek Chaney. I've spoken with the chair of the art department, Patricia Reynolds, but apparently your Miss Vincent is who I really need to speak with. Whatever she read might have been a murder confession about our missing coed."

"Brittney Travis," Rafe said slowly.

Across from him, Janie pressed her lips together and nodded.

Rafe gripped the phone, hard. He prayed—prayed that it was some kind of mistake, some kind of joke, that Brittney wasn't dead, hadn't suffered. He prayed that he could still save her.

This wasn't the kind of closure Rafe had been hoping for.

"Yes." Nathan's voice was terse, guarded.

"Have you had time to—"

"We can't do anything until we speak with Miss Vincent in person."

"I'll escort her myself," Rafe promised. "I can free up my late afternoon."

Katie reached across and took hold of one of Janie's hands.

Nathan immediately snapped, "Late afternoon? I was hoping it would be sooner. And why do you have to escort her? You think she's the type to skip?"

"No." Rafe eyed Janie and Katie. "I don't think that at all." Katie couldn't run, not in her condition, and while Janie was the type, she only ran when she felt no one was listening to her.

Well, if what she'd found was a true account

of a murder, she'd have plenty of people willing to listen to her. Too bad it wasn't Katie who'd read the art book. Solid, businesslike and driven, Katie would be the kind of witness cops dreamed about.

Janie, on the other hand, was flighty, whimsical and always believed the grass was greener on the other side. She acted and spoke without much forethought and a bit rashly.

Rafe said to Nathan, "I intend to be involved in every step of this new lead. So, along with you, I'm Janie's new best friend."

Janie raised one eyebrow and looked askance at her sister.

Actually, Rafe had a home-court advantage over Nathan. He might not be Janie's best friend, but he knew her fairly well. He knew things like she only enjoyed coffee if she had French-vanilla creamer to add to it. That she could sit at a table at the Corner Diner and draw for an hour without being aware of anything that was going on about her. That if the very pregnant waitress happened to serve Janie, Janie tripled the tip.

His mother, Lucille, owned the diner and had noticed these traits first. She'd passed every observation on to Rafe, whether he wanted to hear it or not.

Mom had been playing matchmaker for Rafe

over a decade now. She wasn't very good at it, though admittedly, he'd always found both sisters intriguing. Katie Rittenhouse played with tigers. Janie Vincent painted them from a safe distance. Though the scar on the left side of her face indicated that hadn't always been true.

"Is there something I should be aware of?" Nathan asked. "She ever been in trouble?"

Rafe had twice been called out to Bridget's Animal Adventure, the animal habitat Janie's big sister and husband managed, and where Janie spent much of her time. Once, he'd investigated the plight of two tiny bears, declawed and abandoned. On the second instance, he'd had to make sure the big cats were all accounted for, as there'd been a sighting in town. The cougars, leopards and mountain lions at BAA were all in their enclosures. Rafe never did find out whether it had been an actual sighting or whether someone in Scorpion Ridge owned a very large black domestic cat.

"No, she's never caused me any trouble," Rafe said.

It was a lie.

Janie Vincent had caused him trouble, but it was not the kind that made its way into a police report. No, it was the kind that messed with a man's mind.

During the large-black-cat incident, he'd

asked Janie out. He'd not been concerned about a conflict of interest because he'd been sure by then that the case was merely mistaken identity.

They'd gone out once, but he hadn't called her for a second date.

It had been clear from the start that they were too different—she was a free spirit; he was rules and realistic.

He'd also very clearly gotten the sense that Janie didn't have much use for cops, and that she'd only gone on the date to appease her sister.

"As a matter of fact," Rafe continued, "she just walked into my office. Seems she wants to help."

He wasn't exactly sure *want* was the right word. More likely *felt obligated to help* was a better choice.

Nathan muttered a few choice expletives, all having to do with her being there and not in Adobe Hills.

Looking across his desk at the pretty woman in question, as she so impatiently held herself in check, Rafe thought maybe he'd been an idiot not to call her again.

"Okay, it's good she's there," Nathan finally said. "But please see that she gets here, and soon. I don't want her to forget anything. Apparently Brittney's name and her death were chronicled in that art book. I want to know what it said, every detail."

"I want to see this art book—" Rafe said.

Janie shook her head.

Rafe started to protest, but Nathan, still on the phone, gave a long sigh before saying in a tight voice, "This whole thing's turned into a mess, which is why I need your help. Campus police locked the book up last night after Janie's boss handed it over to them," Nathan said. "Patricia, along with the dean of students and the campus police, opened the safe this morning. Then, they called me."

"And—"

But before Rafe could ask his question, Nathan said, "It's gone."

CHAPTER TWO

NOW RAFE UNDERSTOOD why Janie and her sister had scurried to his office—bypassing the officer on duty. With the art book missing, Janie and her boss were the only people who had read an alleged murder confession. If Derek Chaney had changed his mind about wanting to confess, then he'd be sweating bullets about now, and Janie might be where he'd aim those bullets.

Rafe couldn't cancel his court date, but now, returning the phone calls and the visit to the correctional facility would no longer be his top priority.

Today, Rafe would be spending time with Janie, lots of time.

"Did the campus cop who put the art book in the safe discover it missing, or was it a different campus cop?" Rafe asked.

"Same cop."

"Did he happen to admit to looking at the art book?"

"He glanced at the first couple of pages,

but not the whole thing. It was late and there'd been a report of someone trying to break into parked cars on campus. He wanted to keep his eye on the monitors. Still, he filled out the report, so he knew what was in it."

"Why didn't they contact the police last night?"

Across from him, Janie—ever the teacher—raised her hand. Rafe bit back a wry smile.

"The confession is in Derek's personal art book," Janie burst out. "His art book! It's supposed to contain thumbnail sketches and ideas for the project he was working on. I thought—hoped—he'd decided to write some sort of graphic novel. We had some doubt as to whether it was fact or fiction. Patricia Reynolds, the chair of my department, was going to notify the dean this morning and see what he wanted to do."

"Hear that?" Rafe said into the phone.

"The dean called us just after eight this morning," Nathan affirmed. "Our guy arrived at twenty after. He was there when they opened the safe."

Rafe looked across the desk at Janie. "How did you find out the art book had gone missing?"

"The dean called me."

Turning his attention back to the phone,

Rafe asked, "What does Patricia Reynolds think of all this?"

Nate answered, "She's coming to the station this afternoon to make a statement and try to recreate what she read. She admits, though, that she only scanned the first page then flipped to the last. Once she saw Brittney's name, both she and Miss Vincent headed straight to campus police. Apparently there was quite a bit more to the art book, though, at least six pages."

Rafe could only frown and stare across his desk at Janie. "How much did you see?"

"About six or seven pages. Only four pages had to do with Brittney."

Was there anything after that? Anything you didn't read?"

"Not sure, but I don't think so."

"What's your gut feeling?" he asked. "Does the art book show fact or fiction?"

Her sister squeezed Janie's hand. Janie, for her part, seemed more interested in fiddling with the edge of her shirt, tugging at some unimportant thread.

Janie might not have answered, but on the phone, Nathan didn't hesitate. "I told you this whole thing's become a mess. Kid might have been capable of murder, but not anymore. He died over the weekend in a meth explosion."

Rafe almost dropped the phone. "Accidental?"

"We didn't have reason to believe otherwise until we got the call about the art book this morning. Now there's reason to look at the case again."

"Does Janie know?"

"No."

"Send me what you've got so far concerning Derek Chaney. I'd like a copy of last's night police report, too. I'll be by with Janie this afternoon," Rafe said, ending the conversation and ignoring the raised eyebrow Janie shot him. No doubt she didn't like him making promises for her.

Well, as a potential witness to murder, Janie was about to find out that certain obligations were not negotiable.

He studied Janie's expression: fear battling compassion with a dash of shock at being in such a situation.

He understood that fear and shock, and was glad Janie had her big sister with her. The whole town knew Katie had pretty much raised Janie.

Small towns weren't big on secrets.

"What don't I know?" Janie asked.

He'd hoped she'd let that part of his conversation with Nathan slip by. But, as an artist, details were her life, whether she created them or observed them.

"Well?" she nudged.

As much as he wanted to protect her, he had to prepare her. "You don't know how ugly this case might turn out to be."

Janie and Katie looked at each other. He noted that Katie's expression was starting to resemble Janie's: it was one of fear.

He booted up the computer and retrieved the file on Derek Chaney that Nathan had already sent. Silently, he skimmed the words before turning to Janie, sliding over some blank sheets of white paper taken from the bin of his printer and giving the direction, "Recreate everything from the art book that you remember."

"Everything? Can't I just describe it to you?"

"I want it written and drawn. We can't afford to miss something. And you should recreate it while it's still fresh in your mind."

"Can I do it at home?"

Not a chance. He wasn't about to let her leave. She pretty much lived at a zoo. He couldn't imagine a place with more distractions. Plus, she was constantly rushing back and forth between her own classes at the University of Arizona and her lab assistant duties at Adobe Hills Community College.

"No, I need you here. I want you to copy Chaney's art book as closely as you can—presentation, margin, everything. If he wrote in pencil, I'll get you one. If you need special artist supplies, give me a list."

She looked a bit shell-shocked. "This might take a while."

"Rafe," Katie said, "I can see to it—"

"No, she has to be here."

"But—"

"I'll do it."

Rafe wasn't sure what had put a fire under Janie, but suddenly it was as if she had to get whatever she'd seen out of her.

He watched as she frantically arranged herself so his desk became a drawing table. She brushed aside bits of something he couldn't see and, without asking, moved some of his belongings aside. She then placed two pieces of paper, one on top of the other, in front of her. She held the pencil as if she were afraid it would explode. The point merely broke and he handed her another one.

She made an attempt to draw something on the page. But it only took her a moment to wrinkle the paper and toss it in the trash. Two more pages quickly followed. Her hand was shaking badly—no wonder she couldn't draw.

Katie watched, her lips pressed together.

"What kind of danger is Janie in, Sheriff? Are you going to arrest the kid who wrote the art book?"

Of course that would be Katie's first concern. She knew all about predators, though mostly the animal kind. Being a zookeeper did that. And she and Janie both understood what Rafe knew.

The human predator wasn't all that different.

"Right now," Rafe said, "we just have to focus on finding out what was in the art book so we can take the next steps. Derek's not a threat to Janie."

Janie's fingers tightened around the pencil, but she didn't look at the paper. Instead she stared at Rafe. "What do you mean he's not a threat? How can he not be a threat if what I read is true?"

A case that already set his cop teeth on edge was going to get even uglier. She needed the truth. "Chaney's dead. He died this weekend in a meth-lab explosion."

GUILT PRICKLED UP the back of Janie's neck even as she felt the floor tilt. She started to stand, wanting to run but unsure of where to go. Derek's death wasn't something she could escape from. Nor could she escape her guilt that she'd been relieved by Derek's absence this past week.

She hadn't realized it would be permanent.

She should have tried harder to reach the kid, to find out what made him so unhappy, so dark.

Katie opened her mouth to say something, but Janie settled back into her seat and stopped her. "I'm fine. Really fine. I know what I need to do."

But crowded with three people, the walls of the office started to close in on her. The room was devoid of color.

It made her remember living with her aunt. They'd rented a barren apartment, with no real colors anywhere to brighten the mood of the place. Until she picked up her paintbrushes and created.

Rafe must have picked up on her assessment of his office. "We can do this somewhere else if you'd like? We have a nice conference room."

No, the brown, black and beiges of his office were fitting colors for what she was about to do. If they walked through the police station again, she'd have to see the men in uniform. She'd have to think about how they shone their flashlights while they searched for people on the run. Rafe was dressed like one of those cops, even though he was the sheriff. His badge was bigger, too.

"Here's fine," she managed to say.

Katie excused herself and went to find the ladies' restroom. Janie relaxed a little bit. She should have come by herself, should never have dragged a pregnant Katie along.

"I'm sorry you have to go through this," Rafe said.

She'd heard that line before, from cops even.

Rafe didn't look like any of the cops she'd met, though. His black hair was somewhat short, straight, and only mussed where he'd run his fingers through it in frustration. His piercing eyes were as black as his hair. He gazed at her as if he could see past the facade she presented the public. He was a big guy, solid. He was the kind of guy who would catch you when you fell and not grunt because you weighed more than one-thirty.

She got the feeling he really was sorry.

But many of the cops she'd dealt with had been sorry for what they'd put her through. Rafe was no different. She didn't need his sympathy. After all, he would only be sorry until he didn't need her anymore. Then he'd forget her as the next day, the next crime, dawned.

Typical cop, or sheriff, or person in authority, or whatever.

Janie'd learned at a young age to only trust herself and her sister, Katie. That was why Janie drew animals. They gave no false pretenses, had no ulterior motives.

"Yeah, I get it." Janie's goal right now was the same as it always was when it came to the local authorities. If she couldn't avoid them, do what they wanted so they'd leave her alone.

This time, however, she needed the cops. She just wished she believed, like her sister did, that the men in uniform were the good guys, defenders of the innocent and destroyers of evil.

Because evil had definitely rocked her world.

"It was just a typical evening, a typical class," she muttered, amazed by how quickly normalcy had changed into nightmare.

"I'm sure—" he started.

"And then it wasn't."

How could she explain to him that after reading a few pages of a kid's art book, her world had turned upside down, and she was still clinging to the hope it would right itself, that what she'd read would prove to be just a graphic novel—fiction, and nothing more.

"So nothing happened in class?"

"Nothing. It was after class, in the student union, that everything happened."

"Give me every detail. Brittney's been missing too long."

"You talk as if you knew her."

"Her dad's my insurance agent. Her family attends the same church I do. I've known her since she was born."

Janie couldn't imagine that kind of stability. Rafe had lived in Scorpion Ridge his whole life. She'd bounced from her father's place to apartment after apartment, neighborhood after neighborhood with an alcoholic aunt. In some ways she was still bouncing. Maybe she always would be, as her goal was to paint exotic animals in their natural habitat, and this meant lots of travel. Right now, she was saving every dime and putting together her portfolio and résumé, hoping she would be chosen as a visiting artist in Johannesburg, South Africa.

She could hardly wait.

Rafe, on the other hand, was a third-generation law officer with roots so deeply grounded in Scorpion Ridge that even during his few vacations, he'd rather have been home.

Janie's idea of home didn't match his.

She'd figured that out during their one date.

He'd been all about Scorpion Ridge, its people, the way of life. She loved it here, too, but there were people to meet and places to go.

And pictures to paint of so many different things far away.

RAFE OPENED HIS top desk drawer and withdrew two flyers. These were just the newest. From the day his father entered the Scorpion Hills Police Station to serve and protect, missing persons had received special consideration.

But his father had never solved the one missing-persons case that was the most important to him—his own son, Rafe's brother. Ramon could have been dead all these years… or he could be alive, waiting to be found.

Not knowing he had a family that loved him and that had never stopped searching for him.

Rafe stared at both flyers for a moment before casually placing one in front of Janie.

Three words could describe the photo: young, pretty, happy.

In comparison, Ramon's missing-persons photo had been of a baby not even forty-eight hours old.

Compassion warred with fatigue across Janie's face.

Brittney's white-blond hair streamed past her shoulders. A gray, sleeveless blouse hugged curves that hadn't had time to mature. In her right arm, she clutched a brown-and-white spotted dog, maybe just a puppy, that stared happily at the camera.

Janie leaned forward and began re-creating.

While she worked, Rafe logged onto Cop-Link and learned more about the late Derek Chaney.

The kid's rap sheet was long enough to make Rafe grind his teeth. However, nothing but petty crimes were listed. And yet, judging by the names of those alongside Derek during his criminal activities, the boy was capable of finding himself in the middle of a murder.

Rafe would love to give Brittney's parents some good news. But Derek's involvement only pointed to bad news. For everyone.

He'd just noted the absence of sound, the lack of pencil scratching against paper, when Janie asked, "Do you think Derek died because of the art book?"

"Anything I say would be speculation, and this early in the case, I'd rather not speculate."

She gave him an indignant glare that spoke louder than words. "But if—"

"*If* is a pretty powerful word," Rafe returned.

She gripped the pencil tightly, scratching out words on the paper as if she had to get them out, away from her. Finally, she finished, but not before whispering, "I'm afraid."

"I understand," Rafe said. "I've not slept a full night since Brittney disappeared. Neither have her parents."

She let out a deep breath and turned the last paper so he could see it. "I've re-created everything I remember." She finished by tapping on the last paper. "When I got to her name and then the blood in the dirt, I stopped and headed for my division chair."

Blood in the dirt…

He'd have to, in some form or another, repeat this information to Brittney's parents, so they didn't hear it on the news. Reporters were like cockroaches, they showed up where they didn't belong and were hard to get rid of.

No matter how much Rafe wanted to handle Brittney's case without sensationalism, the media would get involved, would push the envelope, wouldn't care whose emotions got trampled as long as their ratings soared.

"And you're sure you're done?" He nodded toward the paper on his desk.

She glanced again at Brittney's photograph on the flyer and then picked up the pages she'd created. Four in all. Slowly, carefully, she examined each one. After about fifteen minutes, only erasing a few things or adding a detail here and there, Janie scooted the paper across the desk and settled back in her chair. "I'm done."

It took him just two minutes to scan the haunting sketches.

"This is it, all you remember?"

"There wasn't that much more, but after I got to this, I stopped and went to see Patricia."

It had been the right move. The moment she realized what she had in her hand, she should have turned it over to the authorities—too bad it hadn't been the local police. Rafe could only imagine the grief Nathan was giving the campus cops over the art book's disappearance.

Still, he wished she'd read the whole thing, memorized every picture.

"What I'm most sorry about," Janie admitted, "was not paying attention to the numbers on the license plate. He'd included them, but I did no more than glance at the numbers because they were so tiny."

"Could you distinguish the sex of the occupants?"

"They were tiny stick figures but with details."

Still, they could label the occupants—Derek and Brittney were in the back, Chad was driving and Chris was the front-seat passenger.

"I know you've said that nothing happened

in class, but I still want to hear about the last week. All the events leading up to you reading the art book. Don't leave anything out."

Her sister returned.

Janie glanced at Brittney's photo again, then showed it to Katie. To Rafe, she said, "I'm assisting with two classes this semester. Both art. In the late afternoons, if I get an appointment, I work in the Writing Tutoring center. I'm pretty good with English, and it's extra money."

"And she's taking classes at the University of Arizona as well as being employed at Bridget's," Katie threw in.

"My Monday/Wednesday class starts at six. I didn't have a student appointment yesterday," Janie continued. "So last night, I got there right on time."

Rafe noticed a sudden blink of her eyes, a quickening, slightly out of sync. She'd either just told a lie or she'd left something out.

Janie regained her composure, smoothed back her unruly strawberry-blond hair, and went on, "I'd earlier set up the stations and put handouts on the back table. So, when I got there, the students were signing in and already starting to work on their major projects."

"What was Derek working on?"

"It's a medieval battle scene. Very detailed.

He's done two others so far. All pretty much the same focus. Lots of blood, battle, destruction."

"You say you got there right on time. Is being on time important?"

She hesitated before answering, "Yes, for both me and the students. I take points from students who are late. If they're more than twenty minutes late, I count them absent."

Rafe nodded. So, Miss Janie Vincent was a free spirit who also liked rules. "Seems to me that someone as concerned about punctuality as you are would arrive to class early, just in case a student needed to talk to you, or something."

Her lips pursed together before she said, "I used to get there early, but then..."

"Then?"

She looked him right in the eye. "Then Derek Chaney started arriving early, too. At first, it wasn't so bad. He asked questions because he claimed he also wanted to paint murals. I gave him some books to read. He kept them a while, then returned them."

"And this behavior caused you to stop arriving to class early?" Rafe had to give her credit. She was a master lip purser, but she didn't squirm at all.

"Look," Janie said, giving him a haughty

glare that reminded him of his own college days and how a professor could reduce him to age twelve without blinking. Few, however, had made him want to achieve more than a pass in the class. And none had been as pretty as Janie Vincent. "I don't want anything I say here to slant the investigation. I—"

"Slant the investigation?" Rafe sat up. "What do you mean?"

"I mean if I tell you this guy creeped me out, had anger issues, you might believe I'd already condemned him. I can answer impartially, and—"

"Janie," Rafe said carefully, "right now, we can only label Derek as a person of interest, that's all. His art book and drawings are probably just the work of a young adult crying for attention."

She gave a slight shake of her head. She hadn't given her opinion on fact versus fiction earlier, but she clearly had an opinion now.

Not fiction.

He agreed but couldn't let on to that.

"Innocent until proven guilty," was a double-edged sword. In Rafe's profession, his job was to decode, visualize, analyze and interpret. Years ago, a cop's perspective—his intuition—had counted for something. Today, because of politics, Rafe didn't dare share what he thought.

It could later be used against him in a court of law.

Plus, Jane Q. Public—especially in the case of a missing or wayward child—wanted optimism.

"Do you want to know how many people have come forward with information about the disappearance of Brittney Travis? Hundreds. And all of them turned out to be dead ends."

"How many of the hundreds attended the same college?" Katie jumped in.

"More than you'd believe." Rafe leaned forward. "We investigate all leads, and certainly, we hope this one will take us closer to the truth, but chances are it won't. Chances are you have the misfortune of reading some misguided young man's work of fantasy."

"I know fantasy when I read it," Janie muttered. "Derek draws fantasy and his writing was nothing like his usual drawings."

She had him there. And, he figured, by the end of the interview she'd get him a few more times if he wasn't careful.

"Did you tell Professor Reynolds that he creeped you out?"

"Yes." Janie filled him in on some of the suggestions Patricia had made for dealing with a difficult student—like one who invaded personal space, who believed in staring as a way to intimidate, and who got argumentative when given constructive criticisms. She explained how ineffective those suggestions had been and finished with, "Derek left during the break Wednesday, a week ago, and didn't return."

"Any idea why he left?" Rafael prodded.

She grimaced. "No idea. Patricia had me clean and put away his supplies."

"How about the people he sat by? Did any of them leave, too?"

"The students all have their own stations. Pretty much their own worlds. The station to his left is empty. The station to his right is a reentry adult. She ignores him. I've heard her mutter a few times about teenagers with attitudes."

"So you weren't the only person he creeped out?"

"Attitude came off of him in waves."

"Since you were scared to be in the room alone with him before class started, what did you do after class?"

She hesitated but didn't purse her lips. Too bad, he somewhat enjoyed watching her expressions of angst. And she had perfect lips. "Derek was the first one out the door. I don't think the other students even thought twice about what he did after class ended."

"So, no complaints or other students who lingered?"

"Not that I noticed."

She would have noticed.

Katie fidgeted in her chair, but Rafe's attention was on Janie as she stood up and perused his office, stopping to count the softball trophies, smiling at his Baxter the Bobcat keepsakes and studying his photos. Many were of him and his family. His dad had been the sheriff, and his grandpa before that. The photo in the center of the shelf was an enlarged baby picture, the kind taken at the hospital immediately after a birth. Rafe kept it there to remind him. Some of the other photos were of him and his men, or people about town. One showed him holding a fishing rod and a ten-pound bass. She didn't wince at the mess on his desk—a bit messier since she'd rearranged things—although her eyes lingered on his Bible.

He liked her attention to details. She had an artist's eye. It made his job easier. "How many times did Derek miss class?" he asked her.

"Four. He'd used the limit. I can't tell you the dates without the roster, though."

Rafe opened a new window on his computer, punched in a code, and again stared at Derek Chaney's rap sheet. Derek had been arrested driving a stolen car at the end of November. Rafe quickly checked, but neither a Chris nor a Chad had been with him. The judge had given Derek another chance.

Derek should have been in jail, not college.

Maybe if the judge had to knock on the door of Lee and Sandy Travis, instead of Rafe, and tell them that their daughter's car had been found in Adobe Hills Community College's parking lot but not their daughter, maybe then the judge would have been less lenient.

Rafe still called the Travises every two to three days to tell them that there was no news.

Today, his call would be different. He'd have to mention that a student at Adobe Hills Community College had come forward with evidence—a wee stretch of the truth—and that he was meeting with all involved for details.

He wouldn't say anything yet about the nineteen-year-old who had turned in an art book detailing their daughter's murder.

Or that the nineteen-year-old was dead.

He leaned forward, intent, thinking. "The names in the art book were Chad and Chris. Throughout the semester, did Derek mention those names in any other context?"

Janie didn't hesitate. "No, I'm pretty sure he didn't. I haven't taught or tutored any Chads. As for Chris… I'm the lab assistant for two classes on Monday/Wednesday.

There's a Chris in my first one, but she's female. I have two boys named Chris in my second class, Derek's class. But I never saw them with Derek, and Chris is a very common name."

"And you didn't have Brittney as a student?"

"No."

"And you'd never seen her around campus?"

"Not that I recall."

"Was this the first time Derek mentioned Brittney in his book?"

"He usually doesn't draw modern people, so I've never had cause to ask him who he was drawing."

Rafe looked at Brittney's flyer again. Everyone—her parents, her high-school guidance counselor, her teachers—all said Brittney was an easy kid, well-liked and with lots of friends. She'd been a senior in high school and already taking college classes, thanks to dual enrollment.

Rafe's phone rang. It was Justin Robbins, an undercover officer that Rafe trusted. Based on his next words and the emotion in his voice, Justin had known and liked Derek Chaney. A moment later, he told Rafe something he'd already suspected.

Derek Chaney had enemies.

Justin insisted that one of them, and not the meth explosion, had killed Derek.

And now Janie Vincent just might have the same enemies.

CHAPTER THREE

"DEREK CHANEY'S DEATH might not have been accidental. He might have been murdered."

Katie made a sound of shock and Janie collapsed into one of his straight-back brown chairs. For a moment, Rafe again thought she might bolt from the room. Instead, her hands tightened on the chair's arms until he expected her fingernails to leave a permanent mark.

She might look small, but her imagination was big and usually spot-on. She took a deep breath and then, somewhat shakily, asked, "How?"

Rafe only debated a moment before telling them straight out what Nathan had reported to him and what Justin believed. He wanted to see Janie's reaction. Even more, he wanted her to understand just how serious the situation might be.

She came to the same conclusion he did.

"So, do you believe someone was trying to kill him because they knew he wanted to confess?"

"I don't have enough facts to make a judgment," Rafe said.

But he had already made a judgment. He agreed with Justin. Someone wanted Derek out of the picture. And even worse—

Janie, however, didn't give him time to decide what was worse. She did it for him. "And they obviously knew about the art book because it's missing. What if he told them he'd given it to me, before they killed him?"

Years of dealing with witnesses had taught him to be cautious, to not always share the worst-case scenario until he was sure, plus he wanted to reassure her. Aloud he said, "It could have been a drug deal gone bad, it could have been an accident. We don't want to jump to conclusions just yet."

She shot him a dirty look before whispering, "Poor Derek."

Katie gasped. "What? Are you in shock or something? What do you mean 'poor Derek'?"

Katie was right to be worried. Right now there was no poor Derek; there was, however, a poor Janie. Rafe didn't believe for a moment that Derek's death had been the result of a drug deal gone wrong. Not just a few days after he'd turned in a possible murder confession. And, if Derek was killed to prevent his art book from seeing the light of day, then whoever killed him wouldn't hesitate to kill again, had indeed already killed twice.

Another thing that worried Rafe was how the murderer had tracked the art book to the school safe.

Had the killer been on campus last night, watching Janie, waiting to get her alone? Had the killer watched as Janie read the book, watched as she walked to her boss's office and then watched what the campus police did with the book?

So many questions.

But what Rafe found most chilling was that the same someone had been able to get the art book from the safe, quickly and seemingly easily.

Janie must have been thinking the same thing because she asked, "Did they find anything at all in the safe? Are they already gathering DNA?"

Rafe grimaced. Television had given DNA abilities it didn't really have, like the ability to be everywhere. "A safe isn't likely to cough up much DNA. Campus police report that this particular safe is opened by a code that has to be punched in. The crime-scene specialists will fingerprint the push buttons, but, keep in mind, the guard opened the safe this morning, technically putting his prints over whoever had opened it last."

Katie leaned forward, intent. "Did the Adobe Hills police officer say what was inside the safe this morning?"

Finally, something he could answer. "A pair of handcuffs, two wallets and plenty of drug paraphernalia."

Which meant any of that DNA Janie'd been hoping for would be compromised.

It hadn't escaped Rafe's notice that the two women were asking more questions of him than he was asking of them. But before he could form a question, Katie asked, "How long will it take to get back the results?"

"The average is one hundred and twenty days."

The two towns in his county were small, so they were a low priority after both Tucson and Phoenix for the crime lab, located in Phoenix.

A list of who knew the code to the safe could be helpful, yet he doubted an accurate list could be put together. Most likely the college had had the same safe for twenty years, and every officer, past and present, had been given the code. Add to that list the college president, the deans…

Janie started to stand, decided to sit, then

stood again, before finally plopping into the chair and burying her forehead in her hands. "Oh, man! I wish I'd never opened that art book. It was the first time Patricia was trusting me to evaluate the students' work and offer comments."

"If it leads to Brittney's murderer," Rafe said, "then we're glad you did read that art book. Her parents deserve closure."

"And I deserve to live to thirty!"

"You will." Rafe personally intended to keep that promise. His number one priority was finding Brittney's killer while keeping Janie safe.

He glanced at his watch. Ten minutes until he needed to leave to testify in court, and while he didn't want to leave the case or Janie, there was no reason for him to delay the court date. In an hour, the art book would still be missing; Derek would still be dead.

And, for right now, Janie was about as safe as one could be at the Scorpion Ridge police station.

But he did need to keep her busy. He didn't want her to bolt or break down. "I'm going to turn you over to my chief of police," Rafe said. "I'm going to have you look at some photos. See if you recognize any of Derek's friends."

"He didn't have friends," she reminded him. "And I'm supposed to be at the university. I have classes today."

"I'm afraid you'll have to miss them today. And you'll be surprised what you'll remember, the details you'll recall, people and places."

"I should never have opened his art book," Janie muttered again.

"But you did," Rafe said, "So now we'll deal with it." He smiled, trying to communicate that she wasn't alone, that he'd do his job, take care of her.

Then she gave him a glare that almost stopped him in his tracks. He was used to people being grateful, looking up to him, believing him, wanting to be taken care of, trusting him. Janie Vincent didn't trust him.

Before he was quite ready, she stood, practically tapping her foot in impatience. "Fine. Let's do it."

"You want me to stay, Janie?" Katie asked.

"No, you go on back to work. I'll find—"

"I'll make sure she gets home," Rafe asserted.

Janie's eyes narrowed. For some reason, Little Miss Vincent didn't appreciate his offer.

Rafe gathered up what he needed for court, and then followed Janie and Katie out his office door. Katie hurried toward the exit, checking her watch, too. Before Rafe could steer Janie toward the back room, she caught the attention of one of his auxiliary officers. The cop gave her an appreciative once-over before Rafe sent him packing. Then he gently guided Janie to the back room and set her up in front of a computer before summoning his chief of police, Jeff Summerside.

It took her a moment to realize what he planned and then her only question was, "I'm surprised, as small as Scorpion Ridge is, that you're not still using mug-shot books?"

"I'm not even sure they still make Polaroid film," he told her wryly. "As a border community, CopLink is a necessity. It saves time and manpower."

He typed in some keywords and soon Janie was perusing faces. It was all Rafe could do to walk from the room, away from her and what she was doing, and hurry to court. He wanted to be sitting next to her, noting her reaction, and seeing if any of the faces meant something not only to her but also to him.

But he trusted his chief of police.

He wasn't sure he trusted the officer who'd given her the once-over. At least, not when it came to Janie.

And that made no sense at all.

JANIE TOOK A deep breath and looked at yet another young, angry face. Chief Summerside had typed in various bits of information, bringing up the type of people who might be associated with Derek Chaney.

Just as Janie was wondering what type of keywords Summerside had used in his search—*scary, mean, glowerer* must surely have been among them—the officer left to take a private call. Leaving Janie to sit on a hard chair and feel alone. Vulnerable. It wasn't Janie's first time at a police station. It was, however, the first time she'd entered the doors without a police escort. And this time her sister, Katie, had been escorting her in instead of out.

Rafe's words, *I'll make sure she gets home,* had taken Janie back to a low point in her life. Janie had just turned thirteen, and her big sister Katie, now of legal age, had left Aunt Betsy's.

Alone with her alcoholic aunt, Janie had been terrified, and for a solid year the system couldn't be convinced that an eighteen-year-old guardian—one who had a job, was in college and with no police record—was better than a fifty-year-old aunt who couldn't hold a job, keep an apartment, and had lost her driver's license thanks to her best friend vodka.

"I'll make sure she gets home."

Janie closed her eyes. He couldn't have picked a worse declaration. During the year Katie had fought the system, Janie had run away eight times.

Rafe wasn't the first cop to see Janie safely home.

Only in those days, there'd been nothing safe about the home she'd been escorted back to. He also wasn't the first cop to sympathize with her.

Empty words. It was easy to say "I'm sorry." Janie knew from experience that a cop could only do so much, and that when the next call came in, she was just a report to be filed.

And forgotten.

Sighing, she refocused on the screen. After what felt like days, another officer, Candy Riorden, drove her home to her cottage behind the house where her sister and brother-in-law lived.

Since it was only a ten-minute drive, there'd been little conversation aside from the cackle of the radio and a few directions from Janie. Just before Janie closed the police cruiser's back door, Officer Riorden said, "Sheriff Salazar says he'll pick you up later and escort you to Adobe Hills."

It was an order, not a suggestion.

Given by a cop who'd said *he'd* make sure

she got home and then had turned her over to someone else.

Typical.

Yet today, as she took her second shower in under twelve hours, she wondered if she just might have to rethink her own policy. The one she had about not trusting cops. Years ago, when she'd run away, it had always been a cop who had escorted her back to a place she didn't want to go, a place where she didn't feel safe, instead of to her sister.

But in this instance, Katie wouldn't be much help. Janie might actually be putting her in danger. For a protector, Sheriff Salazar might be the logical, and only, choice. And, he did look like someone who could keep her safe. He was tall, over six feet, and had the square jaw that boasted a five-o'clock shadow before noon. Were she the type of artist to paint people, she'd choose him. She'd make sure to emphasize his strong hands, knowing smile and piercing black eyes.

Janie couldn't deny he was easy to look at, if one went for the dark, brooding type.

Appearances weren't everything, though.

Twenty minutes later, she headed through the front gate of BAA, waved at the cashier, and immediately headed for the building that housed her sister and brother-in-law's office.

It was empty; both were in the field.

Good. Janie didn't think she could go over the story again. But because she knew her sister would expect it, Janie took out her cell phone and texted, Where U?

A moment later, Katie responded, Feeding Aquila. U? Aquila was the trained black panther that had brought the Vincent sisters to Scorpion Ridge, Arizona.

Going 2 c George, Janie replied.

Walking next to the employee lounge, Janie suddenly felt a knot forming in the back of her neck. Anxiety boiled through her, ready to send her into a full-blown panic attack.

She wasn't about to let that happen; it had been more than a year. And she'd kept it together last night, as well as this morning and afternoon at the police station. The best thing to do was take her mind off the present situation. When she was younger, she'd always been able to push aside her troubles. All it took was pen and paper.

Today, it would take acrylics and cinder block.

A few minutes later she stood by the Ursus Americanus house. George, the bear that belonged to her father, was sleeping under a tree in the shade. Otherwise, he might have limped over and greeted her. He'd always been an extremely friendly bear, and her favorite.

Crisco, the bear they'd helped nurse back to health more than a year ago, was swimming in a tiny pool designed to resemble a natural pond.

George used to weigh six hundred pounds. Now, he was an old man and starting to shrink. He had arthritis. Crisco was still a youngster, about two years old, and not so friendly.

She didn't blame him. Being mistreated, declawed and underfed was hard to overcome.

At least she'd not been declawed.

The mural for the bear habitat would be the first Janie would complete alone. Adam Snapp, who'd been painting murals around BAA for the last four years, was busy doing other projects outside the zoo. Projects that made him money. He was at BAA today, though, finishing up a few odds and ends, and now showing up just in time to help her.

She'd wanted to be alone, lick her wounds, and try to cleanse her mind.

Within minutes, Adam had already asked her a dozen times if she was all right. Maybe the fact that she'd been staring at the crowds of people—all going somewhere, smiling, acting normal—instead of getting ready to draw the bears gave him a clue something was amiss.

He'd assumed her mood had to do with the mural she was about to start.

He'd never been more wrong.

"You'll do fine," he said, standing back, arms crossed and waiting for her to do something, anything. "You have a whole month to finish."

Until yesterday, finishing this mural and adding it to her portfolio was the most important item on her to-do list. Today, taking the lead on a zoo mural that tens of thousands would see almost seemed frivolous. But Adam couldn't understand her lack of enthusiasm because she hadn't told him about last night, or this morning, or any of what had taken over her life. What she couldn't stop thinking about.

He was her brother-in-law's best friend, and for a short while, she'd thought about making him a bit more. But there'd been no chemistry beyond what they had in common.

They were artists.

Adam was making a name for himself, even as far as California and New Mexico. And now she was aiming to secure a spot as an artist in residence in South Africa.

Just last Friday she'd mailed in the last of her application. For the next month, she'd need to inform the judging panel about her ongoing projects, both in the community and at school. She felt confident about her application.

This was what she wanted to do: paint real animals in their natural habitat. She'd wanted it since the day Tyre, the black panther, had attacked her, since hearing someone say, "You can take the cat out of the jungle, but you can't take the jungle out of the cat."

"Show me your ideas," Adam ordered.

Today must be her day for getting ordered around. First from Katie, who'd dictated, "We are going to see Sheriff Salazar." Then from Salazar: "I will pick you up at two and escort you to Adobe Hills." And now from Adam. "Show me..."

Didn't anyone say please anymore?

Nevertheless, because he was a reference and a friend, she dutifully complied. That had been her assignment from him: come up with thumbnail sketches for the mural. She opened her art book and studied her drawings—done with colored pencils—that were her final choices for the design.

"Crisco's story still makes people cry. It seemed a logical choice." She turned the tablet so he could see that she'd created a time line, starting with Crisco being found with his head caught between the slats of fence, segueing to his rehabilitation and ending with now. Crisco, named because of how they'd managed to free him, now lived in luxury with a pool, plenty of food and a town full of fans who'd read his story in the paper.

"Maybe," Adam said slowly, "you should add something, such as a pelt of real fur. Something for the kiddos to touch."

Janie shrugged. Not what she'd pictured. For the last couple of years, Janie had called BAA home. The place was named after her brother-in-law's little sister, who'd died years ago from complications of Down Syndrome. The real Bridget had loved animals, but Luke had taken the appreciation and healing she'd gleaned from animals to another level. BAA had struggled at first, but Luke had made it into a success story. Next month, BAA would start taking the first Monday of every month's proceeds and donate them to the Down Syndrome research group.

Luke had made goals and kept them.

It was something Janie was trying to learn to do, with her art. She'd always been dedicated to the world her paints created and the projects she committed to. She had to get the bear mural finished by the end of March, plus help Adam finish the orangutan wall. It was his pride and joy, as he'd managed to add 3-D moveable parts to the vague likeness of Ollie, the actual orangutan.

In his heart of hearts, Adam was part caricaturist, part toy maker.

Janie looked at her thumbnails again. She—as always—had been going for realism with just a hint of Norman Rockwell plus a shot of Van Gogh on the side. "Everyone expects cute and fluffy," she argued. "Anyone can draw it."

"We're a kids' zoo. It's what they don't expect but need to know that makes the mural. If you don't want something they can touch, add something interesting like a Seek and Find amidst your time line."

Janie was aghast. "So I'd have a list of words written on the wall, and the children have to find the hidden pictures?"

He brightened. "Absolutely, give the kiddos something to do."

Yup, there was no changing him from his trademark ventures. He did "engaged" murals. Janie hated to think of what he might do if BAA had any skunks.

She changed the subject. "Have you ever heard of Derek Chaney?"

Adam didn't even blink. "No, why?"

"How about Brittney Travis? Do you know her?"

Adam stepped back, no longer looking at the thumbnails. "Yes, I've met Brittney in town. Why? What brings her up? She's been missing more than two months, since Christmas."

"Would Brittney ever run away, do you think?"

"No one who knows Brittney believes she ran away," Adam said. "She's a lot younger than me, so I only met her because she took tae kwon do at my father's studio."

Janie had gone to the studio once with Adam. Even though he'd started her in a beginners' class, one he'd been teaching, she'd stumbled with the most basic of moves. Luckily, she'd been able to laugh at herself.

"That doesn't mean she would never run away."

"No, it doesn't, but she's just not that kind of girl. She was nice to my brother."

Janie couldn't come up with the words to respond. Having siblings with special needs was what had cemented Adam and Luke's friendship all those years ago. Luke had had Bridget; Adam had his twin, whom he fiercely protected.

Being nice to his brother was akin to sainthood, at least to Adam. Right now, Aaron lived with Adam's parents and worked at their tae kwon do studio. He was a helpful ten-year-old trapped in a twentysomething body and was always cheerful.

"What have you heard? Why are you asking this now? Has there been news about Brittney?" Adam asked.

"Nothing I can share," Janie said.

Adam raised one eyebrow. His lips went into a thin line of disappointment. "Look—" he started to say.

And just like that, the anxiety enveloped her again. She couldn't breathe, and the only thing she could do was seek escape. She managed to gasp, "I have to get out of here. I'll talk to you later."

She took off, running, ignoring the echoing shouts of Adam's concern.

Nine years. It had been nine years since the walls had closed in on her, keeping her awake nights and searching for places to hide during the day.

Her sister had never shaken the anxiety. Even today with a husband and a baby on the way, Katie sometimes paced the living room unable to sleep or find peace.

Not Janie.

The minute she'd escaped their aunt to go

live with Katie, she'd pushed the fear to some corner of her mind and fenced it in.

But today, it returned.

Her safe world had crumbled.

CHAPTER FOUR

Two hours later, an hour later than he'd wanted it to be, Rafe pulled into a circular driveway just a mile down from BAA.

Belonging to Ruth Moore, who also owned the land BAA resided on, the minimansion was today a place where fund-raisers were held and where Ruth, along with Katie and her husband, Luke, lived.

Ruth was currently on her honeymoon. She and her new husband, Jasper, were overseas exploring the place where Jasper had lived before Hitler and the war made him an orphan.

Rafe exited the Jeep and walked around to the cottage out back where Janie lived. He had to knock twice before Janie opened the door. She'd changed into jeans and a button-down sky-blue shirt with ruffles.

"Do I really have to do this?" she questioned.

"Yes."

She followed, and soon she sat beside him in his Jeep, no longer looking frightened. Fear had been replaced by exhaustion. They left the property and hit the main road.

"You did a good job with the CopLink photos today. I've given the names of the three students you picked out to the Adobe Hills police. Chief Summerside's gonna go pick up the fourth, our local boy," Rafe shared.

"I wish I could have done more. And I'm still not sure if the people I identified are just people I've seen at school or here at the zoo. Except for Tommy. You know him?"

Yes, Rafe knew Thomas Skinley. He'd been in and out of trouble for the last five years.

"How often does he come to the zoo, and are you sure you never saw him at school?" Rafe asked, trying not to show how disturbed he was by the name.

"No, not at school. He's come to the zoo more than a few times with his sister. As I told your officer, Amanda Skinley is in my Monday/Wednesday class, Derek's class."

The dots were beginning to connect. Amanda was Tommy's sister. Rafe could feel the case turning, gaining ground, starting to move forward. If he didn't lose focus, if he asked the right questions, maybe they'd find Brittney.

"Was Amanda in class last night?"

"Yes, she never misses. She's taking advantage of a dual-enrollment program that allows high-school seniors to take college courses for credit."

Amanda Skinley was a bright girl, born deaf, who rarely made waves and basically avoided the criminal path her brother had taken. Still, she might know something.

"In class last night, did anyone ask about Derek? Did Amanda ask about him?"

"Amanda didn't say anything, but she rarely contributes much. She depends on her interpreters. She did seem out of sorts yesterday, though."

"Go on."

"Truthfully, until after class, when I opened his art book, there wasn't much to tell. We had our break, right at seven-thirty. Class dismissed at nine. I went to the student union to go over their art books and comment on their progress."

"Something you did after every class?" he asked.

"No, Patricia and I usually do it together in her office. Last night was the first time I went through the books by myself."

"And up to Wednesday night, Derek was turning in only what you expected."

"Yes. I don't know why I kept reading. His words made me feel like I wasn't safe, like

I needed to hide, like someone was watching me."

Rafe knew what it was that had prompted her to continue: morbid curiosity. It was the same pull that urged civilians to slow down when they drove by an accident. Derek's life had been a train wreck, and right now, unless Rafe missed his guess, Janie was more or less one more victim tied to the track.

They made it five miles before Rafe got a call from Nathan canceling their meeting and rescheduling it for tomorrow. Seemed Nathan was dealing with a multivehicle collision on Interstate Ten where a tractor-trailer had spilled enough cocaine to imitate a snowstorm.

After hanging up, Rafe hit the steering wheel. Not very professional, but a heck of a lot tamer than what he really wanted to do. "I need something concrete to tell Brittney's parents," he muttered as he pulled into a convenience-store parking lot and turned the car around.

Janie just stared out the window. Rafe couldn't tell what she was thinking, but after Nathan's cancellation, she had visibly relaxed. "The fact that we're not meeting Nathan today," Rafe reminded her, "doesn't mean that Derek or his art book is going away. It's a delay, not a cancellation."

"I'm well aware of that." Janie gave him a haughty look. "It's just that everything's happening so fast. I need some time to think."

Some of his annoyance lessened. He knew he was being unreasonable. Missing persons cases did that to him. And, truly, Rafe understood what she was feeling. It was like a horrible roller-coaster ride, one you'd not meant to get on and one that had no end in sight. The police world was like that. You had to solve a case in twenty-four hours or the odds of solving it decreased by more than half.

A good officer held on to that roller-coaster car and rode it until the tracks collapsed and the park closed.

A great officer knew that at some point you had to exit the roller coaster, step back, watch what others were doing on the ride and then, in just a matter of moments, get back on.

Janie seemed more like the Ferris-wheel kind of girl. The roller coaster? Not so much. She'd probably want to paint the cars.

And look beautiful doing it.

He shook his head, trying to clear the wayward thoughts that were taking his mind off the case. He couldn't afford the distraction. And she was distracting. From the elegant way she held her chin, so stubborn, to the way she crossed her long legs. Again he wondered why he'd not called her for a second date. A date didn't mean committing to eternity. Maybe they'd have found common ground and built, if not a relationship, then a friendship.

"Tell me," Rafe said, bringing himself back to the case, "did Derek share his drawings or writing in class? Is it possible that he showed it to another student?"

She took a moment; her face scrunched in concentration.

"No, I don't think he showed it to anyone. Amanda's the only one who ever showed any interest in his drawings. I doubt any of the other students even glimpsed the one he turned in last Wednesday," Janie said. "It was a new art book. It only had those six pages altogether."

"What do you mean, it was new?"

"All semester he's been handing in an art book. It was full of ideas, projects and such. This time he gave me a brand-new one. I thought maybe he'd misplaced the one he'd been working on previously..." Her words tapered off as Rafe pulled off the road and swung the vehicle around again. This time he didn't wait for a spot on the side of the road, he just did a U-turn, scaring up dirt and revving the engine.

"Hey!" She slid slightly toward him, her left hand reaching out to gain balance. It brushed against his knee. Rafe barely noticed—he knew when a lead was handed to him.

It took only a moment to get Derek Chaney's parents' address from the system.

"We're heading to Adobe Hills," he told Janie. "You'd recognize the previous art book. Maybe he added something to it, something we need to see! If we can get Derek's parents' permission, maybe we'll have some new information within the hour."

He was of two minds about taking Janie along. He hated involving a civilian. On the other hand, she knew what the art book looked like and could save him a lot of time.

Next, Rafe phoned Nathan to get his go-ahead. After all, they'd be on the other man's turf. No luck there; Williamson's number went right to voice mail. The deputy who answered the main number took a message and promised Nathan would return the call. Rafe neglected to tell the deputy exactly what was going on or why the call was necessary. The second call he made was to Derek's parents. More luck there. They were eager to talk to anyone who might shed light on why their son had died. After hanging up, Rafe quickly called his office and got someone to do a background check on the Chaneys.

Janie seemed confused. “Don’t we need a search warrant to go through Derek’s stuff?”

“Not if the person in control of the property gives us permission to search.”

She checked her watch. “It’s two o’clock. I usually don’t help on Thursday night, but an instructor asked if I’d come in. You should take me back to BAA so I can get my own car.”

After returning Janie to where she lived and seeing her safely to her vehicle, Rafe spent the whole drive, nearly an hour, checking to make sure she was still behind him, and getting the dirt on Derek’s parents—there was none, and none on Derek’s much older brother, either.

In the early afternoon, there wasn’t much traffic on Interstate Ten. There was a slight slowdown because of Nathan’s accident that put them in one lane for a while. Nathan didn’t even notice them drive by. He was pacing while looking at a clipboard, talking on the phone and giving orders to a patrol officer.

Multitasking, getting things done. Nathan was doing it. Rafe, too. It was an exhilarating feeling, chasing down a lead, especially one on a case that was personal. It was also bittersweet. His grandfather had been a cop. His father hadn’t wanted to become one but had, all because of a missing child.

Rafe's brother.

Rafe had long ago given up the hunt for Ramon. It had been thirty-six years, after all, and Rafe knew how to shove the memories aside, not that there were many. And today, the memories would only distract him from what he had to do.

The Chaneys' restored two-story home was just a mile into Adobe Hills and in an established neighborhood. A basketball hoop stood guard over the driveway, and a swing sat on the porch.

It looked a lot like the house he'd grown up in.

As soon as Janie pulled up behind him, parked and joined him, Rafe headed toward the porch and rang the bell. It was Mrs. Chaney who answered. Her hair was wild, as though it hadn't been combed in a week. Her yellow-and-red-striped T-shirt was on inside out and didn't go with her orange pants. Her green eyes were watery and bloodshot. She kept dabbing at them with a Kleenex. Judging by the lines on her face, she was about the same age as Rafe's mother.

Rafe wondered what she'd looked like last week—before her youngest son's death.

"Thanks for agreeing to see me," Rafe said. "This is Janie Vincent, she was—"

"Derek's teacher." She held out a trembling hand, and Rafe was glad he'd followed his instincts to bring her.

"He talked a lot about you. I'm Judy Chaney."

"Derek was a talented artist," Janie murmured, shaking Judy's hand.

Mrs. Chaney held the door open so they could walk into the living room. "We're so glad you called, Sheriff. We're desperate to know what's going on and how we can help. This shouldn't have happened."

She didn't invite them to sit but seemed content to let them peruse their surroundings. The couch looked comfortable, inviting and well-used. A television dominated the room. There were two bookcases cluttered with books, knickknacks and photos. Above the fireplace were three portraits. The middle showed a family: mom, dad, two boys.

Derek's father was another tall blond.

Flanking the family portrait were high-school graduation photos. The one on the left showed a craggy blond-haired young man with a crooked grin and kind eyes. The one on the left showed Derek, black-haired, no grin and guarded eyes. On the fireplace mantel was a basket full of sympathy cards.

"We received twenty-two in the mail today." Mr. Chaney entered the room from the kitchen.

"Twenty-two." His voice caught, and he faltered for a moment. "My wife's only been able to open six."

Rafe cleared his throat. Five years ago, when his father had died, they'd been inundated with cards. Rafe's mother cried over every one.

"They're from my friends at work," Mrs. Chaney said.

"Mine, too," Mr. Chaney added.

Mrs. Chaney added, "Some are also from family."

Rafe waited. He wasn't getting the we-received-so-many-cards report because the family felt the need to talk. Both parents were looking at the card basket as if it were an enemy.

"We didn't get a single card or phone call from any of Derek's friends," Mr. Chaney said. "Not one. Or even from the parent of a friend. My wife noticed that first."

"Of course, it's early. Kids tend to take a little prodding. They assume they have all the time…"

Her words faded, and Rafe quickly inserted, "It's early yet."

"We received a few from our neighbors, and even from Derek's past teachers," Mr. Chaney said, "but, they were so generic—'Sorry for your loss. Please know you're in our prayers.' Nothing personal."

Rafe almost said that it had only been a couple of days and that they'd be receiving cards for months yet. Instead, he asked, "Why does this surprise you?"

"Used to be, he was surrounded by friends, kids who laughed, kids who would talk to us. I'm so mad at myself. We could sense something was going on."

"How well do you know the friends he has now?" Rafe continued examining the portraits.

"For the last two years, not well at all." The Chaneys looked at each other. Two people, one emotion: regret.

Mr. Chaney went first. "We mentioned this to the officer who came to notify us about finding Der—" His voice cracked. "About finding Derek's body."

Mrs. Chaney joined in. "We didn't like any of Derek's current friends. He's been in and out of trouble lately, serious trouble, with them. They weren't the kind to knock on the door and be respectful. They honked and Derek ran. The few times one of his friends came in, well, let's just say his new friends didn't bother to curb their language, hide their cigarettes, or even clean up after themselves."

Rafe definitely wanted to show them photos

of the four kids Janie had picked out. Tommy especially.

"We talked to him, gave him a curfew," Mr. Chaney said. "We did what we could. We monitored his computer, found nothing. Whenever we could get our hands on his phone, we went through his text messages. There weren't many. Two years ago, he kept everything. The last three months, it was obvious that he erased his messages as soon as he read them."

Savvy kid, Rafe thought.

"But he's almost nineteen, legal age. Outside of kicking him out, what could we do?" Mrs. Chaney sounded more like she was talking to herself than to them.

"Jimmy, our oldest boy," Mr. Chaney said, taking over, "was worried too. He came home from his job in California at least once a month so we could do something as a family over the weekend. We'd hoped things were changing. Last year, for a while, it was like we had the old Derek back. Then, at the beginning of fall semester, it all went wrong again. He started staying out all night, missing school, taking money without permission."

The Chaneys were doing what most parents did in this type of situation—not so much trying to convince Rafe that they were caring parents, but trying to assure themselves.

"Derek had so much potential," Janie said. "His art was riveting, daring. I could see the artist he could be. If there'd only been more time."

Mrs. Chaney nodded, her eyes filling with tears.

"Would Jimmy possibly know who Derek was hanging around with?" Rafe pressed.

"We asked him. He gave us two or three names, but they were kids Derek had hung around with before leaving high school." Mrs. Chaney shot her husband a guarded look. Rafe waited.

"Jimmy and Derek didn't spend much time together," Mrs. Chaney admitted, "unless we were doing family things."

"Why is that?" Rafe asked.

"There's a ten-year difference in their ages," Mr. Chaney said. "And we adopted Derek. He's my brother's son. By the time the boys got comfortable with each other, Jimmy was heading off to college."

"Jimmy's going to be a doctor," Judy added. "He has little tolerance for anyone he suspects of dabbling in drugs."

Rafe wanted to jump on that comment, but the kid had just died in a meth explosion. He could read about Derek and drugs in Nathan's report without putting the Chaneys through more grief.

"What were the circumstances of the adoption?"

"Derek's mom is in prison. She's not in the picture and she won't be getting out anytime soon. My brother passed away when Derek was six."

Rafe noticed Janie walking over to the picture, staring at Derek, and looking incredibly sad. She'd been taken in by relatives, too, Rafe remembered.

It hadn't gone well, either.

"So none of Derek's issues can be directly related to his birth parents?" Rafe asked. "Maybe something to do with his mother?"

"No, we've had him since he was eight. For the two years after his dad's death, he was pretty much neglected by his mother. Besides, if any of his mother's friends came looking for him, they wouldn't know to search for him under our last name. Once we got his anger issues under control, he fit right in. We were thrilled. We'd wanted five of our own."

The Chaneys were good people. They were doing what innocent people did, sharing everything, trying to be helpful, wanting to understand how things could go so wrong.

"He didn't realize how good he had it," Janie whispered.

Rafe thought the same about many of the juvenile delinquent cases he handled.

Getting back on task, though, he said, "There's a chance that Derek had information about another case we're working on. On the phone, you said you'd let us go through Derek's room?"

"Of course," Mrs. Chaney said. "We will do all we can to help the police so some other kid doesn't become a victim like Derek."

Mr. Chaney ushered them up the stairs and opened the door into a room almost the size of the living room. "My wife can't bear to see all this," he said. "It's exactly the way Derek left it."

A mess, typical teenager. The bed was unmade, the floor littered with clothes and books and video games. A flat-screen television was against one wall. Shelves of books were on two others. A whole row was designated for textbooks. Rafe noticed math, sociology and lots of English. Well, that made sense. According to Janie, Derek also had a gift for writing. Posters, of bands Rafe didn't recognize, graced the wall.

"He used to be a reader," Mr. Chaney said. "Up until about eighth grade."

"What happened?" Janie asked softly.

"First sports, then girls," Mr. Chaney said. "They wouldn't leave him alone. Once he got to high school, it was a strange herd of friends."

There were no photographs in the room, but lots and lots of drawings. Derek seemed to be enthralled by dark castles, fire-breathing dragons and fierce warriors.

"I'd better go check on my wife," Mr. Chaney said.

Janie walked into the room, not a bit put off by the mess. She rubbed her shoulders as if cold, but it wasn't a chill in the air that made her uncomfortable. It was more likely a chill in her heart. He felt it, too.

"I should have tried harder with that boy," she murmured.

"You did make an effort," Rafe reminded her.

"Not enough of one. Sometimes a teacher is the only one who can make a difference, see beneath the grime."

Rafe wondered if a teacher had been there for her, back in her muddled childhood. She'd made it clear that cops hadn't been. Somehow knowing that made him want to change her mind. Not only about cops in general, but about him specifically.

But they were losing precious time, so he asked, “Do you see the art book?”

“Not yet.” Janie walked to the middle of the room, sidestepping a pair of jeans and a skateboard. She turned in a circle, first with her eyes open and then with them closed. After a moment, she headed for a desk.

“The desk is too neat,” she explained. “Nothing else in this room is neat.” She briefly touched the computer’s mouse and lifted the pad. Then, she opened the only drawer.

Nothing.

Watching her, Rafe was again struck by her attention to detail. She was doing what he usually did, had been trained to do, and she was doing it by instinct.

Janie next checked under the bed. He’d already done that and found nothing unusual.

But she pulled out one tennis shoe. “This isn’t his.”

Rafe looked at it: dull brown and somewhat new. “How can you be sure?”

“Derek would never wear this color.”

“What color is it, exactly?”

Janie gaped at him in disbelief. “It’s green.”

Rafe wasn’t one for sharing what he didn’t consider a disability. But, in this case, it might make a difference in what she could see and what he couldn’t.

"I'm color-blind, which means I have poor discrimination with certain colors. Green being one of them."

Her expression went from disbelief to pity. Well, an artist *would* feel sorry for someone who couldn't appreciate every color's beauty.

"That must make your job harder."

"There was some concern that I wouldn't pass the vision test. I did, and luckily, my condition is considered mild. The fact that I work for a small rural county makes a difference. I also wear corrective lenses."

"Derek wore black, gray and white. It's almost as if he was making a statement about his personality. Green is the color of safety."

Rafe dumped the shoe in a baggie he pulled from his pocket and ran out the door to ask the Chaneys what size shoe Derek had worn—Mrs. Chaney said her son was an eleven.

Rafe reentered the room as Janie was bending to check an unzipped backpack that was stuffed to the side, books and papers spilling out. Janie riffled through it for a moment, then she pulled an art book from a side pocket and flipped it open. Derek's inked name was on the cover. She thumbed through the pages.

He touched her arm and angled her so he could read over her shoulder.

"This is his, this is the right one. He's done

most of these thumbnails or scrapped them. No writing yet, but maybe there's something at the end, some reason he didn't want to turn this one in to me."

He noticed how carefully Janie held the book—for a witness, she was getting too involved.

It only took her a moment to make it to the final pages, but it felt much longer to Rafe. Then her face turned white. He took a step toward her. She didn't notice; she was focused on the art book, not on him.

Derek's final drawing told Rafe exactly how much danger Janie was in.

Two dark trees, lots of dirt, and an open grave with a body in it. Derek had penned a few words underneath:

I have to tell somebody. I can't live with this. But if I confess, whomever I tell will be in as much danger as me.

CHAPTER FIVE

THE OLD ART BOOK went into another baggie, which, to Janie, looked like an oversize sandwich Ziploc.

"I'm toast," she whispered.

"No, there's a chance they haven't a clue Derek's even—"

"They! I've got to worry about a they? As in, more than one?" This was going from bad to worse. She'd been thinking of who might be responsible. What kind of person would have access to the school's safe? But it might be a who *all* was responsible, a what kind of *people*.

"You don't know that for sure. All this could just be foolish fabrication."

"Oh, right," Janie said snidely. Since this morning, he'd been a man on a mission. No way could he shift his beliefs now. "Even if the art book hadn't been taken from the school's safe, I'd have a hard time believing you," she finished.

Rafe's hand went to his chin and he rubbed

his thumb on stubble she'd not noticed before. It was dark, the same color as the circles under his eyes.

"So, what are we going to do?" she insisted. "Last night I was nervous about what I read. Today I'm nervous about who knows what I read. This is getting crazy."

He didn't disagree, and he kept rubbing for a moment. Finally, he said, "Everything points to the college. It's where Brittney was last seen. It's where Derek turned in the art book and where the art book went missing. We need to find a friend of Derek's who's willing to talk. And we also need to find out whose shoe is under his bed, and why it's there."

He finally stopped rubbing his chin and lifted the mattress, looking at the mess underneath: old food, socks, a girlie magazine.

Scattered there, too, were a few pieces of Lego bricks—red, blue and yellow. Finally some real color. Nearby was a well-worn baseball glove. Derek Chaney had been a boy, just like the ones who came to BAA and put their fingers in their mouths and made faces at Candy the spider monkey, and who fed pellets to the giraffes while being grossed out by the giraffes' long tongues, and who dreamed about jumping into the pool with Aquila the black panther.

Just like the dark-haired man next to her had at one time been a boy, probably with his head in some Encyclopedia Jones book or insisting on playing I Spy over and over.

She bent down, wanting to move the Legos away from the girlie magazine. As if she could save Derek now.

"Don't touch anything," Rafe ordered.

She rolled her eyes. They'd been in the bedroom for a good fifteen minutes. Her prints were everywhere, and these Lego bricks weren't the calling card for something sinister.

But Rafe was the cop and she the uncomfortable civilian.

When they finished in Derek's bedroom, he led the way back to the living room and the bowl of sympathy cards. Rafe asked for the senders' addresses, and Judy Chaney dug out her book to give him those she knew. Mr. Chaney went looking for envelopes for those she didn't.

Every person who'd sent a card was meticulously recorded in Rafe's little black book. No doubt Officer Candy Riorden would be assigned to find phone numbers and addresses to go with each name. Then, there'd be a visit.

Janie didn't think she'd enjoy Rafe's job.

Way too dark.

No wonder he saw the world in shades of brown.

And, boy, was he good at giving orders. She spent ten minutes sitting on the sofa with Derek's high-school graduation photo staring down at her and listening to Rafe tell the Chaneys what to do. As soon as he and Janie left, they'd be going through Derek's clothes searching for pieces that might not be his.

Clothes weren't the only item. Rafe also asked them to check for out-of-place combs, wallets, books, videos, etc., and to widen the search to Jimmy's old room, the backyard shed, the garage.

They'd be digging up dirt on their son while the undertaker was digging up dirt for his casket.

Morbid.

Janie didn't want to do this anymore.

Without missing a beat, he turned from the Chaneys to her. "Lock your doors before you go to class today. If you feel like something's wrong or someone's acting suspicious, go where there's lots of people. Call me, I don't care what time it is."

"But—"

"No buts. I'm making you my personal responsibility. Give me your phone."

No didn't seem to be an answer he'd accept,

and as sheriff he could pretty much do what he wanted, so she dug it out of her canvas bag and handed it to him. He added his number and two more: those of Jeff Summerside and Candy Riorden.

"You're coming across a little heavy-handed," she reprimanded as she held out her hand for her phone. Delayed reaction seemed to be her standard response when near him. How dare he just take over, without asking? She opened her mouth to give him the you-can't-boss-this-girl speech, but then he looked at her.

Really looked at her.

And she lost her breath. His eyes were smudged coal, ready to ignite, but now only flickering. She'd painted something very much like those eyes years ago. She'd drawn a black panther on the wall of her bedroom—watchful, hurting, helpless, hopeless, as those he loved disappeared.

Never to return.

Rafe was hurting.

She got just that one tiny glimpse of his vulnerability and then the Sheriff Salazar mask slammed into place. He handed back her cell phone and pointedly looked at his watch. "What time does your class begin?"

"Six, and then it's over at nine."

"Great, that will give me a chance to speak

with Nathan," he decided. "I need to bring him up to speed."

Then, he turned to the Chaneys. "I'll make sure he's expecting you to take a look at the mug shots, the same ones Janie went through this morning. Before I show you the pictures she pointed out, I want to see if you pinpoint the same kids. If possible, I'd also like to get another team out here tonight to go over Derek's room."

The Chaneys both nodded. They were willing to do anything to find out what happened to their son.

Rafe held out his hand to help Janie up from the couch. She took it and followed him out the door and to her car. For a moment, she wondered why he hadn't asked for her number to program it into his phone. She easily answered the question: he already had it from their one date. Plus, when you were sheriff of Laramie County, you didn't need to ask for someone's number. You just went to CopLink.

He'd find out a few other things about her on CopLink. Great, just great. Unless it was true that a juvenile's records were permanently sealed.

He opened the car door and said, "I'll be outside the classroom door waiting for you. Ten minutes before nine."

As she pulled out and followed his car down the road, she wondered if she should have just let him drive her to class, as he'd wanted to do. Even scared, she'd been able to breathe while he was by her side. Now, as his SUV idled behind hers as she pulled into a parking space and turned off the engine, the panic started to rise again.

Rolling down his passenger-side window, he said, "You'll be fine. Campus is hopping right now, people everywhere." Then, he rolled up his window and drove off, leaving her alone. The slim hold she had on her emotions slipped even more.

Call Katie?

No, Katie was eight months pregnant and didn't need this hassle.

Call Adam?

No. Sharing the situation with Adam would just mean more talking, no solutions.

Janie followed a crowd heading for the student union and college café. Right now, more than anything, she wanted a hamburger, lots of French fries and a chocolate malt.

She'd just sat down when Rafe called her on the cell phone. "You okay?"

"Now that I'm eating."

"Glad you stayed on campus and with lots

of people. When you're done eating, go right to class. Okay?"

"Yes, sir."

Silence. Then disconnect.

She listened to him, though. After finishing her food—she had eaten every bite—she cleaned her area and headed to the art department. She wanted to talk to Patricia. Her fear turned to surreal introspection as she walked past the parking lot and watched the evening students park their cars and walk to class. It felt wrong; they were so carefree and laughing. They believed they were invincible.

Janie had never felt that way.

Janie continued on to the faculty offices. Patricia wasn't in her office, which was very unusual. It was also too bad because Janie figured, next to Rafe, Patricia was the only one who she could share her ideas and fears with.

Suddenly the hamburger, fries and chocolate shake didn't seem such a good idea.

With no outlet, Janie decided to focus on her duties. She spent her night helping students develop different hues out of just twenty colors. The professor, Estelle Wagner, was a new hire who kept a tight grip on the class and hadn't been too willing to share responsibilities so far. Janie ended the evening covered mostly in green and red and very glad that this class didn't require art books.

When class ended, Janie found Rafe leaning against the wall across from the art room, just as he'd promised. He was watching students leave, studying them, possibly searching for one of the students she'd identified as Derek's acquaintances.

Not in this particular class. Which just showed how much of a loner he was, as most of the students knew each other and considered the class more of a social venue.

A couple of the students recognized Rafe. One or two asked him about Brittney. Most just seemed impressed that they were meeting him. Janie hadn't realized just how prominent a figure he was. Rafe shook their hands whether they agreed with his politics or not.

"Class go all right?" he asked when the last student exited the main door.

"Yes. I was a little jumpy, but I don't think they noticed."

"Smart people get jumpy. Foolish people get lax."

He walked her to her car, bent down to check under it and then waited while she unlocked it. "I'll be behind you. And, yes, that means you should go the speed limit."

Now she was certain he'd looked up her record. Aware that he was watching her every move, she settled behind the wheel, strapped her seat belt, and wished again that she'd agreed to just let him drive. Even with him behind her, she felt alone, traveling in a darkness that had nothing to do with how late in the evening it was.

Finally, she pulled in front of her cottage and exited her car. It took him just a few minutes to open her door, check inside, and wait for her while she gathered what she'd need to stay in the main house with Katie and Luke.

But even after he'd left her in Katie's capable hands, something of him lingered, some remnant of his strong personality that refused to be ignored.

She wished she were that strong.

Maybe then she'd have gotten some sleep that night. In the morning, when Yolanda Sanchez, the college student who kept everything running at Katie and Luke's house, knocked on the door, Janie was still counting sheep.

To be exact, Janie had counted one thousand, two hundred and fifty-six sheep in her head between the hours of eleven and seven. That made two nights without sleep.

Sluggish, Janie changed into her khaki shorts and royal-blue BAA shirt and frowned at the mirror. Even after a shower, her hair was thin and lank. Her skin, normally flush, was pale and splotchy. She felt thirteen again, with pimples and a self-image the size of a postage stamp. Yup, she'd be scaring the customers today. Too bad, Fridays were fairly busy.

Breakfast wasn't even a possibility, so she made her way to the barn. As a rule, she didn't work very closely with animals, but the few that were here at the house were cared for by all. Luckily, Yoda, the hybrid wolf dog, had taken a shine to her.

"You hungry?" she asked. Silly question, Yoda was always hungry. And frisky. He was the only animal in her charge now that wasn't wounded somehow.

Unless loneliness counted as a wound.

"Meredith will be back soon," Janie promised.

Yoda was proof that Meredith had a soft side. BAA's head keeper truly got along better with animals than people. She'd championed the wolf dog, and had trained him to act as an ambassador for both BAA and his species. But unfortunately, because he was part dog and part wolf, he belonged nowhere.

Kind of like Janie.

BAA was her sister's world, and while Janie enjoyed working there, it wasn't her calling.

Janie wanted to travel the animal world and paint it.

Even more, she wanted to know that she *could* do it, alone, without Katie. Katie saw animals as something to take care of; Janie saw them as beautiful, powerful and—if mankind would leave them and their habitats alone—able to thrive on their own, with simple rules for survival.

She'd yet to exist in a world that had simple rules.

She'd yet to exist in a world where she even got to help *make* the rules.

It was her turn.

After filling Yoda's dish, she quickly took care of the other animals in her charge. As they were injured, she wasn't allowed to touch, only to report. She checked the bandage on a barn owl, no seepage. Two sheep stood in a pen, both with stitches from finding the only spot in their usual pen that had a sharp edge. Janie figured they'd go home to the flock today. There was also a family of wild turkey that had been left at BAA's front entrance.

The turkeys were underweight and covered with some sort of tarlike residue that Fred, BAA's veterinarian, hadn't been able to completely remove. They also were all running temperatures, and Fred suspected they might be carrying a disease other animals could catch. Consequently, he'd moved them here instead of using his clinic.

When the animals were all cared for, Janie set off for BAA.

The March weather was gorgeous—her favorite thing about Scorpion Ridge, Arizona, was the temperate climate. Instead of taking her car, she decided to walk the block and a half to BAA.

But a mere three minutes into the jaunt, a car slowed and offered her a ride. This happened just about every time she walked to work. People noticed her uniform, guessed where she worked and offered her a ride. Never before had the act scared her. She was tough, after all. She'd survived Aunt Betsy for a whole year by herself. But today, when the blue Buick slowed, for a moment she'd been poised to run, her left heel in the air, her toes dug into the earth, her body tensed for takeoff.

"No, thanks," she said, backing away from the car. The tone of Janie's voice probably scared the woman more than the woman had scared Janie.

This was why Sheriff Rafael Salazar wanted to guard her, shadow her, keep in contact with her—she was a flight risk.

She broke into a run, striving to get to BAA

quickly. Ten minutes later, happy to be surrounded by people who knew her, Janie was in the employees' lounge and gearing up to start her day.

Today she was filling in for the college student who usually helped in the gift shop on Fridays. Luckily, working in the gift shop was her second favorite job. In the last year, she'd single-handedly turned it into a shop to behold.

"Artistically pleasing," Janie called it.

"Not enough white space," was her brother-in-law's opinion.

Either way, sales increased.

The cashier station was Janie's favorite position. From there, she could people-watch: study facial expressions and the way people held their heads, stretched their necks.

This morning, she'd beaten Gloria, Fred's wife and the manager of the gift shop, to work. Switching on the lights, she first checked to see that everything was in its place. Sometimes the cleaning crew left surprises: stuffed animals on the floor, books flipped so the back and not the cover showed, and candy stocked in the wrong place. She was just heading to the register when the door opened. She turned, expecting to see Gloria, but instead Rafe's body filled the doorframe. Never before had she appreciated his size.

He made her feel safe.

But he was a cop. He'd turn on her the minute she didn't do what he wanted.

"What happened with the case yesterday?" she asked after greeting him.

"I made sure the new art book was tagged and then I spoke to a couple of the men who are familiar with the case. Nathan never made it in. I've called him a couple of times this morning and left messages, but he's obviously busy."

Surprised that he'd shared that much, she said, "That's got to be frustrating."

He stepped into the shop and leaned against the wall stacked with children's books. Next to him a large, stuffed green snake hung. Janie was struck by the urge to tickle his nose with it and see if he smiled.

What an irrational thought!

Tonight she definitely had to get that much-needed sleep, if for no other reason than to keep these strange thoughts about Rafael Salazar from plaguing her.

"Nathan's a hardworking cop. Right now he's not only dealing with a drug ring in his backyard, but also with how it's linked to Brittney's disappearance."

"Good thing he's got you."

Rafe raised his eyebrows. "Nathan doesn't really need me."

"I was referring to Derek."

He left, but throughout the morning, he stopped by again half a dozen times. Occasionally, he passed along some development in the case, like that the Chaneys had recognized one of the students Janie had pinpointed. Other times, he just walked through, making his presence known with a smile or a wave.

"You've got a beau," Gloria whispered.

Janie busied herself instead of responding. If she said no, then she'd have to explain why Rafe was suddenly around so much. It felt surreal to think that there were people at BAA who had no idea that Janie's world was no longer ordinary.

Adam stopped by more than once, too. One time he got there right as Rafe did. No surprise, the two men knew each other and were soon talking and heading toward one of the food kiosks.

Maybe Rafe would tell Adam what Janie couldn't.

"It's funny," said Gloria, right in Janie's ear, startling her. "I thought for a while it would be you and Adam, but that would never have worked."

Usually Gloria couldn't sneak up on her. Gloria could pose for an older version of the Swiss Miss. Stealth wasn't an option.

"Nope, you two would have been competing all your lives and never would have been able to realize that you're both talented at what you do. Rafe, now he's a better match for you."

"Why do you say that?"

"Because you'd be good for each other. He needs to realize that he can't keep the world safe. And you need to realize that the world is yours for the taking."

Gloria had never before showed any gift at fiction. Funny she was sprouting it now.

"What do you mean he wants to keep the world safe but can't? He's a cop, he's supposed to help people."

"His urge to protect stems from more than being a cop, it goes back to before he was born, when his brother was taken and—"

Rafe was back. And he didn't look happy.

He put Gloria in her place with a crisp "Not your story to tell."

RAFE WASN'T SURE why he didn't want Janie to know about his family's tragedy. Maybe because he didn't want her to pity him. Or maybe because he didn't want to hear her echo what others said about missing-kid cases—that they were hopeless.

"She's gonna find out one way or another," Gloria said matter-of-factly. "It's not as if people don't talk."

Usually, Rafe didn't care. If the worst his critics could come up with was: "He gets too involved," or "He takes it too personally," he had no problems living with that. Better that than the cop so hardened he *didn't* get involved, or had forgotten that some things *deserved* to be personal.

And yet, maybe he had let the Travis case become too personal. He had many other things to do, and yet instead he was here at BAA, just in case something happened. Would he have gotten so involved if it had been anyone else except this woman?

"Go ahead," Gloria urged. "I can watch the shop. You two go off somewhere—one of the food courts or, hey, better yet, head on up to the cabin. It's not being used today. You'll have privacy and—"

"He's here on business, Gloria," Janie finally said. "When the business is finished, so is he."

Well, she'd certainly been clear about her feelings.

Before Gloria could make another matchmaking attempt or Janie could remind him of how not interested she was, he left the gift shop and busied himself by returning phone calls and catching up on paperwork in his SUV.

Not a very productive day.

As the afternoon crowd thinned, he decided it was going to be just another typical day at the zoo. So at two, Rafe headed over to Lee and Sandy Travis's. They lived just north of downtown Scorpion Ridge. Lee sold insurance.

Toys were spread across the front yard, neglected. Up until four months ago, Rafe couldn't visit the Travises without having their youngest daughter grab his knees and beg to be carried, or without having their only son toss him a football. Their middle daughter, just a year younger than Brittney, usually sat on the step, watching her siblings, a cell phone in her hand as she texted. Last few times Rafe had driven by, no one played in the yard.

Funny how a house with toys strewn everywhere could look lonely.

He'd just raised his fist to knock when the door opened.

Lee, dressed for work, blocked the door. "Sheriff."

Used to be, Lee had called him Rafe. But

often his job became an entity, defining him, separating him like armor from the man he really was, the friend he could be.

"Got a minute?"

Lee stepped aside so Rafe could enter. Sandy was already standing in the doorway of the kitchen, a dish towel in one hand and a plate in the other. Resignation had thinned her lips. Dark circles had made a home under her eyes.

She reminded him of Derek's mother.

"Can I get you something to drink?" Lee offered. "We've got sun tea or bottled water."

Sandy didn't wait for an answer. She disappeared into the kitchen and returned with the bottled water. Rafe took a long drink, suddenly wishing he'd brought Janie with him. She'd been good with Judy Chaney, praising Derek's art ability. Maybe here she could have been some help, offered a woman's perspective.

"I've got some photos I'd like you to look at." Rafe opened his iPad and quickly went to PhotoFinder. "But first, what size shoe did Brittney wear?"

"Seven," said Sandy, settling down beside him and scrutinizing the iPad screen before Rafe had a chance to scroll to the pictures he wanted them to see. "That's Tommy Skinley," she identified the boy in the first photo. "He sometimes drove Brittney to college, as you'll recall. His little sister was always along, too. Amanda."

"Tommy wouldn't do anything to Brittney," Lee said. "They've known each other forever. He's not an easy kid, but..." Lee's words tapered off.

"Did Brittney own a pair of green tennis shoes, high-tops?"

Sandy made a face. "No."

The shoe they'd found under Derek's bed was a size six, but even Rafe knew that size could depend on brand and width and such.

"Do you mind if I look in her room, at her shoes?"

"Go right ahead." Lee stood, leading Rafe into his oldest daughter's room. It was neat, but untouched since Brittney disappeared. A layer of dust was on the dresser. A math book was open and turned upside-down on a desk in the corner. All Brittney's shoes were lined up on the floor of her closet. She had five pairs, but none of the shoes were missing a mate.

Rafe checked under the bed to be sure: nothing.

"We have a new lead," Rafe shared with the Travises when he joined them in the living room. Sandy still held the dish towel and a plate in her hand. Rafe spoke quickly so he wouldn't give them hope only to have to extinguish it. "A teacher at Adobe Hills Community College read something in a student's art book that might be related to Brittney's disappearance. All I'm doing now is trying to follow a trail. Tommy has been identified as a person of interest. It could be that Tommy knows something and isn't even aware he knows it."

"You questioned him back in December," Lee reminded Rafe.

As one of Brittney's car-pool buddies, Tommy had been interrogated early and often. After all of that, Rafe concluded that Tommy was hiding something but not about her disappearance.

He was hiding his mistress—meth.

The Travises didn't recognize Wesley Clinton, Kyle Easterly or Ramona Turk—the other three students Janie had picked out of CopLink. Rafe wasn't surprised; after all, the three had been Derek's cronies, not Brittney's. They were also older, harder and not even full-time students. Both Wesley and Kyle had already dropped out of the classes they'd been taking. Ramona still attended classes, but she'd been absent this last week.

"What exactly did the instructor come across?" Lee asked.

"I'm not at liberty to say. I personally haven't

seen the art book. It was handed over to the campus police." Rafe wasn't lying; he just didn't want to tell the Travises that they'd found a confession then misplaced it. "I'm just doing some legwork here in Scorpion Ridge to help move things along."

"Is she alive?" Sandy whispered.

On every other visit, Rafe had answered, "I don't know. I'm praying."

This visit… He sat on their worn brown couch, looking at the schoolbooks, deserted shoes and assorted kid projects that made these four walls a home. And the words wouldn't come.

Sandy dropped the dish towel on the floor and ran toward a bedroom at the back of the house, the plate remaining in her grasp. Her soft keen of pain permeated through the walls as she fled.

Then a door slammed, and they heard the plate smash to the ground, shattered like Sandy Travis's world.

CHAPTER SIX

On Saturday, Janie again took care of the animals that were sequestered at Katie's house and then worked in the gift shop at the zoo. It was boring, and Rafe had clearly decided that tailing Janie wasn't his priority. Instead he'd sent Officer Candy Riorden, who loved animals.

"Can I help feed the camels?" was Candy's first question. Followed by: "Can I pet the lion?" She got that wish, but only because Terrance had the personality of a poodle, very few teeth left and not enough energy to work up a good swat.

When Candy left, Chief of Police Jeff Summerside appeared. It only took Janie a few hours to realize that he and Candy were taking turns on guard duty. Chief Summerside was definitely the more serious of the two. He followed Janie, never interfering or getting involved, mostly nodding at what she did but mostly scanning the crowd.

She got the idea crowds made him nervous.

But it bothered her that she felt abandoned by Rafe. She obviously didn't rate very high on his list of priorities.

"Where's the sheriff?" Janie finally asked when Summerside showed up—for the third time that day—just before closing.

"He's with the governor working on some commission to deal with border issues."

For once, Janie felt a little sorry for him. That didn't sound like fun. No wonder he hadn't even managed a text. Cops did, indeed, walk a rigid line.

Sunday wasn't much better. Katie ventured out to the barn Sunday morning as Janie was feeding the turkeys. In a brown shirt and waddling, she looked a bit like a turkey herself.

"Luke took off for Young, Arizona, at two this morning."

"Why?" Janie asked.

"Got a call about some guy who has a black panther as a pet. Guy can't keep him anymore. Luke thinks we can afford him."

Luke thought they could afford elephants and rhinoceroses, too. Until Katie talked him down. That was something she did for both of them. Through Janie's whole life, Katie had been the beacon keeping her sane. There'd been one year, though, when Janie had been alone with Aunt Betsy, and no one had been there to save her.

Closets.

Cigarette smoke.

Not enough food.

"Janie," Katie said. "Did you hear what I just said?"

"No."

"Stop worrying," Katie advised. "You turned the art book over to the police, told them what it said. It's their job now to figure out the truth."

Janie nodded, gazing past Katie to the Santa Catalina mountains, the blue sky and the white clouds. Everything about Scorpion Ridge, Arizona, appeared perfect.

But appearances were deceiving.

Both Candy and Jeff Summerside were again on duty, each popping in at the gift shop every hour or so to check on her.

It annoyed Janie to no end that she looked for Rafe from the moment she left the house. It annoyed her even more that she was disappointed when she didn't find him.

This time when Janie asked, she was informed that "Rafe has the day off."

Janie didn't get the day off. And she certainly didn't get a day off from being scared. Maybe she wouldn't ever stop feeling scared until she was far, far away from here, in South Africa.

She needed to remember that and work harder toward her goal.

On Monday things went back to normal. Janie spent the day working on the bear mural. Crisco didn't seem to mind being her subject and ignored her. The zoo's visitors didn't. They stopped, asked questions, and mostly complimented her work. At noon, the bear exhibit emptied as mothers took their children to the food area. Janie figured she'd have quiet for about thirty minutes—kids didn't waste much time eating when they were at a zoo—but instead a lone man came to lean against the edge of the bear exhibit.

Used to be, Janie wasn't spooked by lone men.

This one looked vaguely familiar, but Rafe wouldn't assign a cop she didn't know. She certainly didn't recognize the man from school; he was just attractive enough that she'd remember him. After a moment, he rolled his shoulders and then made his way to her.

That's when she recognized him.

"You're Derek's brother."

"I am. I wanted to come by and thank you."

"Thank me? For what?" She doubted he wanted to thank her for bringing the art book to light. After all, that art book was a journalist's dream. Once it hit the evening news, the Chaneys would have the media camped in their yard, clogging their telephones and digging for any secrets the Chaneys had, whether they were related to Derek's story or not.

"My mom said you told her Derek was talented. It really meant something to her. She's pretty convinced that everyone will think she was a poor mother. She wasn't. She was a great mother. Derek just..."

"Often the most talented are the most troubled," Janie tried.

"That pretty much sums it up."

Janie glanced around to see if either of her cop watchdogs were nearby. They weren't. She wanted to text Rafe, tell him that Jimmy Chaney was here, but taking out her phone seemed rude.

"Derek loved your class," Jimmy finally said.

"I'm just the lab assistant."

"Yes, but you were someone close to his age who was doing something she loved."

"Did he talk about the class, or about any of his friends and what they were doing?"

"He didn't talk to me about his friends. He knew I didn't care for any of them. He talked about your class and a girl he liked."

"Brittney." Janie nodded, not bothering to correct Jimmy about Brittney being in the class.

"I don't remember the name. The cops asked me about her but I couldn't say much. Neither Derek nor I are talkers."

As if to prove his point, he took out his cell phone and checked the time. "I need to get home. Mom's trying to find out when Derek's body will be released to us so we can bury him."

"I'm sorry."

"Me, too."

He walked away, leaving Janie feeling unsettled.

That evening Janie went to school where an empty chair in her class accused her of not caring enough.

It wasn't just the chair that was empty. All Derek's belongings—his paints, his paintings, his trash—it was all gone.

"The police took it," Patricia said when they had a chance to talk as the students worked. "They came in with a warrant."

"Rafe?"

"No, the other one. Nathan Williamson. It was this morning. He asked if you were around, but I said you'd be here this evening."

"He ask you questions?"

"For over an hour." Patricia spoke softly, not wanting the students to overhear. Even if the students didn't know all the details of what was going on, thanks to the news and campus grapevine, they knew enough to be scared. It made for a silent night, with lots of furtive glances toward the windows, and even the students who usually worked with bright colors were drawn to browns, blacks and grays.

When class finally ended, Janie helped clean up and then headed for the door. Rafe was leaning against the wall, exactly as he had last week. He appeared just as relaxed, just as cocky. She had to fight to keep from smiling. She was glad to see him, but he didn't deserve it.

This time her students didn't make small talk with him. Maybe because another officer, young-looking and clearly nervous, stood next to him.

"You waiting for me?" Janie asked, glancing from one to the other.

"Miss Vincent, we'd appreciate it if you'd come down to the Adobe Hills police station and answer a few questions." The young officer spoke quickly, his words stumbling, as if he had a job to do and no one was going to usurp him, not even a sheriff.

"Finally!" Janie said. "Did you find the art book?"

The young officer didn't look at Rafe and quickly said, "Do you need an escort or shall I—"

"I'll escort her." Rafe took her elbow, nodded to the young officer that he was done, and guided Janie into the dark blue night. There was a slight chill in the air, carrying a faint scent of a nearby creosote bush. But Rafe's hand, still cupping her elbow, provided a warmth that spread through her until she couldn't keep the smile from her face.

The campus was emptying, and Janie didn't mind. Not with Rafe walking by her side. She felt safe again—finally—because Rafe was here. He wasn't just doing his job; he was making the world, her world, a better place. So right now, in this situation, for a while, she could put away her distrust of cops.

Or at least of Rafe.

He kept coming back for her, he was constantly the one who took control and made her feel…well, special, as well as safe. She'd never felt special to a cop. Or anyone, actually, except for Katie.

Once they left the sidewalk and hit the parking lot, they had the added safety of the young officer already trailing them in his squad car.

In the distance came she heard easy laughter and the sound of someone being chased. And enjoying it. Rafe stilled, listening to the noises and gauging how he wanted to react. Suddenly, the laughter seemed to take on a sinister tone, but Rafe didn't so much as twitch.

Had Janie imagined the threat? Or had her involvement in a missing coed case suddenly changed the way she viewed the world?

She certainly hoped that wasn't it.

Once the laughter died, Rafe relaxed.

"Just kids having fun," Janie suggested.

"Yes, something Brittney Travis will never do again."

Was he reminding her of this so she'd do more? Or was he reminding himself so *he'd* do more?

"You'll solve this case."

Rafe raised an eyebrow. "I certainly hope so."

"By the way, you scared that young officer," Janie accused.

Rafe smiled. "Which is why I didn't talk to him while we waited for your class to end. He's been on the force for two weeks and it's the first time he's had to deal with a sheriff."

"I thought the police were one big happy family, working together both on and off duty."

"Who told you that?"

Janie couldn't answer that. She remembered all the times she'd sat in the holding rooms of the police stations in Big Smith, Texas, and listened to the cops as they bantered back and forth.

She'd felt so inconsequential back then, almost invisible, and they'd been a huge, unified force against her. They certainly wouldn't listen to her.

"Be nice to him," she ordered gently.

Rafe looked surprised at her request, but said, "I'm always nice."

Janie didn't bother to respond.

"Okay, I'm not always nice, but sometimes it isn't an option. I've been trying to meet with Nathan since last Wednesday. First he had the accident and the DEA and feds to deal with. But ever since we've been playing phone tag around my commitments and his. We should have been able to connect, somehow."

"Is he avoiding you?"

"No, we're just busy, and the immediate takes precedence over the past. In this case, however, the past seems to be very much alive."

The young cop pulled up beside them, rolled down the window, and said, "I'll see you in ten minutes."

"He may be new," Janie noted, "but he's already good at telling people what to do."

"It comes with the territory." Rafe opened the passenger door and gestured for her to get in.

"Typical cop," Janie said.

"I take it," Rafe responded, sounding oddly subdued, "that's not a compliment."

Before Janie could retract her statement, or even feel guilty about making it, the young officer stopped and called Rafe over.

Janie climbed into Rafe's Jeep and pushed aside the folders left on the passenger seat. Pulling her phone from her purse, she texted Katie her whereabouts and settled in to wait.

When he returned, he was smiling. She waited until he'd started the SUV, exited the college parking lot and merged into traffic before asking, "What's so funny?"

Pointing at the squad car that was already pulling onto the street, Rafe said. "Kid's worried. He hasn't yet told Nathan that I'm along for the ride, nor that you and I seem very comfortable with each other."

"We're not comfortable—"

"Oh, yes, we are. We're on a first-name basis already. In cop-speak, that means you consider me the lead on the case, and Nathan very much considers *himself* the lead. Except

I'm the one who had you look at CopLink for people who had connections to Derek, and I'm the one who found the second art book."

"I'm the one who found it, technically."

"Yes, and Nathan very much wants to be involved in whatever happens next, especially if it's some sort of clue or lead provided by you. Nope, he's not happy that I'm along for his very first face-to-face with you."

"But you're helping him." Janie was amazed. "You're trying to work together. You're the sheriff."

"I'm not *his* sheriff," he reminded her. "So my involvement is starting to annoy him. Still, you gotta admire his backbone. I mean, we have a police escort. Wow."

She'd never understand the male species. Rafe acted somewhat rejuvenated by the situation. All Janie wanted to do was find Nathan Williamson and give him what for. He should have met with her last Thursday, as he'd requested, and asked his questions then. He should have found time to work with Rafe, at a reasonable hour, instead of waiting until now, when she was tired and wanted to go to bed.

Rafe didn't seem to mind the late hour at all.

While they drove, Janie filled him in on Jimmy's visit to the zoo, paused, and then asked, “Do you think there’s more to Detective Williamson’s recent actions than just being busy?”

Rafe surprised her with how fast he answered.

“Brittney’s case is interfering with an ongoing investigation into a local drug ring. In the last year, someone’s been bringing an increasing amount of cocaine into the area from Mexico. We’ve had double the arrests, and the hospitals have reported more drug-related visits. You remember Justin? My undercover friend? He’s afraid that with the recent police pressure to bring down the drug ring, whoever’s behind the operation will relocate. Meaning all his work would be for nothing. Which is why the art book hasn’t been high on Nathan’s list of priorities.”

He continued to speculate for the rest of the drive, mostly about what was inside the art book.

“The kid would have made a good sketch artist,” was Rafe’s final summation after Janie exhausted every detail she’d put to memory.

“A decent writer, too, if he’d been given the time to straighten up. He had me on the edge of my chair even before I realized what I was reading might be true.”

"Too bad you didn't read the last two pages," Rafe said.

There it was, the one thing that had been eating at Janie. Derek had handed in the art book on Wednesday, he'd died three days later on Saturday, and she'd she read his work the following Wednesday.

Four days too late to change the course of fate.

The ending of Derek's old art book, the one they'd found in his room, was the work of regret; he was facing the truth. The pages at the beginning of Derek's new art book, the one he'd given to Janie, was the work of redemption; he was confessing.

She stared out the Jeep's window as they passed through Adobe Hills. It was a typical college town, basically Scorpion Ridge times ten. Adobe Hills had two bowling alleys, two box stores and a water park.

All Scorpion Ridge had was BAA and a couple of resorts.

When they reached the station, Rafe parked his truck next to the car of their police escort. After the last few days, Janie knew he was an open-the-door-for-the-lady kind of guy. He did so now, but before he helped her from the truck, he reached under the seat and pulled out an evidence bag.

"What is that?" Janie asked.

"The art book we found in Derek's room."

This whole time she'd been sitting above the book that read: *I have to tell somebody. I can't live with this. But whomever I tell will be in as much danger as me.*

Without a word, Rafe directed her through the front door. Their escort disappeared almost immediately. The Adobe Hills police station's waiting room was decorated in wanted posters, dirty handprints and aged flooring that had probably seen too many incoming and not enough outgoing. It boasted a somewhat restrained atmosphere of rigid professionalism combined with harsh reality.

Near a desk, an irate woman demanded her son's release. On a chair, head back against the wall, a man who looked drunk snored and drooled. Next to him, completely comfortable and making herself at home, was an overweight woman reading a book. Every once in a while the woman nudged the man upright. In one corner, a group of young men—all sporting tattoos—sulked while impressing each other with loud four-letter words. All except one eyed her in a way that made her wish she had on more clothes, carried pepper spray and was anywhere save here. The one who didn't stare had a completely different emotion in his eyes, an emotion Janie couldn't read, one she wasn't sure how she'd paint.

Her steps slowed.

Rafe didn't seem to notice. He continued on with impressive single-mindedness, opening a door and ushering Janie into a hallway. As the door slammed behind them, the irate woman's voice muted somewhat and soon blended with the behind-the-scenes sounds of a busy police station.

This late on a Monday night, there were few officers present. One officer was on the phone. In a cubicle, another officer spoke to a young couple. The woman was softly crying.

Rafe guided Janie into somebody's office. She'd just sat down when the door opened.

She expected Nathan Williamson; surely this was his office. At the very least, she expected another man in blue. Instead, Janie's mouth went dry the moment an officer delivered one of the sulking kids.

But…why wasn't he handcuffed?

She scooted closer to Rafe. He noticed, smiled and, of all things, gave the tattooed man a back slap.

Tattoo Guy grinned—surprisingly he had all his teeth—and said, "Looks like this case is blowing wide open," he said. "And, you were right, most of it is going down here."

"Glad you could make it. I notice you brought your entourage."

"One of the perks of the job." Mr. Tattoo turned to Janie and held out a hand. His nails were short and dirty. For that matter, so was the sleeve of his shirt.

"I always wear long sleeves," he said. "It hides the needle marks."

Rafe laughed. "Go ahead and shake his hand. He's not contagious, and I know for a fact he faints when confronted with a needle. The tats are fake. This is Justin Robbins, one of the best cops I've ever met. I mentioned him to you earlier."

"I feel like I've been punked," Janie said.

"I feel punked every day," Justin said, "when I look in the mirror."

"Do I need to worry about you blowing his cover?" Rafe asked.

Before Janie had a chance to respond, someone cleared his throat. Loudly. Nathan had entered.

Justin moved aside to let Nathan in.

To Janie's surprise, Rafe motioned her toward one of the chairs and took the other while Justin perched on the edge of a half-size file cabinet. Williamson was beefier, older and grouchier than Rafe, yet in many ways very similar to Rafe. He appeared very unhappy about the crowd in his ultraclean office. Outside of cop paraphernalia—awards, newspaper articles—and one small photo of him and a chubby young woman with a lot of hair, there was nothing in his office to prove the man had a life.

He held out his hand to Rafe. "I hear you have something for me."

Rafe gave him the art book. Williamson walked around them to sit at his desk and then put on a pair of gloves before pulling the book from the evidence bag, flipping it open and skimming a few pages. He started to close it, but then stopped, one finger marking a page, every muscle in his body tensed. White-lipped, he said, "This should have been turned over to my department immediately."

"Read the last page," Rafe suggested, ignoring the other man's assertion.

Nathan's lips stayed pressed together in a thin white line as he read. He uttered a curse word. "Okay, this changes things. I'm glad I asked Justin to stop by in case there's something the two of us…" He paused, looked at Janie, then included her by saying, "…the three of us, can piece together about Derek Chaney."

He'd left Rafe out. How interesting.

Before Janie could decide if she wanted to

stick her tongue out at him or nod, Nathan continued, and it was clear he wasn't happy. "I understand Justin's already spoken with you more than once."

Rafe nodded. "Justin called me the morning the art book disappeared. Then, I called him yesterday with some more questions. He never believed Derek's death was accidental."

Janie glanced at Justin, waiting to be filled in.

"I knew Derek," Justin explained to Janie. She detected a slight tremor in his voice, the briefest glimpse of sorrow. "Kid wasn't as stupid as most. He didn't make meth or sell it, just experimented with it. Didn't use crack, either. I met him three years ago. I was pretending to be a senior in high school, he really was a junior.

"Thanks to Derek," Justin said, "in the last three years, we've put at least two small-time dealers behind bars and confiscated almost a million dollars of marijuana and cocaine. I'm still trying to find the person who is the connection to the cartel. When I find him, the streets will be a bit safer."

"Derek was a narc?" No way could she have missed that.

"No," Justin said. "All I had to do was hang with Derek and I'd find what and who I was looking for. He wasn't as jaded as most. He still trusted people, trusted me."

"Why didn't you try and help him?" For some reason, Janie felt indignant. Maybe because it was easier to feel than guilt. After all, she'd had a kid in her class who'd expressed himself through drawing, a kid who'd maybe been honestly trying to change his wayward life, and she'd not reached out to him. Instead, she'd done everything to avoid him.

Because he wasn't easy to like.

She'd not been easy to like, either. She'd taken to wearing black. She'd been miserable and sullen. Yet, she'd managed to drop a sentence here and there, a plea really, to certain teachers, hoping someone would see past her facade and into the nightmare she was living.

One teacher had seen, and it had been her testimony that had swayed the judge to grant Katie custody.

What if the teacher hadn't cared?

Janie continued, "Why weren't you helping him if he still trusted people? Was it because you didn't want to lose your in with the dealers?"

Justin shook his head, suddenly appearing as the mature professional he was instead of the immature kid he was pretending to be. "I did try to help. I liked Derek. I might have even called him a friend. It was my advice that led him to Adobe Hills Community College, and for six months, I didn't see Derek at all."

"Then what?" Janie queried.

"A few months ago, I run into him at a rave. Next, he shows up at a minor drug deal. Pretty soon, he was back in my scope, and I'm running into him just about everywhere. We turned this kid around for a while, and then someone else dragged him back down. I want to find out who."

CHAPTER SEVEN

RAFE WANTED TO find out who it was, too.

And now it wasn't just because of Brittney, it was because of Janie and how she'd stumbled into a dangerous situation.

Still, Rafe couldn't help but notice the expression on Janie's face: indignant. It amazed him that throughout the whole investigation, she'd started to sympathize more with Derek than with Brittney.

Somehow, Rafe needed to make Brittney more real to Janie.

With that in mind, Rafe guided the conversation back to the missing girl. He asked Justin, "Did you ever run into Brittney Travis at any of those places?"

The other man shook his head. "No. Nathan showed me her photo when she went missing. I came in thinking I'd go through the evidence bag from her case."

Because Brittney had gone missing in Adobe Hills, their police force had jurisdiction. All the evidence from the case was stored here, no matter what Rafe preferred.

"Good idea," Rafe said. "I'd like to take another crack at the evidence bag, too."

"There's not much there." Nathan's words were gruff, clipped. "After I left the school Thursday morning, I came back here, called you and then dug out everything we'd gathered on the Travis case. It was the first time I'd looked at it in over a month. All the evidence was circumstantial."

Rafe understood that. "So there's nothing there to link her to Derek."

"Nothing," Nathan said. "There's one note, written to her, obviously from a boy, asking her out. But the handwriting's not Derek's. Plus, whoever wrote it sounds young and fairly innocent."

"Do you have any new evidence that connects to Derek?"

"Friday morning, I got a call. A meth bust right inside county lines. At the scene, one of my deputies was handcuffing a female when she told her husband, 'Hey, it could be worse. We could be Derek.'"

"Meaning it's better to be busted than dead," Rafe told Janie.

Before she could say anything, the phone

on Nathan's desk rang. He answered it, interrupting their conversation.

Settling back, Rafe crossed his legs and waited for Nathan to finish. He wasn't sure how much attention Janie was paying to the call. She appeared to be studying Justin, who obviously enjoyed her appraisal. Rafe wanted to caution him that Janie was just sizing him up with her artist's eye, and that she didn't really like cops.

Then she turned her attention to Rafe, and not in an appraising way. She gazed at him with the same do-something expression she'd worn earlier. He'd seen that plea often, from victims of crimes, from parents of missing children, and even from his own officers who wanted to do more than the law allowed.

But Rafe was good at his job, and part of being good at his job was understanding when to act and when not to.

Right now, waiting was their only choice. If Nathan got any more agitated, Rafe might sever their tenuous partnership

At thirty-two, Rafe Salazar was the youngest man to earn the title of Laramie County Sheriff. He'd been elected because of how he'd campaigned, what he'd accomplished during his eight years on the force, and yes, because of his last name. When Rafe's father had died in the middle of his term from a heart condition, Rafe was the only one who'd been willing to take the position. Still, his youth was something people talked about. Since winning the election, though, he'd more than won over the people of Scorpion Ridge—most of whom had known him from birth.

It was the neighboring towns that presented more of a challenge. A good four years older than Rafe, Detective Nathan Williamson clearly did not appreciate a much-too-young sheriff, especially one who made his office in the much-too-small neighboring town and who butted in on what Nathan considered to be his turf.

Finally, Nathan hung up the phone. His mood had gone from annoyed to testy. "I spoke to the woman we arrested. She admitted to knowing Derek, but not a Chad or Chris."

"It's as if they are ghosts," Justin said.

"Speaking of people who personally knew Derek," Rafe said, "when were you going to tell me about Justin's connection to Derek?"

"I wasn't going to," Nathan admitted. "I was thinking you'd get to read it in a report stamped SOLVED."

The testiness gone, Nathan suddenly looked tired.

"Anything else you're withholding?" Rafe asked.

"Just how mad I am about drugs in my town and police evidence going missing," Nathan said, unhappily. "I mentioned that I was at a meth bust on Friday. A landlord decided to stop by his rural rental property for a surprise visit. When the tenant took a shot at him, he called us. We found their meth lab. The renters were a man, his girlfriend and their two children, ages one and two. We took both children to the hospital. The one-year-old has respiratory problems."

Rafe felt the burn begin.

Justin said something under his breath before saying, "You'd be talking about the Tanners. I've been to their place. They're small fry. The bust is probably the best thing to happen to them because it might be a wake-up call."

"Their children should be the wake-up call," Nathan snarled. "They're making drugs where their children breathe! I didn't call you back right away, Rafe, because besides the respiratory problems, the one-year-old also had a few broken ribs and a long burn on his arm."

Rafe watched as Janie's eyes teared up. She'd not had much of a childhood, either.

"For the past two days," Nathan said soberly, "those two toddlers were my priority. I just don't understand those people. Family is the most important thing."

Rafe agreed.

"But then again," Nathan continued, "the love of family didn't keep my ex-wife from doing anything and everything she could to secure her next fix."

He seemed to get a hold of himself and refocused on the case. Nathan showed Rafe what his cops had been doing, who'd they'd spoken to and where they'd been. Rafe read the reports on the campus police officers. None had criminal records; all were ex-police. Janie was once again scanning photos and going over her re-creation of Derek's art book to see what she could add, change, delete.

"He'd included the license numbers on the car, but I just can't remember them," she mourned. "I mean, he had so many details."

She'd redrawn the pages three times in fifteen minutes. With each likeness, she grew more and more frustrated. Finally, Rafe held out his hand to help her up from the chair. "You've done enough tonight. Let's get you home. Tomorrow's a new day."

She took her purse from beside Nathan's desk and slowly draped it over her shoulder. They said goodbye to Nathan. Justin had already left with his pretend buddies, all cursing at the top of their lungs about the Adobe Hills Police Department.

As Rafe bid good-night to the desk sergeant and held the door open for Janie, he relaxed a bit. The lobby was silent. "I'm not sure I needed to be a part of all that," Janie said after Rafe escorted her back to his car and after she'd climbed in, took his place behind the wheel.

"It's not how we usually do things," he agreed.

"Then why are you doing it now?"

He hesitated, unsure of what to tell her or if he even should tell her. He figured spouting some empty platitudes would only piss her off.

He gripped the steering wheel a moment, then reached over to put the key in the ignition. Before turning the car on, though, he said, "You're the one who read the art book. You're the one who works at Adobe Hills Community College. You're the one who might recognize some name, some obscure reference, some connection we might miss."

"I'm only at the school a few days a week."

"Yet, you were the one Derek chose to confess to," he reminded her, then finally started the car. "You've made a difference. It's not just me losing sleep over Brittney's disappearance anymore. You've brought her back into Nathan's and Justin's focus."

She stared out the window, silent. He tried to imagine what she was thinking. Probably that she wanted to run screaming from the whole situation.

Then, after a moment, he felt the gentleness of her hand as she reached over to touch his shoulder. She gave him a slight squeeze, letting him know she understood what couldn't be understood.

IT WAS AFTER midnight when Janie finally walked through the door of her cottage. After she picked up her car from the school, Rafe had again followed her all the way home, walked her to her door and checked inside.

"I just need to grab some clothes and then wake up my sister and her husband."

"There's nothing else you want to share with me?"

She shook her head, although it wasn't quite true. She hadn't shared with Rafe that she was battling her attraction to him, even while she disdained his profession.

Though it was hard to keep that disdain after she'd listened to a cop bemoan the plight of two little children. Still, Justin admitted to knowing the couple, knowing what they were doing with two little kids in the house. Why hadn't they taken the kids away months earlier?

But she understood now that cops had to weigh the short-term risk versus the long-term reward. But she didn't have to like it. After walking her to the main house, Rafe seemed to realize that it was time to go. "Lock the door, and if you hear anything suspicious, call me."

His footfalls sounded against the hush as he strode to his car. The cool late-night air stung her cheekbones. Or was it tears at what she didn't want, couldn't have.

As she listened to the departing sound of his engine, the silence of the Arizona night settled around her.

And she felt alone.

Usually she enjoyed being alone, especially in her own space. She appreciated the freedom of it all, being able to do what she wanted when she wanted to do it. And no one could make her do what she didn't want to do.

The commanding Rafael Salazar threatened that. So why was it that the more time she spent with him, the less she wanted him to go away?

With no answers, Janie headed for the shower to wash the grime of the day off her body. Being at a police station still made her feel invaded. Turning the shower to blistering hot, she tried to analyze her attraction to Rafe.

With Adam, the only thing they'd had in common was art. Not enough to build a relationship on.

Rafe, however, was one conversation after another, from dealing with grieving parents to shaking hands with people who had voted for him, to putting a neighboring detective in his place.

She was starting to understand his world. And starting to question her too-little-too-late opinion of cops.

She'd always prided herself on her self-reliance. But now, the fact that she was in more danger than ever before, added a new dimension to everything she held close.

She couldn't simply head for a wall and some paints anymore. There would always be a window—a window that allowed Janie to view her newly endangered world, but also allowing a killer to view Janie.

So, right now, she was thankful that every time Janie looked out the proverbial window, Rafe stood guard.

It didn't take a rocket scientist to figure out Rafe's motivation: he hadn't been able to keep Brittney safe, so he'd for sure keep Janie safe. After all, that was his job.

And she had to remember that's all it was to him, no matter how personally involved he seemed.

JANIE DIDN'T SEE Rafe again until Wednesday. He sat in the back of the classroom where he could see the door, the students and her.

It was strange, having him there. On one hand, it was unsettling because he watched her every movement. She was also aware that he was very human and very male.

About halfway through class, he took a phone call and then left. The students barely noticed. Not so, Janie. She was on full alert until he returned.

The class seemed to take forever, but finally the last brush was cleaned, put away, and the last students exited the classroom.

Rafe joined her at the front of the room and cut straight to it. "We've got a leak somewhere," Rafe started. Then he backtracked, looking a bit annoyed. "That is, Nathan has a leak. The main television station in Phoenix aired one of your re-created drawings on the news tonight. I guarantee the rest will be broadcast soon. Candy says we've been getting calls nonstop. My guess is the Adobe Hills station is getting them too."

His anger simmered just below the surface,

though he somehow managed to keep it in check, barely.

"This could be good," Janie suggested. "One of the calls might give you a new lead."

"Yes, but Nathan was already working with one of the major stations to control what would be released and how. He had a specific hotline number. Now people are calling Scorpion Ridge, Adobe Hills, Tucson, Phoenix, Gesippi. Calls are going everywhere. When calls are this disjointed, this spread out, it leads to mistakes."

"Any idea who leaked the page?"

"Nathan's looking into it. After I make sure you're safely home, I'll—"

"I can see myself home. I promise I won't stop. I'll have my cell phone right next to me with your number showing, and I'll call you the minute I walk through my front door." It didn't make him happy, but he finally agreed.

Not ten minutes after Janie walked through her front door and phoned Rafe, the first police car drove by. Every thirty minutes, all through the night, she was monitored.

At 6:00 a.m., the regular patrol car was replaced by Rafe's SUV and Janie fell into a sound sleep, no longer awakening every half hour.

She was safe.

"YOU MIGHT AS well admit that you miss him."

The problem with sisters, Janie realized, especially a sister who'd taken on the role of both sister and mom, was they saw too much.

"I don't miss him. It's just that the Brittney Travis case has pretty much taken over my life. I can't stop thinking about it."

"That's only natural."

For a moment, Janie hoped she'd succeeded in taking the focus off Rafe, but then...

"What's not natural," Katie continued, "is the way you look over your shoulder, as if expecting someone—"

"Every time I turn around, Rafe is there!"

"Not every time," Katie teased, "and when he's not there, the smile on your face disappears and the light in your eyes dies."

"Oh, pooh," Janie retorted. "You've been reading too many romance novels."

Katie grinned. "That's because the man who puts a smile on my face and the light in my eyes won't let me do much of anything else until this baby is born."

"And that same man—" Luke came up behind her, slipping his arms around her belly and holding both her and their soon-to-be baby in his grasp "—thinks it's time for you to go and put your feet up. I'll keep tabs on Janie."

He ended his request with a gentle kiss to Katie's forehead.

Katie'd gotten lucky. There weren't many men like Luke Rittenhouse around.

Janie could almost believe Rafael Salazar might be one.

Someone she could trust.

If only he wasn't a cop.

CHAPTER EIGHT

THE ART STUDENTS signed in quickly and nervously. They didn't usually have to sign their names to anything, except their paintings. But Detective Nathan Williamson wasn't usually at the front of their class. As they passed, a few whispered to each other and Janie heard disjointed words, phrases, questions.

"Did you see the drawing on TV last night?"

"Scary."

"You think she's dead?"

"Bad news."

Janie was scared, too, and she well understood their discomfort. At one point early this morning—usually her favorite time of day—she'd sat in front of the bear's habitat, a half-finished wall mural waiting in front of her, paintbrush in hand. But she had no idea where to begin, no idea how to continue, and the thought of what to do next terrified her.

Lately, memories of her childhood were tapping her on the shoulder quite often, reminding her that she still owned them. They hadn't gone away as she'd pretended they had.

She was dry, empty. And this time, there was no one to run to. Katie was pregnant. And as for Rafe…

Well, she shouldn't be considering running to Rafe. The trust still wasn't there.

It wasn't even six yet, but her whole class was in place. Instead of standing before their easels, they were sitting still at their desks. Gone were the smells of fresh paint, the sound of brushes dabbing on canvas and the quick intakes of breath as creations developed.

No one complained about the weather or not having enough time to get things done or the price of gas. No one made plans for the weekend. Typically, Amanda's two interpreters would be joking with each other and watching something funny on their iPad. But they were silent, too. Two of her students, who'd quickly become a couple, should be comparing notes by now, debating whether to use watercolor or acrylic. Instead, they were far away from each other.

From the emails they'd sent her, she knew they all were aware of what was going on. Her re-creation of Derek's art book was now both local and national news.

Janie no longer answered her cell without

checking caller ID. She'd had eight people call to hire her as a muralist. Only one was serious. Six had been thrill seekers wanting gruesome details. One had suggested something Janie still blushed about.

The blinds were closed, per Detective Williamson's order. Janie could hear the wind outside. It was the only sound in the room.

The detective stood at the front, a stern, silent, imposing man. He wouldn't recognize a smile if it tapped him on the shoulder. She got the sense he wanted to believe that Derek's art book was a hoax.

Detective Williamson cleared his throat and her students went still. Then, he began. "I'm Detective Nathan Williamson, and I'm investigating the death of Derek Chaney. Because of his participation in this class, we're hoping you can help tie up a few loose ends. We'll be doing interviews with all of you during tonight's class. If you have something to share, don't hesitate."

Janie looked to the back of the room at Rafe. He probably didn't realize that he could almost pass for a student, one sitting perfectly still and paying attention. Except Rafe's attention was on her instead of Nathan.

He didn't glance away when their eyes met.

Something fluttered in her stomach. He was

too powerful, too in control. He was unlike any cop she'd ever met. He didn't shy away from doing what he considered right, and he didn't care what people thought of him. He tried to keep his word.

So far.

Because of him, his commitment to Brittney and to Janie's own safety, she was willing to help. Detective Williamson, however, didn't inspire her at all. He reminded her too much of the cops she'd run into in the past. The ones who believed that a twelve-year-old runaway didn't know what was best for her.

Williamson was nothing like Rafe. The detective was by the book, impersonal. Her students, almost as one, leaned back in their seats as if distancing themselves from the man.

He started by mentioning Derek's death and the concerns surrounding it, and no one seemed surprised. He segued into Brittney's murder and Derek's connections to it, and finished by mentioning Derek's personal art books, including the one Janie and Rafe had found in his bedroom.

Everyone stared at Janie. The media hadn't shared that.

Before he could continue, Janie's youngest student, Amanda Skinley, who was also from

Scorpion Ridge, let out a cry, followed by loud, hiccupping sobs.

Amanda's interpreter stopped signing for a moment and glanced at Williamson before scooting closer to Amanda, signing to her frantically. Janie left her seat and knelt by Amanda, saying to the interpreter, "Tell her it's okay. They'll find who did this."

That only made Amanda cry harder.

A few students started to leave their seats, with whispers of "Can I help?" and "Do you need a tissue?" Finally one of the interpreters escorted Amanda out of the room.

Her best friend in class, Max Carter, shrank into his chair.

Looking at Rafe, it dawned on Janie how closely the threads of a small town were woven. Amanda—and Max, too—would have known Brittney from high school. They were close to the same age, so they probably went to the same church, public pools, movie theater.

Slowly, Janie lowered herself into the seat Amanda had just vacated and she reached over to pat Max on the hand. He didn't look at her, just blushed red.

Her fingers brushed against the blank sheet of paper Detective Williamson had passed out. He was giving the class the option of writing, anonymously, any information they had.

As if the drama had no effect on him, he passed around photos of both Derek and Brittney. He also taped a few to the dry-erase board. Then, he added, "I'd also like your art books so the Adobe Hills Police Department can look at them."

Janie saw aghast expressions on some of her students' faces. For many, the art books were as private as diaries. Others obediently gave in their art books with no qualms at the thought of starting anew.

"Where's Patricia?" a student asked. The older woman had taken this same class a dozen times, each taught by Professor Reynolds, and was clearly agitated by the idea of parting with her art book.

"She's at the station going through some pictures," Nathan said. "She's doing all she can to help us find whoever killed Derek." The admission caused most of the holdouts to retrieve their books and hand them over. Then Rafe made his way to the front of the room.

With just a few words, he owned the room.

"Many of you know me as Sheriff Salazar. I'm the one you hear on television talking about what we're doing to strengthen our borders, or talking about the pitfalls of drunk driving. You probably read about me in the paper, especially in regards to our battle with drugs."

He ran a hand through his black hair, mussing it slightly. It made him appear older, worried, sincere.

When Williamson did the exact same thing, it just made him seem older.

"When people ask me why I want to be sheriff," Rafe said, "I tell them the truth. I want to make my corner of the world a better place, a safer place. I do that by battling everything I just mentioned—borders, drugs, drunk drivers."

He gazed across the classroom, and Janie got the sense he was seeing beneath the students' appearances. Instead of an older man whose fingers shook from all the medications he was on, he saw a Vietnam serviceman who missed his late wife and his comrades, and who took art at a community college as a way to keep living. Instead of a woman who'd already had her cell phone out twice and who'd dropped both her purse and her notebook on the floor, he saw a single mother who'd left her children with a new babysitter and who'd only gotten five hours of sleep the night before.

She was aware of all of this because being a teaching assistant had its perks. She wasn't in charge of their grades or the classroom curriculum, so sometimes they confided more to her than they would with the real teacher. They viewed her as a peer.

Rafe continued. "Brittney Travis is the first young person to go missing since I took my oath as sheriff. This class and that art book of Derek's is the first break we've had in months. I want to establish open communication with all of you, and I want to eliminate, as much as possible, any false leads. With your help, I can do that. Please do as Detective Williamson has asked. While you're writing down information, he and I will be calling you into the next classroom one by one to speak to us privately. As this is going on, I ask that you not talk to one another so I hear what's on your mind first, before anyone else has had a chance to comment."

With a few more words, Rafe made Derek almost seem a victim; he made Brittney seem a saint. He didn't mention that Janie might now be in danger, as well.

When he finished, he leaned against her desk, managing to appear both in charge and approachable. Not an easy balance.

Amanda had returned and was now sitting in the back. She had calmed down and was quickly writing. Her interpreter was doing the same. Janie wished she could get a peek at what they were working on. Amanda, who had known Brittney and Derek both, might actually have a lead. The only other person in the art class who might have something to add was Max Carter.

Tall, shy Max wasn't writing a word. He mostly glanced at what the others were doing, a bewildered expression on his face. Janie watched as Rafe did one last sweep of the classroom, his gaze lingering on Amanda and Max.

In alphabetical order, student by student, he and Nathan pulled them out of Janie's class and into a room across the way where a table and chair waited. They'd cull any memory the students had of Derek or Brittney, no matter how minute.

The room felt somewhat empty, and a little eerie, without Rafe's presence.

She watched as the different personalities dealt with the assigned task. Most were more than a little hesitant, some determined, but a few seemed angry.

She didn't blame them. They were remembering Derek. How he got too close to them when he wanted to argue about comments on his art. How he interrupted them and even cursed. Petty things, somewhat typical of a young man his age, but for some reason, a degree more sinister.

The first student returned, packed her bags and left. Rafe was right behind her, already calling the name of another student. Then Detective Williamson did the same.

Eventually, Rafe and Detective Williamson neared the end of the alphabet. The handful of students remaining were getting antsier by the minute. Janie hoped none of them had to go through the hours of questions that she had this last week. Some were single mothers, others just kids. The rest were people who worked hard during the day and used this class as an outlet, a way to escape.

Janie was in a situation she couldn't escape.

She gazed down at the blank piece of paper in front of her. Last week, she'd re-created Derek's art book pages, but surely there was something else she could do.

Closing her eyes, Janie tried to remember the drawing of the car—it was an older model, four-door. For the last week, she'd been focused on the tiny jagged lines that had made up the license plate numbers, as well as on the words, those life-changing, life-ending words. She had to accept that she wasn't suddenly going to rearrange her memory and figure out the numbers or change the ending to the story.

So instead she pictured the tiny drawings of the car's passengers. She didn't need to draw Derek or Brittney; everyone was very familiar with what they looked like as well as where they were in the vehicle.

The front passenger driver…that's where she'd start.

The white piece of paper in front of her was clean, pristine, and she picked up Amanda's stubby pencil. Derek's drawing had given her a side view of the passenger. He'd sketched a head of spiky hair behind the closed window—it couldn't be rolled down, she remembered from what she'd read.

She drew the figure, bigger than the original, remembering the way his nose had been shaped, how he'd had straight hair that flopped over his forehead and was long in back. Derek's sketch had been in black and white, so she wasn't sure of the color, but her gut instinct said black.

Somebody set a sharpened pencil next to her. She took it without hesitation.

The passenger had had the barest hint of whiskers on his chin, a chin that had been more pointed than round. He'd fit solidly in the window, not overly tall or overly short. His shoulders had been of a size that suggested strength, not bulk.

"You're good," someone whispered in her ear.

Janie turned to find Rafe kneeling beside her, his eyes on her drawing and a look of appreciation on his face.

She wanted that look to be aimed at her instead of the drawing.

"I'm glad he was wearing a T-shirt instead of a jacket or a hoodie. A simple T-shirt lets me pinpoint his size."

"I'm done with my interviews and all your students have left. You were so involved I didn't want to disturb you. Wow. I had no idea you could do something so precise. We enlarged the drawings you made that first morning, but they weren't as sharp as this. Can you draw the driver?"

"No, in all of Derek's sketches, the driver always appeared next to the passenger, so the passenger blocked the view of him."

"Suggesting that Derek was more scared of the driver."

Detective Williamson joined them, appearing just as he had at the start of class: angry and annoyed. He glanced down at the recreation and frowned.

"Recognize him?" Rafe asked.

Williamson shook his head. "He looks like a million other kids."

One sentence took her all the way back. She'd been a twelve-year-old runaway with a story the cops didn't have time to hear. After all, they'd heard it from a million other kids.

She'd like to believe that Rafe was different.

But she was already very aware of how many directions he was pulled in, of his full calendar that he'd compromised because of Brittney, because of Janie. How long until he had to switch his priorities?

"I was about to ask Janie what happened in class while we were busy interrogating," Rafe said. If he sensed the effect of Detective Williamson's words on her, he didn't let on. "Anything surprising happen while we were out of the classroom?"

"Like someone disappearing?"

Rafe shook his head. "Like someone acting out of character."

"Just Amanda, and you were here for that. May I go now?" Janie took a step toward the door.

"Wait a minute, Miss Vincent." Detective Williamson blocked her way. He shot Rafe a glare that clearly read "Back off."

Behind her, Rafe tensed.

"There a problem, Nathan?" he asked.

Janie's cheeks grew warm. Rafe—no, she had to think of him as Sheriff Salazar—was acting like her protector.

But her earlier gushy feelings about him were gone, thanks to the reminder of her past. She could take care of herself, thank you very much. "Do I need someone on my side, like a lawyer, detective?"

"Maybe you do," Detective Williamson said. "You said you didn't know Brittney Travis."

"I didn't."

"Well, three of your students wrote about seeing the two of you together."

"What?" Janie was so surprised, her knees almost gave out. "They're wrong."

"No, they're not. I verified the connection."

Detective Williamson pulled a piece of paper from a folder. Janie squinted at it.

"A copy of an appointment calendar from the tutoring center?"

Detective Williamson nodded. "And according to this, you met with Brittney Travis quite a few times."

CHAPTER NINE

IT WAS AFTER midnight when Janie let herself into her cottage. She hurried to the front window, waving at the sheriff to say she was safe, and then watching as the rear lights of his vehicle grew dimmer and dimmer before disappearing.

He'd wanted to come in, stay awhile, make sure she was okay.

But one way or another, all her life, she'd been trying to find that elusive "safe." For a while, she'd believed she'd had it here, in Scorpion Ridge, with her sister.

She didn't believe that any longer. And, once again, it was because of her experience with the police. It had taken Rafe, Janie and the supervisor from the tutoring center a good hour to convince Detective Nathan Williamson that Janie'd helped an average of ten students a day, and that average doubled during midterms or at the end of a semester.

Janie only remembered the students she tutored if there was something about them that stood out. The kids who came, asked questions, listened and then went away weren't so easy to remember. There were too many of them, marching in a line, always one to take the place of the one before.

Janie let the curtain fall from her hand. One light blazed from the living-room lamp, but suddenly one wasn't enough. Janie went through the whole house and turned on every light.

Then she changed from her school clothes—blue dress pants, white blouse, blue-and-white smock, for once not covered with paint—into pajamas. She was an oversize-T-shirt-baggy-shorts kind of sleeper.

Though tonight she wouldn't sleep at all. It wasn't even worth trying, so Janie headed for the kitchen, poured herself a glass of tea, and sat at her round table with a sketchbook open to a blank page. She spread out colored pencils in front of her, all newly sharpened.

She'd already re-created Derek's art book twice.

Tonight she wanted to do something else: the actual crime scene. Derek hadn't drawn it. Maybe he hadn't been able to.

Since the age of ten, there'd barely been a day when Janie hadn't drawn something, be it places, things or an animal. The one thing she'd never drawn was people.

If she drew an individual, she wanted to make them physically flawed, like she was. Not much of an audience for scarred beauty. And she never drew a family because she didn't believe in them.

Family let you down, fathers gave you away, aunts ignored or punished you. Drawing a happy family would only make Janie mourn something she could never change.

And Janie wondered if maybe that's why Derek hadn't been able to draw the crime scene.

Picking up a black pencil, she sketched a side of the road. She knew it was rural because Derek had spoken about hating nature. So she added trees, thinking about the few rural areas she'd explored just outside Scorpion Ridge.

Using her pointer finger, she smudged the background and then added a bit of gray. It was night; he'd mentioned the darkness. And it was December. What would rural December in Arizona look like? No leaves.

She drew the car far enough off the road so that anyone driving by wouldn't notice it. She put Derek near the car, hovering, staring down. She put Chris a few feet from Derek, looking away from the road and toward the trees. Chad she placed in the thick of the trees. He held a gun, pointed at the ground.

In front of him, Brittney lay sprawled on her stomach, shot in the back.

Derek had mentioned blood. There must have been a full moon, maybe. That would have allowed Derek to see all the details. She'd have to check.

Finished, she examined her work. Suddenly, every light in the house wasn't enough. "Oh, my," she whispered. She should never have undertaken this endeavor alone. What she had in front of her was the most frightening thing she'd ever created. Yet she knew her work was good. So good that she needed to do more.

From the moment she'd accepted that Derek's sketches had been fact and not fiction, she'd realized she was involved in something she couldn't control—something that would make her put all her other endeavors, like painting, on hold.

After studying Brittney's picture, meeting Derek's parents and hearing about the two toddlers at the meth lab, she didn't just want to draw bears swimming in a lake. She wanted to understand Brittney, get into Derek's mind, walk where he walked, see what he'd seen so she could end this nightmare.

Painting animals no longer worked as a

means of escape. She'd have to find another refuge.

Rafe could yank her anywhere he pleased if it would help solve the case.

She went and got her laptop, setting it up at the kitchen table. She taped her drawing to the wall so she could stare at it while she wrote.

She started re-creating the words in Derek's art book, her fingers erratically dancing across the keys. With the computer, she could cut and paste, play with words, and even choose a font that resembled Derek's original handwriting.

Away from Detective Williamson's pain, Justin Robbins's grief and Rafe's eagerness, she could take her time. After a while, she started to write with her eyes closed, trying to picture Derek's dark handwriting, imagine how tightly he'd held the pencil, attempting to feel the texture of the art book—a book that had just one week ago belonged to a living, breathing boy.

She could almost taste his fear.

Derek had done a good job of creating tension in just a few pages. That he'd died making poor choices and in poor company only made Janie even more angry.

He could have made a difference!

In her mind's eye, she could see the beseeching look Brittney had aimed at Derek and feel the suffocating fear in the air. She could hear the crunch of their boots breaking through the brittle grass and the deafening sound of the bullet.

She could smell the metallic copperness of Brittney's blood as it stained the dirt black.

After an hour, she was done, both literally and figuratively.

This morning, in the predawn hour—still dark and spooky—Derek's words settled around Janie like a blanket forcing her to accept the desperate truth.

She'd witnessed a murder through the words of one of her students.

Janie hit the save button on her computer and headed for bed. She didn't expect to sleep, but she did—the dark, unnatural sleep of someone who wanted to hide from the world and wasn't quite succeeding. No matter where she hid, the killer found her.

When someone started pounding on her door, it blended into her dream. Only it sounded like howling, like Yoda the wolf dog. It wasn't until the pounding increased in volume that she awoke. Janie slid from her bed, threw on a robe and headed for the door.

"You should fix your doorbell," Rafe said.

"You should get a life," Janie muttered.

The expression on his face didn't change,

and Janie regretted her words. Rafe wasn't looking too hot. Dark stubble peppered his chin. His hair, in need of a haircut, was today decidedly spiky—as if he'd run his fingers through it so often it had taken a different shape. But it was the dark circles under his weary eyes that changed Janie's mind about what to do and say next.

"What do you need from me, Rafe?"

"I'm heading over to see Brittney Travis's parents this morning. I was thinking it might be a good idea to have you along. You did a great job of connecting with Derek's parents. Maybe you can do the same with the Travises. They'll let you in her room. Maybe you can go through her things and identify anything that might connect her to Derek or—"

"I'll go. When?"

"Now."

"Rafe, I just woke up. I'm hungry. I'm a mess. I—"

"Well, I didn't sleep at all. But I'll feed you first. And, by the way, if what I'm staring at is what you consider a mess, then I'm a firm believer in mess." Something in his expression changed, softened, pulling at her and making her want something she reminded herself was totally wrong for her.

Especially when he added, "You look perfect."

"The Travises already think I'm coming," Janie guessed.

"They don't care about your appearance," Rafe said. "They're willing to do anything for just the chance you'll connect a dot, see a T that isn't crossed. You'd be surprised at how much a stranger can glean from a room. And you're a master of observation," Rafe added.

"What?"

"If I handed you colored pencils and paper, could you draw my office?" Rafe asked.

"As if that would be hard. I'd only have to draw fish photographs followed by football and baseball stuff. And then that decrepit Bible that's on your desk."

"Which do I have more of, football or baseball?"

"Baseball."

"You're right, baseball. And that 'decrepit Bible'," he said slowly, "belonged to my grandfather, then my dad and now me. *Decrepit* is not the word I would use to describe it."

It was a treasure, an honored treasure, handed down through generations, something Janie didn't have. "I take back the term *decrepit,*" she offered.

That got her a smile, followed by another

question. "How about Nathan Williamson's office? Could you draw that?"

"It would only take me two minutes. There's really nothing there." What she didn't say was that his office was almost as barren as her cottage. At least he had one photograph.

"Instead, why don't you take two minutes, get dressed and we'll stop at the Corner Diner before going to Brittney's."

"And let your mother see us together?" Janie's stomach gurgled. She wasn't sure it was from the thought of dealing with Rafe's mother or from hunger.

"I wondered if you knew she was my mother." Rafe followed Janie into the living room.

"How could I not know? She showed me your picture the first time she waited on me. The second time she showed me a few more pictures and told me you were single. On my third visit, she ran down your list of accomplishments. And on the fourth—"

Rafe held up his hand. "I got the same treatment about you, sans the photos."

Not wanting to explore that further, Janie hurried to her bedroom, wondering what Rafe would notice about *her* space.

Her paintings were everywhere, most stacked against the wall with only a few of her personal favorites hanging. As for family photos, there were two. One from when Janie was very young and the whole family had posed. In it, baby Janie, her eyes unfocused, stared at the world from her mother's lap.

The other was her high-school graduation photo. It depicted Janie decked out in a blue robe, cornered hat and tassel, holding a diploma in the air. Katie stood next to her, all smiles because she'd been the one to raise Janie, the one to make sure this step in life had been taken.

Janie needn't have worried about Rafe's opinion; he wasn't interested in her decor. After she dressed, she found him at her kitchen table, leaning forward and studying her drawing of Brittney's murder.

"You think Derek was by the car, turned away?"

"I do," Janie said, "but it might be because I knew him. And because he said he didn't approve of what was going on. Didn't have the stomach for it."

"I'd put them farther in the woods, away from the street."

"But they were scared and wanted it over with."

"Is she still there?" Rafe asked softly.

"I'd say yes," Janie said, "and I believe they

buried her deep because they didn't want her found. They proved that when they got rid of Derek."

"You made them all look young," Rafe noted.

Janie stared at her drawing. She'd been so purposeful in representing their feature, but she'd not consciously realized she'd pinpointed their ages.

"You think they're all students, don't you?"

PANCAKES HAD NEVER smelled so delicious, and Rafe's mother outdid herself in the charm department. If Rafe hadn't been so tired, he might have protested more.

"That's my boy," she told two of her regular customers. "He's got good taste, and I'm not talking about his choice of restaurants."

"Mom, don't get any ideas," Rafe ordered as he guided Janie to a booth. "We're working on something."

His mother nodded. "The Travis case, yes. I'll get the usual for both of you."

"Where's the other waitress?" he asked. Usually, there were two waitresses handling the floor.

"She called in this morning. Doesn't feel well. Don't worry. I've got everything under control."

Before Rafe could say anything else, an older man slid in beside him. "Glad to hear something's happening with Brittney's case. Got anything to report?"

"Now, Bob, you know I can't share anything with you right now. What I can do, though, is introduce you to Janie Vincent. Janie, meet Bob Hossnell. He spends his day pretending to be a lawyer. Secretly, he wants my job."

Rafe could read a facial expression; Janie wasn't any fonder of lawyers than she was of cops.

"Nope, you can have your job," Bob said, after shaking Janie's hand. "Unlike you, I don't get calls in the middle of the night too often. The wife appreciates that."

For some reason, Bob was gazing at Janie and smiling. Janie looked relieved when Rafe's mother arrived, delivering two glasses of orange juice. Rafe waited until she left before asking Bob, "Has the name Derek Chaney ever appeared on our court docket?"

"Not that I recall. He's not from Scorpion Ridge. I'll do some checking, though."

Rafe took a small sip of juice before asking, "So, Bob, Tommy Skinley still working for your brother's construction company?"

Now Rafe had Janie's attention. She sat up straight, fully engaged. Rafe was getting the idea that while she wasn't exactly comfortable around cops, she was starting to be more comfortable as part of their world.

Strange, but he wished she was more comfortable because of him, because of how he made her feel. He wished it had nothing to do with this case and everything to do with her desire to be with him.

"TOMMY'S BEEN WITH them almost two months now," Bob said.

Janie made a mental note to ask Katie if she knew Tommy. Amanda, Tommy's sister, was a regular at BAA, especially since Katie signed. The teenager regularly volunteered at fund-raisers and such.

Janie didn't remember ever seeing her brother, though. Or even hearing about one.

"He a good worker?" Rafe asked.

"His probation officer reports that Tommy shows up to work about five to ten minutes late every day, he's usually hungover, and he leaves the moment his shift is done. My brother's a bit more careful in what he says to me because he's aware that Tommy will go to jail if he gets in trouble again. So, tell me, why do you ask?"

Apparently, Rafe hadn't slipped the question in as slyly as Janie had thought. "His little sister goes to Adobe Hills Community College and was friends with Brittney Travis. I'm wondering how well Tommy Skinley knew Brittney."

"If Brittney's parents had any say, not too well," Bob guessed. "Tommy's a bit older than Brittney, who was the same age as Amanda."

Rafe's mother showed up with two plates, and Bob, somewhat reluctantly, excused himself.

After taking a few bites, Rafe said, "A few days ago, we got lucky at Derek's. Usually it's like looking for a needle in a haystack." He looked Janie full in the face. "We got lucky because of you."

"You'd have found the art book eventually."

"But it would have taken more time. You sped things up. And, I was thinking of the shoe, not the book."

Rafe finished his last pancake before Janie had managed one. He ate without glancing at his food—his entire attention was on Janie.

If Janie were to describe Rafe, she would use the word *driven*. Driven to solve the case of Brittney's disappearance, that is.

She was starting to wonder what kind of man he'd be without the badge. Or did he ever put it down?

He checked his watch. Janie put down her fork, appetite gone.

"Where do the Travises live?"

"About five minutes from here. Right behind the high school."

Which was right across from the police station. Janie just knew there'd be a side trip and probably more mug shots to pore over. She'd already looked at hundreds of Chads and Chrises. One thing was for sure, those names were ruined for her. She'd never meet a new Chad or a new Chris and not consider him a suspect.

She stood. "What time, exactly, are the Travises expecting us?"

"Twenty minutes ago," Rafe admitted.

Before he could stand, his cell rang. "I expect that's Mr. Travis. They… Well, they're really hoping you can find something that will help." He quickly answered the phone. "Salazar."

Janie sat down again. She'd be walking into a room to face two people—terrified parents—desperately hoping she could make a difference, when in all likelihood, she'd accomplish nothing. There was no body, so they had to be hoping that somewhere, somehow, Brittney was alive. Since there was no reason for Janie to lie, they had to be terrified she'd read the truth in Derek's book.

She considered the drawing she'd left in her

kitchen. For the first time, she'd created something she didn't want the world to see, didn't want Brittney's parents to see.

"You're kidding." Rafe was half-turned from the table. His whole body had gone rigid. He clutched his phone as if it were a weapon.

Janie had to remind herself to breathe.

"Janie's here with me," Rafe said. "We're at the Corner Diner." He stopped talking and listened, then snapped. "Please say you're kidding."

Finally, Rafe glanced up from his phone and noticed her eyes were on him. Janie had to admire his grit. He didn't even seem flustered. Finally, he ended the call with a terse, "I'll get back to you."

"Who was that?" Janie asked. "Not the Travises?"

"It was Nathan. The call was about your boss, Patricia Reynolds. They found her body about an hour ago."

CHAPTER TEN

THE SECOND FLOOR of Adobe Hills Community College housed many of the faculty's offices. Right now the whole floor was in panic mode. As Rafe and Janie arrived, the dean of students and a police officer stood guard at the door to the elevator, ever so careful not to cross the cordon tape.

"Everyone knew she was allergic to nuts," was all the dean had a chance to say to Rafe before his cell phone rang. The police officer had both Rafe and Janie sign their names in his notebook.

Rafe pointed Janie to a chair in an empty student waiting area off to the side which had already been set up as a command post. She continued to amaze him. Tears shimmered in her eyes but she didn't let them fall. She clenched her fingers, and he knew she wanted to hit something or scream at the injustice of it all, but instead she stayed calm, intent on helping, on making a difference.

On their way to the school, he'd called the

Travises to say he and Janie wouldn't make it over, and as he talked, Janie had been checking her calendar to find time to go there, even if she went by herself.

Not that he'd let her.

He didn't even like leaving her alone now. But at the moment, Patricia Reynolds was his priority.

He ducked under the tape, heading down the hall to Patricia's office. Thanks to Janie, Rafe probably knew as much, if not more, about Patricia Reynolds than Nathan. On the drive over, she'd chattered—as people in shock are prone to do—almost nonstop about her boss.

She'd told him Patricia's real age, how long she'd been chair and that *beloved* didn't begin to describe how her students viewed her. She was also severely allergic to nuts and she'd made everyone aware of that.

Including, it seemed, the person who'd left her a plate of brownies.

Rafe didn't even attempt to enter Patricia's office. He rattled off the most important questions to the officer at the door, and then glanced in and groaned. As far as crime scenes went, this one was a nightmare. Usually the floor offered the most in way of evidence. But he couldn't even see Patricia's floor. Books, canvasses, boxes of supplies—some open, some not—and other paraphernalia took up all the space except for a narrow walkway to her desk.

And that's where he found Patricia, slumped back in her chair.

Rafe took in every detail, from the position of her office window to the type of light on the ceiling. He'd just started examining the pictures on her wall—mostly abstract art but a few personal photos—when Nathan appeared.

"You're not part of the immediate investigation, Rafe," Nathan said.

"You're stuck with me. I didn't enter, didn't disturb anything, and I have Janie with me."

"Good, I want to talk with her."

Nathan looked like a man on a mission. Rafe had seen other cops take cases too personally—himself included. Nathan was doing that now. He was so tightly wound that those around him gave him a wide berth. Rafe had watched the man bring suspects to their knees, but even then he'd never displayed this much intense determination.

"So, what do you think happened?"

Nathan's gaze moved from Patricia's office to down the hall, where the dean of students again was on the phone, to the other end of the hall where yet another officer blocked an entranceway. "I think this killer is in some way connected to the college and to the police."

"Then you've got your work cut out for you," Rafe said. "I've got a few people to question, so I'll get out of your way. You've got this under control. We'll meet later when the medical examiner arrives. I want to hear what he has to say."

"I'll keep you informed."

Rafe walked down the hallway, noting the office doors on each side and their corresponding nameplates. Most of the faculty had personalized their doors in some way, such as taping up cartoons, kids' pictures, news articles about the state of education in Arizona, etc. Soon, Nathan's officers would open every one of these offices, search them, and question the occupant.

He ducked under the tape again, nodded to the officer and the dean, and sat down in a chair next to Janie. He angled his chair so he could see past the elevator.

"Did they say when she died?" Janie whispered.

"Why are we whispering?" Rafe whispered back. He couldn't talk to her about the crime scene, not while he could be overheard, anyway.

She narrowed her eyes.

Rafe simply whispered louder. "The medical examiner hasn't arrived yet to give an estimated time of death, and I've learned to never guess."

"If I were a cop," Janie said at her normal volume, "I'd always be trying to guess."

"It's only on television that a time of death is given as a fact," Rafe said. "In real life, it's a guess, nothing more." And he didn't want guesses, he wanted facts.

But Janie was pale and tired, so Rafe was willing to cut her a little slack. "I'll tell you as soon as I find out."

The chairs in the students' waiting area were as uncomfortable as the chairs in his police station's waiting room. Rafe shifted his weight, trying to get comfortable and forcing himself to remain seated. He was a guest on this case. He had to let Nathan take the lead.

Students came and went, all pressing against the cordon tape that blocked the double doors to the art department. Some were clueless about what had happened, but most wanted to find out what was going on. Many were in tears. An officer dutifully copied down each and every name. Rafe didn't envy Nathan having to run down so many long-shot leads. But if Patricia's death was deemed a homicide—and there wasn't an officer involved, including Rafe, who believed it was an accident—murderers too often came back to the scene.

At the moment, Nathan was busy questioning Georgia Stratton, the liberal arts division secretary. He'd not invited Rafe to join in. That turf thing again. Of course, it might have to do with numbers: two's company; three's a crowd.

Rafe shifted on his chair again, reminding himself that the more he pushed Nathan to work with him, the less chance he had of getting any cooperation.

It wasn't easy. From his vantage point, he could see Georgia through the glass windows of the private office. She looked about ready to faint, not good for a woman of her age. She'd been here when Rafe was a student.

"You on a first-name basis with Georgia?" he asked Janie.

"I go to her whenever I need supplies, or have a question. We get along fine. I gave her one of my paintings."

He noticed the painting then. An acrylic of a lion, standing still, chin raised and mouth open. Behind him was the pride. They all faced the main lion.

"Georgia has all the answers," Janie supplied, as if she sensed what Rafe was thinking. "Everyone comes to her. One day I was waiting my turn to ask her a question, and I decided she needed a painting."

"You painted it from your imagination."

"No, I used Terrance the Terrible at the zoo as a model, and then just painted him fat, skinny, squatty, regal, young, old."

Rafe was amazed. "One lion over and over."

"From different angles, at different times of the day."

"Amazing."

Even more amazing than her talent was the lady herself. Rafe forced himself to look away from her because all he could think was about the last line in that art book.

...whomever I tell will be in as much danger as me.

The kid had been right.

The brownies had been left in Patricia's office, on a paper plate covered with a paper towel. Georgia insisted that she hadn't brought in brownies yesterday, and that whenever she did bake brownies, she never added nuts.

But they'd been left on a plate from the teacher's workroom. A note with the word ENJOY had been left beside them. The letters didn't resemble Gloria's handwriting.

However, even though everyone, including Nathan, believed Gloria innocent, he continued to ask her question after question.

Finally standing up, Rafe excused himself and walked to the end of the hall, away from the noise. He pulled out his phone and dialed.

"I was expecting your call," Justin answered without a hello. He wasted no time. "So, who discovered Patty's body and exactly when?"

"The division secretary found her this morning. She got here about six and noticed her boss's car in the parking lot. After she did her morning routine, she went down and knocked on Patricia's door. When she got no response, she got curious, unlocked Mrs. Reynolds's office door and found her."

"This case is taking on a life of its own," Justin muttered. "A couple of kids Derek hung out with have suddenly had a change of life-style."

"What do you mean?"

"They've either left town or gone home to live with their parents. And they're the same ones Janie picked out as Derek's friends. I've kept track of them. Right now his old crowd, well, it's a different kind of scared. They're itchy."

Rafe could tell by Justin's voice how disturbed he was.

"It's as if," Justin said, "the carpet is being rolled up, and some kids had the brains to get off the carpet while others got trapped inside.

We need to figure out who's controlling the carpet."

It was a pretty decent analogy, even if it wouldn't stand up in court.

"Then why isn't Nathan willing to let me assist? He's always been one to appreciate help."

"I'm not sure," Justin admitted. "But I suspect he feels he wants to redeem himself. There's also the time element. Once this latest death hits the airways, everyone we're investigating will disappear into the night. That's why we're taking it slow. I'm following Nathan's lead, but he's frustrated. And, I've never seen him quite like this."

"I've never seen *you* quite like this," Rafe pointed out.

"I knew Derek personally," Justin said, slowly. "I wish Nathan had, too. Maybe then he'd have believed Derek's death was murder from moment one, and he'd be doing things a bit differently."

"Why?"

Justin cleared his throat but didn't answer, struggling with his grief.

"Why? Why would he do things differently?" Rafe asked again.

"I've been undercover now for over five years," Justin finally said. "In that time, I've had three kids die. One OD'd, and let's just say the other didn't fulfill an obligation. Then there's Derek. None of them were yet twenty-five. Their deaths made the streets safer and my job easier. I went to their funerals. I understood why they'd died and I didn't worry about blowing my cover by attending their funeral."

"You did all you could, and—"

"See," Justin continued, not waiting to hear Rafe's platitudes, "there's a few things I haven't shared with you. Things that I only reported to Nathan because we don't want to blow my cover if we don't have to. You should know, though, that I was at that farm an hour before it exploded. They'd finished making the batch for the day. They'd cleaned up."

"Who cleaned up?"

Justin named a few names that meant nothing to Rafe.

Justin continued, "After they cleaned up, a couple of the guys went smurfing for materials for the next batch, but there were no plans to head back to the house that night. We all knew it would be awhile. See, it was no longer safe for the boys to simply walk into a nearby store and buy the stuff. They'd been in there buying supplies already that week. They couldn't afford to be recognized trying again. They had to find a third party, someone who hadn't bought the supplies in the area before.

So Derek and I headed to a burger place, ate, and then went our separate ways. We were supposed to meet at a party later that night. Derek didn't show."

"Because he'd died in the explosion."

"Right," Justin said bitterly. "But there was no reason for him to return to the house, none. There were no plans to start the next batch, and Derek wasn't the cook anyway. The kid could barely make a grilled ham-and-cheese sandwich. So he must have been lured back or forced back and then…"

Before Justin even said the words, Rafe knew what they would be. Justin had uttered them once before, clandestinely, just two days ago, over the phone.

"…he was murdered."

No doubt about it. Now that Patricia had been killed, Derek's untimely demise would receive a bit more attention.

And so would Janie.

"So," Rafe said, "theoretically, you were the last person to see Derek alive."

"Except for whoever murdered him."

Rafe hadn't put any thought into Justin being the last, besides the killer, to talk with Derek. It added a new angle. "What did the guys who went to buy more supplies say about Derek's death?"

"It's amazing how much kids can talk and still say nothing," Justin said. "I can tell you they never made it back to the farm. They'd found a guy to do the buying, but when they got to the store, he chickened out. By then, it was getting late. The store would be less crowded, and they were afraid somebody would notice how often they came in, so they went home."

"What else?"

"They said Derek never cooked up any meth. But they're not going to talk to the police. Most are just glad they weren't in the house when Derek bought it. The rest simply hope whoever came after Derek doesn't come after them."

"None of them have any idea who killed Derek?"

"If they did, I'd be the happiest man in Adobe Hills. Then I'd either have the connection to the cartel, or at least someone who reports directly to him. When this case finally breaks, I can start an investigation, testify and go back to being a street cop."

Frustration edged his every word. In order to get the kingpin, Justin had to wait. But the longer he waited, the bigger the drug ring grew, like a flood, swallowing Adobe Hills Community College first and then lapping against Adobe Hills High School and Middle School.

"Are any of the kids you're talking about in Janie's class?"

"No. I have a list of names I've given Nathan. I'll email you them tonight and put an asterisk around the ones I believe are most involved. Both Nathan and I would appreciate any help, since you are more familiar with the kids who live in Scorpion Ridge."

"And you don't know any Chris or Chad?"

"No."

Rafe finally hung up and headed back to Janie. He hadn't really gotten any answers, but at least now he'd decided which angle to investigate first: Derek's murder.

"Important call?" Janie asked.

"Yes."

She wanted more details. He could tell by the myriad of expressions that crossed her face and the questions in her eyes. He'd give them to her because she knew more about the college than he did, almost making her his inside man.

He muttered, "Later, not here."

That satisfied her. "What do we do next?"

"We?"

"Yes, we. Up until this morning, you'd considered yourself my personal bodyguard. My life hasn't been my own for days. Now, with Patricia's death, I'm stuck with you, aren't I? It's a 'we' whether you admit it or not."

"I could assign a deputy to guard you."

Janie rolled her eyes. "Right."

Just then, Georgia left the office, grabbed her purse and stomped to the restroom. The officer who'd been gathering names headed for Nathan and turned over a stack of papers.

"He's giving Nathan the names of the students who stopped by, plus the names of anyone Patricia might have spoken with last night," Rafe told her.

But Janie didn't pay any attention to him. Funny, she'd been hanging on his every word until then.

"I have to visit the ladies' room," she said.

Rafe opened his mouth to tell her not to interfere with Nathan's investigation, but he closed his mouth before the words came out. She would do with Georgia what he'd just done with Justin.

They really were a "we."

The chair was no more comfortable now than it had been an hour ago. It creaked as Rafe leaned forward to get a better look at Nathan.

Rafe often felt angry when investigating a senseless crime. So he understood the expression on Nathan's face. It could best be described as fury.

The presence of drugs did that to a cop.

Janie came back.

"Spill," Rafe ordered.

"Georgia arrived just after six, her normal time. It was close to six-thirty when she opened Patricia's office with her keys."

"Where does she keep the keys?"

"I think she has them on her key chain. There's also a set in the top desk drawer, but Georgia keeps that door locked and the key is on her key chain."

That didn't mean much; desks were notoriously easy to break into.

"Georgia phoned campus security, and an officer got there about three minutes later. He stepped in, checked Patricia for a pulse and then called the local police.

Rafe had never shared information this easily with a civilian. It felt right; Janie had said it correctly earlier. They were a "we," whether it was a good fit or not.

Janie's face seemed a bit paler than it had been just five minutes ago.

"What else did Georgia say?" Rafe asked.

"That Patricia's EpiPen was missing from the top drawer of her desk, where Patricia kept it. There's no sign on her body that she used it. Nor can they find it on the floor or underneath anything. Georgia says if it's missing, someone took it."

CHAPTER ELEVEN

"WHAT ARE THEY going to do about Patricia's classes?" Standing in front of the elevator with Rafe, the dean and Detective Williamson, waiting to go down and hopefully home, Janie wasn't sure why she felt obligated to ask, especially now.

Patricia Reynolds, the only other person to have read Derek's art book, was dead.

But the twenty students in Intermediate Canvas partially belonged to Janie. She knew their names and their stories. Some were truly gifted. "The students have already had to deal with Derek's death," she continued. "For some of them, it's their fifth or sixth time taking Patricia's class. Many of them consider Patricia more a mentor than a teacher."

"You're just the lab assistant, right?"

Janie didn't appreciate how Detective Williamson said "just," but that didn't matter now. "I haven't got the credits to be the main teacher."

She could do the job, though, probably better than a sub as they were halfway through the semester and Janie had been there every day.

"And," Rafe said, "it's probably not a good idea for you to continue teaching right now. It's not safe."

The dean of students, standing next to Detective Williamson, nodded. "He's right. It's not safe for you, and it's not safe for the students. You and they are our top priority."

Before he could say anything else, the elevator door opened. More students poured into the hallway. Janie recognized two of them.

"Is it true?" they asked. Their eyes, however, weren't on Janie. Their eyes were on the cordon tape.

Rafe's arm gently gripped her elbow, and he answered when she couldn't. "Right now, we're in the middle of an investigation. As soon as we have something definite to report, we'll make an announcement."

"I received a text," one girl said. "Classes are cancelled for the rest of the day. We've been asked to remain off campus."

Janie reached out and took the girl's hand. "That's what you need to do. The police will do their job, but it's easier without a crowd."

As quickly as they arrived, the students left, shepherded by the dean of students. Rafe, Detective Williamson and Janie waited for the next elevator to take them down.

When the elevator opened onto the first floor, the dean was waiting for them. "We've never had a suspicious death happen on campus before. Or any deaths for that matter. I should see what our legal department advises."

"Two people in the same class," Janie said softly, heartsick.

"And we don't want there to be a third." Rafe looked at Janie when he said the words. Last night, she'd considered her students unwillingly involved in a criminal investigation. Now, it seemed as if they were more than involved; they could be considered in the line of fire, casualties of the war on drugs.

Or was she the last name on somebody's hit list?

The reality of Patricia's death, along with Derek's confession and fears of reprisal, suddenly hit Janie full force. "What am I supposed to do? Hide? Will you put me in protective custody?"

Nathan's expression turned guilty. "First we need to prove that Patricia's death was actually a murder. And, harder still, that her murder has something to do with an art book that we no longer have."

"You no longer have it because you lost it."

"Janie," Rafe cautioned.

Funny, she hadn't noticed that his hand was still gently gripping her elbow. Somehow, being with him, being connected to him, was starting to seem natural.

"Sorry," she managed to say. "I realize that you didn't lose it. But, really, if it hadn't gone missing, Patricia might still be alive."

Both cops glanced at each other.

"I know, I know," Janie said next. "You're thinking of the butterfly effect, but this change isn't small."

Nathan appeared confused. "Butterfly effect? What are you talking about?"

"I'm talking about the missing art book, and it being responsible for Patricia's death. You know, one event leads to another and—"

Nathan just shook his head, stopping her explanation, clearly unconvinced that the two were related.

"We'll find out who's doing this, Janie," Rafe said firmly. "You have my word."

And how long will it take?" Janie felt the tentative grasp she had on her emotions start to slip. It had only been a little over a week since she read the art book. A week!

It felt like a year.

If she didn't do something, she'd wind up in

her bedroom, wearing pink fuzzy slippers and afraid to leave the house. "I'm scared spitless."

"Good," Detective Williamson said. "You should be scared. It will make you careful. It's not necessary for you to be on campus."

"I need to finish out the semester. It's part of my college course load, and if I don't complete my courses, there's no chance I'll win the art internship in Africa. Spending a semester in a teaching situation is one of the requirements." Even as she said the words, part of her was screaming in fear. Another part, though, was focused on her future and how an incomplete could hurt her career.

Hurt, not kill.

Detective Williamson's expression didn't change. "What you do is up to the college. I can only recommend a course of action."

"Not a chance I'm letting you out of my sight," Rafe said.

She took a breath. Life was coming at her too fast, too out of control. She needed to find stability, make some decisions. "I don't want to stop teaching."

"There's always next semester," Rafe pointed out.

"That would put me a whole year behind."

"There are worse things."

"I'll be careful."

Rafe and Williamson exchanged looks again.

"From here on out, every move we make is for your safety," Rafe said. "With all that's happening, there's not a chance I'm letting you be in the classroom without a police escort."

Williamson agreed. "And if you're in danger, your presence puts the students in danger."

Rafe turned to the dean. "Janie's just the teaching assistant. Who do you have that can take over for Patricia?"

There it was again. That word *just*.

"Georgia would know best, but I'm not willing to disturb her further by asking that question just yet. We'll probably meet sometime tomorrow."

"Cathy Michaelson subbed for Patricia when she went to a week-long conference," Janie said. "It won't be hard for her to take over with my help. I'm even familiar with how the students have been graded so far."

No, the everyday routine wouldn't be hard for Cathy to take over, but it wouldn't be the same. Something sinister was going on, something evil simmered under the cover of a peaceful southwestern college campus, and inadvertently, Janie'd become part of it.

Rafe's phone sounded. He checked the caller and said to Nathan, "We've got some things to discuss. Have someone escort Janie to my car and stay with her while we chat."

Nathan motioned to an officer. Then, he walked down the path and pulled out his notebook before stopping to talk to two teachers. With a young cop on her heels—the same one who'd escorted her and Rafe to the police station earlier in the week—Janie made her way out the front door and headed for Rafe's SUV.

"This is turning into quite a case," Janie said.

He nodded.

"You like working for Detective Williamson?"

"He's a good cop."

She could tell the young officer believed those words, too. "What's your name?"

"Brandon Long."

"How long have you been an officer?"

"I graduated from the academy three months ago."

Brand-new, and not that much younger than Rafe.

"So far, you enjoy it?"

"It's what I always wanted to do. When I was little, I used to watch *Adam Twelve* reruns with my mom. I liked that Reed and Malloy helped people."

As if to prove his words, he opened Rafe's

passenger-side door with a key Janie had not seen Rafe pass to him.

She climbed in as he said, "It's a job that makes a difference."

Funny, Janie'd heard of the show but never watched it. Based on her experience, cops only did what they had to do: stop fights, give tickets, take runaways home without caring *why* the twelve-year-old had run away.

At least, that's what she'd always believed. But Janie was starting to change her mind about cops. She didn't believe for a minute that Brandon Long would hesitate before protecting her. He might come across as a bit too serious, scanning the area as if he expected a Rambo wannabe to drop from the sky, but he had heart.

Just as Rafe did.

Around her, the campus looked lost and lonely. It was supposed to ring with the sound of young voices of kids who were vibrant with life and ready to take on the world. Instead, it was as if someone had, with one giant sweep, robbed the glorious place of all color.

For the second time today, Janie felt the urge to draw something other than an animal. And again, she wanted to draw a place, this place. Using black, white and gray.

"I'll bet your mom is proud of you."

He leaned against the SUV, glancing left and right, his hand staying near his gun holster. “She would be, ma’am, if she were still alive. She died last year of cancer.”

Janie’s mom had died of cancer, too, but Janie had been very young. Her only memories of her mother were of a laughing woman who used to sweep Janie into the air and laugh while they twirled together.

“Sorry to hear that.”

He simply nodded, watching as two figures approached them—Rafe and Nathan.

Rafe stopped speaking before he reached the SUV, so Janie didn’t get to hear what he and Detective Williamson had been discussing. Maybe *discussing* was the wrong word. It was more like Rafe was ordering and Williamson was agreeing.

“I’ll have everything ready first thing in the morning,” was Williamson’s parting line.

“See to it.” Rafe nodded to Brandon Long as the officer stepped away, and then turned on the ignition. With no other cars to maneuver around, it only took a moment before they were on their way back to Scorpion Ridge.

Rafe gripped the wheel so hard his knuckles were white. And he was speaking to himself under his breath. He probably didn’t even realize he was doing it.

"Solving the case?" she asked.

He jerked, started to deny it, and then said, "Lots of rabbit holes on this one." He paused, and for a moment, she feared he wasn't going to share. But finally he said, "There's got to be a college connection. The campus police are investigating every angle, trying to figure out how they lost the art book."

"They were lax."

They left the city limits of Adobe Hills and entered a nearly empty Interstate Ten.

"Most of them are retired cops. Two of Adobe Hills' campus police worked with my dad. They're savvy. Plus, we have someone who not only knew that Patricia had a nut allergy but knew exactly what to do to make her think the brownies came from Georgia."

"Lots of people were aware of her nut allergy."

"Students included?"

Janie nodded. "Art's a relaxed class. Students would often bring in food, so everyone was told that she couldn't have nuts."

"But they wouldn't know about the plate from the teacher's workroom, or about putting a note that said ENJOY."

"Most wouldn't," Janie said slowly.

"If we add students to the list of suspects, we'll be investigating for a year."

"Do you think Chris and Chad are students?"

"Chris, possibly. Chad, no. Chad's name is unusual enough that we could eliminate him from the first day. Chris is a little different. It could refer to a male or a female, be a nickname, or his full name. It could also be spelled with a K."

"Derek wouldn't misspell it."

"Why not? Maybe he didn't know."

"Artists pay attention to details. Derek didn't have a single misspelled word in his art book."

Rafe didn't seem convinced, but he did seem to be considering her words.

"His attention to detail," Janie pressed out, "is why I was able to create the crime scene."

"Which would never stand up in court, as you created it from a perception that cannot be documented."

"That's because you—"

"Don't say it."

"Aw, you're no fun." She threw out the words in jest, but to her surprise, he didn't respond in jest.

Instead, he stared at her, and she stared back, taking in his black hair spilling down his forehead and his piercing dark eyes which now held weariness, purpose and something else. Something that made her shiver. His next words, though, made her shiver more.

"I can be fun."

IF HE HAD to do it over again, he'd not toss back an innuendo with an even more loaded innuendo. At his words, Janie started fidgeting with the hem of her shirt, something he noticed she only did when she was nervous.

Rafe got another phone call. Then, three more in quick succession. The final call was from Justin.

"You got your radio on?" he asked.

"No, Janie's in the car with me. We just left the college. I haven't had time to think."

"Well, somebody's had plenty of time to think. Seems a reporter covering the murder for KLBG heard about the missing art book and the confession it held. He sniffed around and reported the possibility that two students, along with Derek, kidnapped and murdered Brittney. He insinuated that the students were known to Brittney, maybe she even considered them friends. According to the news, you're not responding to attempts to reach you."

"Did he name names?"

"No, but it's going to be an interesting Monday when classes resume. Every male who shared a class with Brittney is going to feel under the spotlight."

"I'll start damage control when I get to my office."

Rafe couldn't hide the conversations from Janie. Usually, having a civilian overhear police business disturbed him. But she'd been such an integral part of this investigation since reading the art book that he valued her opinions. In a way that surprised him. Had his own mother been in the car, he'd have stopped, gotten out and carried on his conversations on the side of the road. Oh, he valued his mother, too, but she'd be little to no help.

Because a missing child, no matter the age, could put his mother in bed for a week.

Halfway to Scorpion Ridge the phone calls stopped. He glanced at Janie. She'd stopped fidgeting and was staring out the window.

"I take it," she said softly, "that Derek Chaney's involvement in Brittney's disappearance is no longer a secret."

"No, and that means your involvement is no longer a secret. You can expect the reporters to start calling."

She took out her phone and said, "I have five missed calls from the same number. I think it's safe to assume they've found me. Great, just great."

"It was bound to happen."

She didn't answer and her eyes stayed glued out the window.

"You okay?" he asked after a few miles.

"I'm trying to imagine whether they brought her this way. Every once in a while we pass an exit, and I wonder if she's out there, within our grasp, just waiting for us to find her."

"I wonder that, too."

She turned from the window and looked him full in the face. Even after such a draining day, she was beautiful. Her blond hair still had a bit of curl. Her eyes stared at him as if they could see inside of him, as if they could change—or at least limit—his pain.

A pain that stemmed from not being able to prevent a second death.

"I don't think Nathan's heard of the butterfly effect," he said conversationally.

"He doesn't have that kind of imagination."

"He's a good cop."

Janie went back to gazing out the window. "That's what Officer Long said. Williamson might be a good cop, but he sees everything in black and white. He'd be a great cop if he used a little imagination."

"A cop isn't supposed to read more into a crime scene than what's there. It clouds the picture." Now he had her attention. Then, he added, "You've only met the man twice. Neither of which I'd call the best situation. Cut him a little slack."

"I'd paint him in black, gray and white. No bright colors. He's an unhappy man."

Rafe couldn't disagree with that. Right before Rafe took over the job of Laramie County sheriff, Nathan had gone through an ugly divorce. It had changed him. Before that, he'd been the slap-on-the-back kind of cop you went to with your troubles. After his divorce, he became a by-the-book, let's-get-this-done and quickly, kind of cop.

"You and Long seemed to be getting along quite well," Rafe observed.

"He's a nice kid."

"He's older than you."

"It's because he's always so nervous. Makes me think he's just a kid."

"And here I'd hoped you were relaxed around him because you'd gotten over your mistrust of cops. Instead it was because you see him as a nervous kid."

To his surprise, she didn't answer. Just went back to staring out the window.

"What happened? What made you so distrustful of cops?"

"Katie didn't tell you?"

He knew she was thinking back to how her

sister had set up their one date. "No, not really. She just said you'd had a bad experience. I figured it had something to do with what happened when you lived with your aunt. She was an alcoholic, right?"

"There are all kinds of alcoholics. Some can function, go to work, take care of a kid. Others..."

"Such as your aunt," he commented.

"Others, such as my aunt, are neglectful and..." She paused before finally saying, "Hurtful."

A sign reading Scorpion Ridge, twenty-five miles, flashed by. They were almost home, and this might be his only opportunity to find out what made her so hesitant when she was with him.

"Did a cop somehow make things worse for you?"

"Yes, more than one."

Rafe whistled. "More than one. No wonder I had my work cut out for me to convince you I'm a nice guy."

She didn't laugh, or smile, or anything. Rafe got the idea she still wasn't sure what to think. Her mistrust of people had kept her safe. Changing her perceptions meant taking a risk. And with all that was going on, what a time for Janie to take a risk.

When Janie did begin to speak, it was in the direction of the window, toward the dark cobalt-blue that made for an intimate Arizona night. He could see her reflection, though. It made her words ethereal, somewhat ominous.

"Katie moved out the day she turned eighteen. I was twelve, and she took me with her. We honestly didn't think Aunt Betsy would care. Boy, were we naive. We moved into a tiny apartment above a garage. There wasn't even a wall to hide the toilet, but I loved it. I started painting the walls the very first day. Katie didn't mind. On the third day, the cops arrived. Aunt Betsy had called them, and they had come to get me. Both Katie and I tried to describe what living with her was like, but Katie—according to the cops—didn't have custody, or means to take care of me."

"Why didn't your aunt Betsy just let you go?"

"At first, Katie and I believed it was because my dad sent her money."

"Then why didn't you call your dad and tell him that she was mistreating you?"

"We quickly found out that money—Dad's money, anyway—wasn't the issue."

"You still could have called your dad and told him how things were."

"Katie tried to, right when we first moved

in with Betsy. He screened his calls and never answered the phone, and after he died, we discovered that he'd never opened our letters, either. He didn't want to know."

Rafe had no idea what to say. As a cop, he'd witnessed all kinds of neglect. Dads who beat their kids for no reason, dads who spent grocery money on beer and dads who walked out without saying goodbye. He pitied them. But, he pitied the kids more.

"So why didn't your aunt Betsy let you stay with Katie?"

"Because she didn't want to be alone. She liked the attention I brought. And because she got more handouts. Can you believe it? I was an extra box of food to her. And if she had free food, she could spend the money she didn't spend on food on beer. She made me miserable all for an extra box of food! Try telling that to a cop."

"So you did try?"

"Yup."

"And those cops pretty much ignored what you were saying."

"Yes. And at least one of them knew how bad it was. He'd been called to Betsy's apartment a time or two when one of her parties got out of hand."

It wasn't right, but Rafe understood what the

cops had probably been thinking—there was a fine line between neglect and abuse. Neglect had to be pretty pronounced in order for the cops to intervene.

He left the highway and turned onto one of Scorpion Ridge's main thoroughfares. The Corner Diner was still open. Inside he could see his mother as she wiped down a table. "But you were being fed."

"Spaghetti and peanut-butter-and-jelly sandwiches, mostly."

"And you went to school."

"Perfect attendance until Katie moved out and they forced me back to Betsy's."

"And you were clean."

"Katie made sure of that, and I prefer things neat, myself."

"So the cops took you back."

"And I started running away. I always ran to Katie. Every time, a cop found me and returned me to Betsy. They threatened Katie with kidnapping, with contributing to the delinquency of a minor, with harboring a fugitive."

Rafe wanted to say they were doing their job, but he couldn't form the words.

"How bad was it at Aunt Betsy's?"

"There were the lonely times. Those I could take. Then, there were the hard times. Betsy would steal any money I didn't hide. If I didn't have money, she'd sell my things. She sold my paints."

"Did anyone ever hurt you?"

He wasn't sure he could take her answer. If she said yes, he'd head for Texas, find this Betsy and…and what? Slam her against the wall? Yell? No, he'd been raised better than that. He'd never in his life hurt a woman, not even one resisting arrest with her teeth and fingernails. And what would yelling get him? Just a sore throat.

And if Janie said yes, then he'd have to acknowledge that he was part of a system that didn't always work, didn't always do what it was supposed to do: serve and protect.

"No, I was very lucky. I knew when to disappear and how. Plus, I was only there a year on my own. Before that, Katie was with me, and she'd call the police the minute Betsy started to turn ugly."

"And the police came. So, they were helpful."

"Just for Katie."

"Did you ever call them when you were by yourself with Betsy?"

"Once."

"What happened?"

"Two cops showed up, the same two cops

who'd driven me from Katie's the first time. When he recognized me, one of them rolled his eyes and checked his watch."

Rafe made a mental note to never roll his eyes while she was looking. "And you never called the police again."

"Katie gave me a cell phone the minute she had extra money, and I called her when I got scared. She'd come and get me, and I'd stay with her until the next day."

"You're a strong woman. You survived."

"I didn't feel strong, still don't," she admitted. "When Katie left Betsy's, I started failing school. No one was around to make sure I did my homework. Some teachers noticed a difference and pulled me aside. Others didn't care. One, though, Mrs. Freshia, she cared."

"So teachers are a bit like cops. Some are better than others. And," he puffed up, exaggerating, "some are great."

That earned him a low chuckle from her. "I never thought about it like that." She continued, "I stopped sleeping at night. I'd just get this sick, knotty feeling in my stomach. Anxiety. That's when I really started drawing. I couldn't stop."

"And you drew animals."

"I must have remembered animals being around when times were better."

"Then you should be pretty happy right now." He turned his SUV into the driveway of Katie's house.

"Why? What do you mean?"

A pack of wolves sounded in the distance. The scream of a peacock echoed in the wind. He'd not even parked or switched off the engine before Katie had the front door open and was hurrying down the front steps. Her husband was right behind her.

"What do you mean?" Janie repeated.

"You've got animals again. And here comes your sister. Times are better."

Janie opened the passenger door and exited before he could get out of his side and assist her. Waving at her sister, she came around the SUV and met him.

"You're right. Times are better, and I need to remember that." To his surprise, she came close, stood on her tiptoes, and gave him a quick kiss on the cheek.

On the cheek!

But what bothered him most wasn't the kiss. No, it was that he wanted more than a quick kiss on the cheek.

CHAPTER TWELVE

"AMANDA'S HERE, AND she'd like to talk to you."

Janie glanced up from her work on the mural. Crisco, as if sensing he no longer had an audience, rolled over and fell asleep. Katie looked tired, and Janie felt a moment's pang knowing she was the cause.

"Why didn't you text me instead of walking all the way over here?"

"I was afraid you'd ignore the text. You have that habit."

Last night Luke and Katie had ganged up on her. *You can't keep working as the lab assistant for that class. Your life's worth more than the internship in Africa.* In the end, Luke, her brother-in-law, volunteered to pay her way to Africa. She could start the residency now. Or, if she didn't get the residency, she could create her own program.

But Janie knew he didn't have that kind of money.

Meanwhile, Rafael Salazar had lounged on one of the armchairs in the living room, as if he belonged there, and agreed with every word her brother-in-law said. It was just like when Janie had been a teenager, with adults making decisions for her, some of them wrong, and not taking her desires into consideration.

This time, though, there was more at stake. There was a murderer lurking on the campus of Adobe Hills Community College, and Janie was sure she was his next target.

"Give me a minute to clean up," she said, snapping her attention to the present. "I'm done on the mural for the day."

"We'll be upstairs in my office." Katie rubbed her stomach, a pinched expression crossing her face.

"You all right?" Janie asked.

"Outside of ankles that look more like Cheeky's than they should, I'm fine. It's Amanda I'm worried about."

Cheeky was a three-cheeked camel whose name more than summed up the personality of BAA. Amanda was Janie's art student as well as a friend of Katie's. Before taking over as director of BAA, Katie had been an interpreter for the deaf. A few years ago, Katie had given Amanda a private tour of the zoo just for the chance to do one of the things she loved: interpret. It turned into a win/win friendship, as Amanda herded all her friends to BAA and they helped with fund-raisers.

And Katie championed young Amanda much the way she championed Janie.

"What's wrong with Amanda?" Janie started to stand. She could leave her supplies. Amanda was more important, and with everything that had been going on…

"It's okay, she can wait a minute. Luke's with her, and she's got Tinker in her lap. He's calming her down. He's good at that."

For a moment, Janie wasn't sure if Katie was talking about the cat or about Luke. Then Katie got a wistful look on her face and Janie knew she was talking about Luke. The man was a saint. After dinner last night, even while he'd almost hyperventilated over Janie's day, he'd held Katie's feet in his lap and given her a massage.

What was it like, she wondered, to have a man love you that much?

To love a man that much…

Katie hadn't dated much, if at all, before Luke. That was partly Janie's fault, as Katie had single-handedly taken over raising her. Janie, on the other hand, had dated often. None of the relationships lasted, though. And no one had ever put a wistful look on her face.

Katie waddled away, one hand rubbing the small of her back.

Last night, Rafe had said that Janie was a survivor. But Janie had always believed that the only reason she'd survived is because she'd had Katie's hand to hold.

Getting the residency and going to Africa would accomplish one thing, for sure. Janie would finally be on her own, away from Katie. She'd finally discover if without her sister she'd sink or swim.

If she survived her current nightmare.

Once her art supplies had been washed and put away, Janie headed for the main office. It was one room, with windows on every side, and stood on top of the gift shop. The walls had been a dull brown when Janie had first showed up. Not long after, she'd painted the walls blue and added trees and BAA animals. She'd included all of the animals' names and the year they arrived at the zoo. Now, when Katie and Luke took guests or business partners up to the office, they could show them the place's history.

Today, Amanda, her mother and Katie were crammed into the office. Amanda was sitting on the couch, clutching Tinker the cat and crying. Katie was signing to her frantically, words like *calm you, no afraid, brave, job need done.*

Janie could sign, too, just not as well as Katie. They'd learned ASL at a neighborhood church when they were both young and searching for a safe place to escape to. So anytime the church offered a community workshop or class, the Vincent girls signed up. Consequently, Janie could sign, read music, build birdhouses and complete any obstacle course for ages twelve and up.

If possible, Amanda's mother looked more scared than her daughter. Katie, who always knew the right thing to do, relayed to Janie, "Amanda heard about Professor Reynolds on the news. She thinks maybe there's something about the case she should share."

Amanda started signing frantically, too fast for Janie to follow. Katie did lots of nodding. Amanda's mother rested her head in her hands and moaned, "I was sure Tommy was getting into trouble."

Amanda kept signing, and Katie interpreted for Janie. "Tommy and Derek were friends. Sometimes, Tommy would give her and Brittney a ride home from school. Often, Derek would be in the car. That's how Tommy and Brittney met."

This was no surprise to Janie. Rafe had shared as much. "Did they date?" Janie asked.

Katie didn't even bother posing the question to Amanda, as she'd already given her the answer. "No, Brittney liked someone else. Amanda's not sure who." Apparently, in the time it had taken Janie to get from the bears' enclosure to the main office, Amanda had done nothing but sign her story.

"Did the police ask you about all of this?" Janie signed to Amanda.

Again, rapid-fire answers came from Amanda's fingers. Janie gave up trying to follow.

Katie spoke. "Amanda told the police that they were all in a car pool together. Nothing else."

Janie pulled a chair up so she sat in front of Amanda. She didn't touch the girl. She wasn't comfortable doing that. Katie already had the emotional part under control. Amanda still cried, but she'd stopped signing. She glanced at her mother through shimmering tears.

"I think," Janie said, "that Amanda doesn't want to go on if you're upset, Mrs. Skinley."

"Oh, my goodness, Janie. You've called me Helen since you met me." With that, Helen turned to her daughter and signed, *Doing right thing.*

Amanda nodded and wiped her nose on the sleeve of her shirt. Katie reached in her pocket and pulled out a tissue. She was going to be an awesome mother.

And she'd already had plenty of practice with Janie.

Amanda's fingers started flying again. *One time before we left college town, we stopped at store for drinks. Derek was friends with someone in next car. Tommy and Brittney were inside store. I was in the backseat. Derek maybe forgot I was there. He maybe didn't know I read lips.*

"I should call Rafe," Janie said. "He should hear this."

Amanda read her lips and wailed. Her mother pulled her close. "I don't want her to go to the police. Brittney's probably dead. Her art teacher and Derek are certainly dead. I'm not putting my girl in danger. She'll tell you everything and you can repeat it to the sheriff. You don't have to mention where you heard it. Say you read it in an art book or something. That's how this whole thing started, right?"

Whatever Amanda was about to share, Rafe would certainly have the smarts to figure out the source. And he'd not settle for secondhand reports or hearsay. But for now, Janie made herself settle back and urged, "Go on."

For the next five minutes, as Katie translated the tale Amanda's fingers spun, Janie studied Amanda's facial expressions and body movements, noticing she held her stomach a lot.

"Derek's friend drove a blue car, four doors. Old. Two people in it. No coats."

"When?" Janie asked. "When was this?"

"A few weeks before Brittney disappeared. I remember Halloween decorations on the window of the store.

"One got out. Tall. Almost man. Short hair, big, strong. He put his arm around Derek, led Derek away."

There was no word for Derek, so Amanda signed each letter.

"The man told Derek to leave us alone. We cause trouble. The man said someone could get hurt."

"Why didn't you tell Rafe this?"

This time, Amanda signed right to Janie.

Man also said Tommy could get hurt.

Helen Skinley wasn't crying anymore. "That does it. We're taking a vacation, moving, something. I'm not sticking around here for my children to get hurt."

"Tommy's no longer a child," Janie pointed out.

"He's not acting like an adult, either."

"But Helen," Katie said, "what if taking away the only person who witnessed this man's words, saw this man, causes someone else's child to go missing? Can you live with that?"

"What I couldn't live with," Helen said, "is something happening to Amanda or Tommy."

"Mom." Amanda hardly ever attempted speech. That she did so now was what Janie needed to break through the wall she'd put between herself and the girl.

Reaching forward, Janie put her hand on Amanda's arm. "Can you draw him? This man?"

Amanda shook her head.

"Can you give me the details, so I can draw him?" Turning to Helen, Janie added, "And I'll sign my name to the drawing. That will keep Amanda safe."

Amanda apparently didn't care what her mother thought because she was already nodding.

It took the rest of the afternoon, every magazine that Katie could find and fifteen pieces of paper. Janie didn't even count the pencils she went through.

They used *People* magazine to get the body type, settling on a young Bruce Willis. The nose was Bruce Jenner's but a little wider. The forehead was Hugh Jackman's. While Amanda asserted that the hair color was similar to Jackman's, the style was not. They went through seven magazines before switching to the office computer and the internet. Finally Amanda reacted when they came to the picture of an army man with his hat tucked under his arm.

Military cut? Interesting.

The internet photos also helped Amanda identify bushy eyebrows, close-to-the-head ears and broader shoulders than even Bruce Willis boasted.

All the while, Janie drew. Because Amanda was a budding artist herself, she added her opinions and sometimes wielded her own pencil.

In the end, they had the image of a twenty-something male, slightly stocky, probably just under six foot, with short brown hair and an angry expression.

Amanda nodded.

Janie reached for her phone. The image was very similar to the one she'd re-created from Derek's sketches. Maybe, just maybe, she and Amanda had just drawn Chad or Chris.

"I'LL GET THIS to the campus police Monday morning," Rafe said, standing beside Janie in the now very crowded office. "They can show it around, see if they have any student ID photos that are familiar."

What Rafe didn't mention was that he'd

personally deliver the drawing. He wanted to watch how each member of the campus police reacted to it. Somehow, Derek's art book had been lifted from the safe in their office. One of them might know more than they were letting on.

"So," Amanda signed via Katie, "this guy will be someone under suspicion."

"Yes," Rafe said. "This might be one of the best breaks we've had." He'd been about to say *if only you'd come forward sooner,* but the red-rimmed eyes of both Amanda and her mother stilled him. Then, too, there was Amanda's recounting of the threat to Tommy. When this was over, he was going to have a little talk with Tommy Skinley. And, if his parents complained that Rafe had overstepped his bounds as sheriff, let them. The boy needed to hear some hard facts and hard truths. It could just as easily have been Amanda as Brittney.

He thanked Amanda and shook her hand as she and her mother left.

"I think that girl stood a bit taller on her way out the door," Katie said.

"And they'd both stopped crying," Janie added.

"You should have called me the minute she started talking." Rafe studied the drawing again. He didn't recognize the man. It wasn't someone who called Scorpion Ridge home.

"They would have bolted," Janie said. "Amanda's mom was talking about the whole family leaving, going on vacation."

"I hope not. I may want to talk to her again," Rafe said.

Janie quickly filled him in on what they'd done to arrive at the final sketch. He was impressed. He'd only watched a sketch artist at work once before, and that woman had come with lots of stock pictures of noses, eyes, ears, facial shapes.

"You're good. Maybe painting animals is not what you're meant to be doing."

She frowned.

"Just giving you a compliment."

"He's right," Katie said. "I had no idea you could draw people quite this well."

"I'd have nightmares," Janie said finally, "if I had to listen to people describing criminals who'd done horrible things. It was hard enough with Amanda. She kept crying, and I felt helpless."

"You're not helpless," Rafe said. "A helpless woman wouldn't have put this, my first real lead in days, in my hands."

Unfortunately, even as he said the words,

Janie backed away, shaking her head, rejecting the compliment.

Rejecting him.

CHAPTER THIRTEEN

"DID YOU KNOW," the student standing next to Janie said, "that art students accrue more debt than students with any other major?"

Janie believed it. And, because it had been more than two weeks since she'd been able to work at the Adobe Hills Community College, she'd essentially just taken a salary reduction. Speaking of her major life change, she glanced around. Officer Candy Riorden leaned casually against a wall, checking something out on her cell phone, keeping Janie in sight.

Janie only liked being cosseted when her bodyguard was Rafe, and lately, he'd more often been sending Candy or Chief Summerside to watch over her.

The around-the-clock bodyguard detail was getting old, and unnecessary. With Patricia Reynolds's death, the news media had seized on the story like a dog on a bone. They, more than anything or anyone, assured Janie's safety.

Too bad the stories hadn't aired before the

murderer decided to eliminate Patricia. Over three hundred people had attended the funeral. Of that number, at least a hundred had sought Janie out afterward, wanting to talk about Patricia. In the end, Rafe had put a protective arm around her and escorted her to his SUV and then home.

A chill peppered Janie's spine and she looked over at Candy. Having a bodyguard wasn't all bad.

Still, she was attempting to get her life back to normal. This morning, along with about thirty other university seniors, she was helping set up an art exhibit that she was participating in. Not just any art exhibit, but one that came with a prize.

That Janie was desperate to win.

"I'm glad you could help," said one of Janie's instructors.

When she'd first been asked to be part of the exhibit, she'd had to refuse. Her tutoring and lab-assistance work kept her from doing any extras here at the university—she needed the money more than she needed to raise her profile. Truth was, sometimes she felt more like a visitor than a student at the university in Tucson. She did most of her art at BAA and she interacted more with students at Adobe Hills Community College.

This event, the John Tompkins Exhibit, was part fund-raiser, part spotlight. Most of Janie's peers were into abstract. Janie was the sole wildlife painter. She didn't mind. It made her work stand out. She had three pieces in the exhibit, all boasting residents of BAA. The one of Crisco the bear was her best, but she'd painted him the most. She'd titled the offering *First Step,* and it showed Crisco walking out a door—no one had to know it was actually the door of the zoo's infirmary. Her next piece depicted Cheeky. He was standing by the biggest tree in his enclosure, looking up at a hot-air balloon. It was a vantage-point painting, and a scene Janie had glimpsed on a crisp morning before the first visitor had come through BAA's doors. She called it *There's No Place Like Home,* because she was sure Cheeky was wishing himself somewhere else. The last painting was of her sister's black panther, Aquila. He was dancing, up on two legs, and looking both regal and predatory. She'd entitled it *One Owner Heart,* and intended to give it to Katie for her birthday.

Aquila, as a black panther, was a breed that didn't tame. And yet, Aquila had always been Katie's, just as Janie had.

By three that Friday afternoon, they'd finished setting up the exhibit. Tables were ready for food, chairs were ready for people and the director of the art department was already figuring out more ways to get patrons to part with their money.

In this case, most of the "patrons" were parents who had already parted with their money. It was called tuition.

At four, Janie's phone rang. It was Georgia, and she sounded a bit frantic. "We lost Gabriella, Patricia's temporary replacement. She fell off a ladder as she was painting a wall. Four broken ribs. Her doctor says she can't return to work for six weeks."

"That's almost to the end of the semester."

"Yes," Georgia agreed. "She only taught the one class."

"My Monday/Wednesday."

"The students have made their wishes very clear to the school president. They want you as their teacher, or they want their money back."

"I'm not qualified—"

"They can do it as a special assignment, one semester only, emergency contract."

"Is it safe?"

Even over the phone, Janie could hear the gush of breath that Georgia released. "I'm not sure I'll ever feel safe again. But the campus police haven't relaxed. They're persistent. And now we have community-watch volunteers driving through the parking lot and handing out whistles in the cafeteria."

"But is it safe for *me* to return?"

"I can't answer that. One of the deans will be calling you shortly. I'm just supposed to make you aware of the job offer. You'll need to make a choice by four-forty-five so I can get the paperwork started."

"Let me call…"

No, she wasn't going to call Rafe. He wasn't her boss, only her protector, and she could make her own decisions. She'd worked hard to get to where she was: living with Katie, majoring in what she wanted and giving her dreams a chance to become real. She didn't need a man to mess with her mind.

She had goals.

He was already getting in the way.

If she gave him a toehold, he'd take over. Cops were like that; it was the way they were wired.

Even though he kept trying to make her forget that.

"I'll give you an answer now—yes." Janie followed her yes with a quick call to the dean. Then, she was once again gainfully employed as a teacher—one of the stipulations for getting the summer artist-in-residence position in South Africa. She was back on track.

"I DON'T LIKE IT," Rafe said that evening when he came to the exhibit to take over as her bodyguard. "They can get someone else to take the class. Your safety is more important."

Janie stood next to him, wondering at his taste in art. He seemed drawn to a watercolor of seven horses running toward a sunset. Judging by the details, she doubted the artist had ever been near a real horse. These animals were too perfect. And besides, pastel colors could never catch the real essence of a living, breathing equine.

Rafe was somewhat color-blind, she reminded herself. That could be the only reason he found the watercolor remotely interesting.

"It's been two weeks, nothing's happened."

"Yes," Rafe agreed, "and we've worked hard to make sure nothing *did* happen."

Janie hadn't seen him dressed up before. Mostly, he'd been outfitted in his uniform—brown khaki pants, a tucked-in tan shirt with sheriff patches on both arms. His badge was usually over his left breast. He finished up the attire with cowboy boots.

Maybe he was a closet cowboy.

Tonight, though, for her exhibit, he'd dressed up—dark gray pressed slacks, a tucked-in white shirt and a gray-and-black sweater. For once, his hair didn't look as though he'd just run his fingers through it.

She'd always been aware of how black his hair was, just not how thick. Even in different clothes, however, she was sure he still carried a gun, and she noted his police radio clipped to his belt. Other than that, he could have been her suave date for the evening.

"Whoever was worried about Derek's art book has probably realized that if something substantial was in it, the police would have discovered him by now."

Rafe frowned. "Or you were out of sight, out of mind. Heading back to the Adobe Hills campus could put you in his sights again. Remember, we're working under the assumption that there's a connection between the school and whoever killed Derek and Patricia."

Rafe had told her earlier that Derek's body had finally been released to his parents. To Janie, it felt like closure. Going back into the classroom would cement that feeling even more.

"Yes, but messing with me would keep him in the spotlight when he should just slink away."

"That's how a rational person would think. Killers aren't always rational."

She had no argument for that, and, luckily, Rafe let the subject drop.

"Yours are the best," he said, stopping in front of her drawing of Aquila dancing.

"You're prejudiced."

"No, cops aren't allowed to play favorites. It gets us in trouble."

"We certainly wouldn't want that."

She almost missed his response because he muttered it under his breath. He, however, had a deep voice, rich and full. It was like hot chocolate on a cool night, wrapping her in a cocoon that promised safety and something else.

Something she'd never let herself dream about.

Making that toehold she'd worried about earlier an even bigger reality.

He said, "I'm already in trouble."

A GUITAR QUARTET, made up of two men and two women, stood behind a microphone and started strumming. The tune was upbeat, something Spanish-y, but they kept the volume low enough so the people milling through the John Tompkins Exhibit could still talk. Rafe just wanted to grab Janie and get out of there.

Some of the displayed art had price tags displayed; others had bid sheets nearby. Janie clearly was in her element as she spoke to the people admiring her work. The picture of Crisco got her the most attention, as his story had been in the news. Rafe and Janie had both been there when the young cub was discovered.

Keeping his eyes on Janie as she sipped from a bottle of water and answered questions, Rafe remembered that the day he'd met Crisco was actually the first time he'd met Janie. He ambled over to study the painting of the bear. The highest bid was seven hundred and fifty dollars.

Rafe couldn't remember if he'd ever purchased any art to go on his walls. He lived in a small house just north of the Corner Diner. He had two bedrooms—one that he used for an office—plus a living room, kitchen and bathroom. He'd decorated in two ways. One, with stuff he'd carried over from his childhood. Or two, with stuff his mother had bought him because she couldn't bear his sparse bachelor's pad.

If his mother had her wish, he'd still be living at home.

She should have had ten children instead of just Ramon and Rafe.

And all she wanted now was grandchildren.

Taking the pen attached to the stand holding the bid sheet, Rafe wrote eight hundred on the paper. Then, he crossed the number out. Without another thought, he wrote one thousand.

He wanted the painting.

But what he really wanted was the woman.

She possessed the one trait he really valued in a woman—she was willing to change. She'd been open to viewing cops in a different light. Plus she could be soft and creative when necessary, but then switch to sturdy and focused if need be. And she did it with courage and beauty.

If he didn't watch out, he'd fall in love. The annual policemen's banquet was fast approaching. Rafe usually took a date. This year, there was only one woman he wanted to invite. And yet, he hesitated to blur the line between business and pleasure.

Falling for her, right now, wasn't a good idea. It meant questions he wasn't ready to answer, commitments he wasn't prepared to make, feelings he wasn't prepared to share. Not to mention the fact that she distracted him so thoroughly that he could miss something important in the case.

So, after battling with himself, he decided not to invite her, taking the joy out of his evening.

By ten, the finger food had vanished, the quartet had packed up and the last of the art students hurried around making sure nothing was left behind.

Janie had earned almost two thousand for the art department; half of that came from Rafe's now protesting checkbook. She'd also, because of the painting Rafe now owned, earned an honorable mention.

"The judges were blind. You should have won the award," was Rafe's comment.

"The competition was fierce. The program has a lot of talented artists enrolled."

"Yes, but first place went to a watercolor of weirdly colored horses."

She stopped hustling about, picking up bid sheets, broken pencils and such. The look she shot him then was priceless, and for the first time in his life, he realized he'd said exactly the right thing to a female.

At exactly the right moment.

The Arizona moon glittered in a blue velvet sky. The slight breeze seemed to nudge him closer to Janie. Close enough so that he could bend down and kiss her.

So he did.

His fingers cupped her cheeks gently, tilting her face upward as his lips met hers, hesitantly at first, but then claiming ownership and something else, something that spread warmth right to his heart and made him want.

If someone hadn't dropped an easel right behind them, he'd have explored more, touched more, gotten lost in the feel of her lips on his. If someone hadn't dropped an easel right behind them, he'd have had to admit that he wanted her, like he'd never wanted before.

And that was exactly why Janie was dangerous.

AS A LAB ASSISTANT, Janie had taken whatever classes Adobe Hills had offered her. Thus, both classes she'd helped in were evening classes. Even her tutoring stint was in the late afternoon. But now suddenly Janie was on campus during prime time, and the days were different. There was a liveliness to the campus that was missing during the evening.

Today, her return to campus, she'd dressed with a little more care than she had as the lab assistant. After all, it was her first time as the actual instructor. Surely there was no other reason.

And her disappointment that, instead of Rafe, one of Nathan's police officers was her escort around campus had nothing to do with Rafe not seeing her on what she considered a big day.

Though he'd promised he'd be here as soon as he finished in court. Maybe he'd be at the door when she ended her class. He could take her out for ice cream or something, to celebrate.

Her ultimate goal was not to be a teacher, but it would look good on her résumé. Just this morning she'd sent off her virtual portfolio to the search committee in South Africa. She hoped they were wowed by it. An honorable mention from the John Tompkins Exhibit at the University of Arizona was something to be proud of.

Funny, she'd spent the whole weekend not thinking about the award but instead about the sight of Rafe carrying her painting to his SUV.

And the fire in his eyes that said he wanted to carry *her* to the SUV.

Since moving to Scorpion Ridge, she'd had a few dates here and there. For a while, Adam had seemed like the perfect guy for her. And he was—the perfect guy friend. For a while, Georgia had talked about her son, but Janie had only joked about enjoying her single state.

She'd even, at Katie's insistence, gone out with Rafe well over a year ago. Janie had only done it to appease her sister and prove to Katie that a cop would never be the perfect male, and she hadn't been disappointed when he didn't call for a second date.

Maybe she should have given him more of

a chance. She'd been overly flippant with him, purposely distant and somewhat rude.

She'd had her defenses up, for sure.

A whole year later, she realized those defenses had been unnecessary.

Once this investigation was over, she was going to get more of a life. She'd not just teach and spend her days either lost in her art or with family. She'd start socializing. Maybe she'd even listen to what Katie had to say about falling in love, how it changed your life but didn't have to change your dreams.

Then again, Rafe was so committed to Scorpion Ridge, and nothing was keeping Katie from her dream of actually painting a lion in its natural habitat. She was so close.

First, though, she had to get through the next month—alive.

The cop tailing her offered to carry her bag, but Janie turned him down. It would only draw more attention to her. She didn't want that. As she made her way to the art department before her class, she saw a few of her students and nodded her head but pressed forward. If they'd been curious before about what she knew concerning Derek's death, she could just imagine their questions about Patricia. The sub had only been privy to the most superficial of details.

And thanks to being at Rafe's side for hours on end, then watching and listening as Detective Williamson investigated Patricia's death, she could answer just about every question—except the identity of the killer.

That information eluded everyone. So far, all Detective Williamson had been willing to share was a rough time line. He had a good-size window for the time of death. One of the social-science teachers remembered seeing Patricia getting off the elevator and heading for her office just after 8:00 p.m. The last thing Patricia had done alive was place a phone call, at exactly nine-thirty, to one of her adjuncts. She'd left a message asking if he'd be willing to sub. Patricia hadn't mentioned what class or when. And then Georgia had found her the next morning. The hours in between were a mystery.

Janie switched her art bag from one shoulder to the other and waved at one of the other faculty members as she headed for the stairs. The two-o'clock classes were ending and classrooms were starting to empty. Suddenly the stairway became very crowded as students made their way to their next class. Janie moved closer to the handrail as she headed up the stairs against the flow of exiting students. The cop was just a few steps behind her.

She made it to the top, waited for a group of students to move out of the way, and stepped around a Brittney look-alike to reach for the door.

She didn't make it.

Even as her knees hit the top step, she couldn't figure out what happened first. Had someone grabbed her bag? Had someone managed to tangle their foot under hers? Or had she really felt someone push against the back of her left knee until she fell?

By the third step down, she knew it didn't matter.

This was going to hurt.

CHAPTER FOURTEEN

"IT COULD HAVE been much worse," Katie said.

Gazing down at Janie's sleeping form, complete with taped ribs, assorted bruises, an impressive goose egg and one black eye, Rafe didn't blame Katie for not sounding convinced. Still, she was ever the optimistic sister, always searching for the positive.

"And you say Max Carter is involved in all this?" she asked with wonder. "He's helped out at the zoo a time or two during events."

"He claims he didn't mean to push her. He was trying to get her attention and grabbed her book bag. Max didn't leave the scene and started confessing before she hit the first step. There's no reason not to believe him." Rafe could still see the kid. He'd practically been crying. It had only taken a phone call to discover he didn't have a police record, not even a speeding ticket. He was, however, a student in Janie's Monday/Wednesday class—Rafe remembered interviewing him—and one of the few students who had known both Brittney and Derek.

In class, he palled around with Amanda.

Rafe checked his watch and then looked out the hospital room's window at the setting sun.

"And you believe him?" Katie asked.

Had they been at the station, or back at the school, Rafe would have refrained from giving an opinion. Too often the picture of innocence was an illusion. But in this case… "I believe him."

Katie pulled her chair closer to Janie and stroked her sister's arm. She probably wasn't even aware she was humming a lullaby.

Janie resembled her big sister in many ways, except Janie was a bit taller, more willowy, graceful.

Exactly what Rafe preferred.

Janie wasn't moving. Her blond hair lay listless against a white pillow. The color of her face matched the pillow. All traces of makeup had been wiped away, and with a start, Rafe realized how little she needed the makeup.

Not with her eyes. Through this whole ordeal, they'd been a vibrant testimony to annoyance, anger, indignation, disbelief, realization, fear and quite a bit more.

Camaraderie?

He hated that her eyes were closed now and

she wasn't sitting up, narrowing her eyes at him and sharing her opinion on what just happened.

Rafe had been at the college, but he'd missed the most important part: the actual fall. He'd heard the commotion and gotten to her side, praying all the way, just as she'd landed. Janie had been barely conscious. A thin drop of blood had slowly dripped from the corner of her mouth. She hadn't been moving, but she'd managed to say, "Somebody pushed me," before he shushed her.

He had to give Nathan credit. He'd arrived in minutes and had done what Rafe should have been doing. Even after Max's confession, the detective had pushed the crowd back and was taking names within a minute. The dean of students had called for an ambulance.

Rafe's eyes had been on Janie and only Janie. His hands had been reaching for her yet afraid to touch her.

He'd felt helpless. Not his usual reaction.

From the moment Janie unwillingly walked into his office, this criminal investigation had taken on a life of its own. One very different from the usual missing-persons case. And Janie Vincent wasn't a typical witness. She'd already managed to worm her way into his world with her drawings of imagined crime scenes and attention to detail like the green shoe.

He stood on the other side of her hospital bed. He touched her hand, so small and cold. Cupping it in his, he traced her fingers and then lifted them and gently kissed each one.

"Rafe?" Katie began.

"I'm so glad she didn't break her arm or anything that would keep her from her art. She'd hate that." Maybe if he changed the subject, Katie wouldn't mention what she'd just witnessed.

He cleared his throat, and added, "Especially now, when she's so close to finding out if she's going to South Africa."

Away from him.

Well, at least she no longer seemed to be in pain. That had killed him the most: the blood on her chin, the agony in her eyes right before they closed and his unwanted, unwelcome sense of helplessness.

"Rafe!"

"What?" He'd been in a land all his own, just him and Janie. But Katie's exclamation brought him back to earth.

"I was going to ask if you'd gotten any farther in your investigation into Patricia's death, but now I'm more interested in what's going on between you and Janie."

"Patricia? Were you on a first-name basis with Patricia Reynolds?"

"Of course. A few years ago, some students did a documentary at BAA. Patricia brought her art students to design the sets. Now, what's going on with you and Janie?"

"Nothing's going on, except she's involved in an investigation."

"Yeah, right," Katie said, switching from the lullaby to "Here Comes the Bride."

Rafe ignored her—it was the pregnancy hormones, that's all—and addressed Katie. "By all accounts Patricia accidentally ingested nuts that were in some brownies left in her office."

"Who would leave brownies with nuts in Patricia's office? She's allergic."

"You knew that?"

"Everybody did. She keeps an EpiPen in her purse as well as in the top drawer of her desk."

"Georgia mentioned that she carried one," Rafe said. "They found Patricia's purse locked in the cabinet in her office. Exactly where Georgia said she put it. The EpiPen was there. Nothing appeared to be disturbed. And while the EpiPen was missing from the top drawer, the key to the cabinet was there, right where it was supposed to be."

"You think she ran out of time?" Unspoken were the words *or was someone preventing her...*

"That's a question we hope the medical examiner can answer."

"Well, one thing's for sure..." The words were throaty, as if the speaker needed a drink.

"Janie!"

If Katie wasn't occupying the chair by Janie's hospital bed, Rafe would have slid into it. Good thing, because he'd have taken Katie's place and clutched Janie's hand, and Katie would have started asking questions all over again.

Janie opened her eyes. They were dark and brooding. Not typical for her, but better than closed. And throaty had never sounded so good.

"What's for sure?" Rafe asked, retreating to lean against the wall, by the window, away from the bed.

"My life's in danger."

"No," Katie said quickly. "They've already spoken with the kid, Max Carter, who grabbed your book bag. It was an accident. He's beside himself."

"It wasn't the grabbing of the bag that sent me down the stairs," Janie protested. "It was whoever tangled their feet in mine, found the back of my knee and gave a little push."

"You're sure?" Rafe questioned.

"I'm sure. I felt someone messing with the book bag, but I didn't fall until someone kicked in my left knee."

"You see anyone?" Rafe was already taking his notebook from his shirt pocket.

"Just a bunch of students, mostly young."

"Four classes were emptying," Rafe said before Katie could ask. "We've had the instructors supply their attendance charts. Maybe you know the teachers—Burt Taylor was teaching an economics class, and CeeCee Harrington was teaching an English class."

"I know CeeCee."

"To be safe," Rafe added, "we're also talking to the students who were filing into those same classes for the next period."

"That's a lot of kids," Katie said. "Plus, some of them have boyfriends or girlfriends who walk them to class."

"It's a long shot, I agree, but right now it's all we have."

"Okay!" Katie held up one hand. "No more case talk. Janie, how do you feel?"

Janie closed her eyes as if she had to think about the answer. Katie met Rafe's eyes and grimaced.

"I feel like someone tried to kill me," Janie said, and promptly drifted back to sleep.

"And," Katie said, eying Rafe, "I'm sure the sheriff of Laramie County is going to make sure that doesn't happen again. Right?"

Before Rafe could answer, his radio sounded. For the last four days, every time he got a call, it had something to do with the Brittney Travis case.

Almost as if God understood he didn't need other distractions.

No, almost as if God understood that Janie Vincent was distraction enough.

THEY'D KEPT JANIE in the hospital overnight, just as a precaution. Now, breakfast was over and she'd already had her blood pressure taken twice. She wanted to go home. For the fifth time she texted Katie. U almost here?

Katie didn't respond and Janie hoped that meant she was busy driving.

Janie hadn't been in the hospital since the day seventeen years ago when Tyre, a young black leopard, had taken exception to her walking into his enclosure.

She'd been looking for Katie. Even back then, she'd known to go to Katie. The cat had taken two steps in her direction, leaps really, and she'd not been afraid. After all, she'd watched Katie work with both Tyre and his brother, Aquila. At age six, Janie hadn't figured out the difference between pets and wild animals.

That changed in a twinkling.

Tyre had swiped just one paw at her, claws digging into the side of her face, and took her down. It lasted maybe ten seconds and then Katie had been there, making noise, getting Tyre away from her, subduing him.

It had been Katie and Jasper, her father's right-hand man, who'd stopped the bleeding and called the ambulance.

Her father had picked her up from the hospital the next day. He'd not commented on her stitches, not asked her how she was feeling, or anything. A month later, when the stitches had been removed and the doctors had concluded she'd be fine—no damage to her eyesight—he'd shipped both Katie and her off to live with his older sister.

Neither girl had met Betsy.

"It will be safer," he'd explained.

Janie had more respect for Tyre than she had for Betsy. She'd figured out quickly that the leopard had been behaving exactly as a leopard should.

Aunt Betsy had no inclinations to act like an aunt, let alone a mother figure. The scars from Tyre's paw were now light pink, and only two claw marks had left standing puckers, and now that Janie worked at BAA, she figured her scars were the mark of a true animal handler.

The marks left by Aunt Betsy weren't visible, but were harder for Janie to get over.

"The doctor will be here momentarily," a nurse said from the doorway to Janie's room. "He'll sign your release form and you can go. You feeling okay?"

"Fine. I'm fine." Yes, Janie had a nice-size lump on the back of her head, but it didn't bother her. Her ribs, on the other hand, hurt. Every time she breathed, her ribs ached. The flesh around her left eye was tender and swollen, but her ribs were the only real reminder that yesterday she'd pretty much plummeted down an elevator chute without waiting for the door to close or pushing the bottom-floor button.

"Good," the nurse said. She'd barely exited before someone else showed up in the doorway.

"Miss Vincent, I'm sorry." Max Carter stood in the door to her hospital room. He was a gangly kid who managed to always say the wrong thing and ducked his head a lot. Sometimes Janie wanted to assure him that he'd grow into his shoe size, but she imagined that family and friends had been telling him that for years, and that as a college freshman, he suspected that it should have already happened.

There were late bloomers.

Janie was one, at least by her big sister's standards.

Janie had never held a job for more than a year, didn't worry about social security and retirement, and was now living with her sister instead of on her own. She was saving all her money for the visiting-artist possibility in South Africa.

Katie didn't understand.

"Come on in, Max. What are you sorry for?"

"I'm the one who caused you to fall."

Janie swallowed. "You tangled your feet in mine and pushed my left knee?"

"No, I grabbed your book bag because I wanted to ask you a question. Someone bumped into me and I bumped into you. I think the way I pulled your book bag threw you off balance."

"No." Janie shook her head. "Someone pushed into my knee and I felt a hand in the small of my back."

"I didn't touch you. Only your book bag."

"Then you can stop beating yourself up. It was whoever tripped me that caused me to fall."

"I promise. That couldn't have been me." Relief didn't begin to describe the expression on his face.

Janie looked at the clock. Just after ten. The doctor should be there any minute and so should Katie. She wanted to pick Max's brain before her sister or the doctor arrived.

"Did you see anybody you recognized in the crowd around the stairs?" she asked.

"The cops asked me that. I was at the police station for hours answering questions. I knew probably half the people in the stairwell. I'd just gotten out of my communications class and was heading to the student union to grab something to eat. I saw you—"

"Tell me the names of the students in your class?"

"I'm not sure I can remember all of them. Some never talk."

From her art class, Janie knew that Max was a talker, but he usually chose the wrong thing to say and then spent five minutes saying it. It took him an hour to go through the twenty students in his class. In the end, he remembered all their names *and* their quirks. Janie only recognized one name: Amanda Skinley. But apparently she'd been absent that day.

Well, Rafe would certainly be interested in that if he hadn't already discovered it.

"How close are you and Amanda?" Janie asked.

"My mom and her mom are friends. I'm supposed to watch out for Amanda while she's here because she's only seventeen."

"She needs watching out for?"

"That's what I wanted to ask you yesterday!" Max suddenly became animated. "I haven't seen or heard from her since the Wednesday night two weeks ago when the cops came and she left the classroom crying. She hasn't been coming to school at all. She's not answering her cell phone or returning my text messages, and no one answers at her parents' house, either. Even my mom tried calling."

Janie closed her eyes. Fatigue took a brief hold. Unbelievable. She could fall asleep right here, right now, with Max fidgeting in the hospital room's doorway. Forcing her eyes open, she stared at the young man. She couldn't tell him about Amanda's visit to the zoo and the drawing they'd made. She couldn't tell him that Amanda's mother had said she would take both her children on a vacation just to get them away from Scorpion Ridge and Adobe Hill.

Janie knew so much and yet so little. She suddenly wished she'd pressured Rafe about what he'd gleaned from his interviews with her Wednesday night students.

He'd not been willing to tell her. So, she'd have to ask her own questions.

"I usually hear from Amanda about ten to twenty times a day," Max continued.

"Did you know Brittney?"

He sobered. "I did. Last semester she was in two classes with Amanda and me. We took a basic math class and then a college success class."

"So, the three of you hung around?"

"No, not really. Brittney's really pretty and kinda cool. Since Brittney and Amanda are from the same high school, Brittney's mom would drive them to the college. Mrs. Skinley or Amanda's brother would pick them up. Once Brittney got to school, she pretty much ditched Amanda. I think she was trying to hide the fact that she was still in high school. She ignored me."

"Why?"

Max made a face. "I can't believe you're asking that."

"I can't believe you're not giving me an answer."

"Brittney was blonde, gorgeous and guys were all over her from day one. Amanda and I cramped her style."

"Did she know Derek? Was Derek in any of those classes with you?"

Max sighed, reminding Janie of how she'd felt that Thursday morning—only three weeks ago—in Rafe's office when he'd wanted her to repeat all the information she'd already given.

"He was in our math class. He sat in the back row and I never saw them together. But, as I told the cops already, that doesn't mean anything. She did mention once that she thought he was 'scary interesting'. Her words, not mine. Even Amanda seemed fascinated by him."

Finally Max, looking resigned, stopped fidgeting and came to sit in the guest chair. He was no longer apologetic. He just seemed young.

"This is hard for you," Janie observed.

"You have no idea. Ever since Brittney disappeared, it's as if Amanda's my responsibility. I don't have a choice. I like being Amanda's friend, but being her protector is a bit much. This semester, my mom told Mrs. Skinley my schedule and right away, Amanda's enrolled in the same classes."

"The Skinleys are overprotective?"

"No, not really. It's just that they've already realized that Tommy's not heading for college. He's working at some construction job in Scorpion Ridge. I think they're afraid

Amanda's gonna mess up if she doesn't have someone to guide her."

"Well, would she?"

"That's just it. Not a chance. Amanda's a good girl. She's good without even trying. She'd rather draw than eat. And she's really smart."

"Was Brittney smart?"

"I couldn't say," Max admitted. "She was more interested in impressing her friends. That was easy for her to do."

The way he said that indicated to Janie that Brittney'd sure impressed Max. If he'd been assigned to protect Brittney, he'd have considered it an answer to a teenage boy's prayer. He scooted the visitor's chair closer to Janie's bed. "You don't really think Brittney's dead, do you? I mean, she could have just run away."

"I'm not sure. Was she the type of girl to run away?"

For the first time, Janie saw the man that Max would someday be, and she was very impressed. Soulful brown eyes carefully studied Janie. Janie figured her face revealed the truth.

"No, she wasn't the type to run away. She had it too good." Max rose and backed a few feet away from Janie. "She's dead."

Janie opened her mouth and wished she'd let whatever drugs they'd been giving her put her to sleep. Anything so she wouldn't have to tell Max she agreed with him.

"Max Carter, you've saved me a trip," a voice cut in. Detective Williamson stood in the doorway, making it look both small and blocked.

Max froze.

"We've got a few more questions for you, but first I need to talk with Janie here. Wait for me in the lobby."

Max started fidgeting again. Still, it didn't reduce his speed. He slid past Detective Williamson, and Janie could hear his feet hitting the polished floor as he ran down the hallway.

"He's going to be fine," Detective Williamson said. "He's not involved in whatever's going on at Adobe Hills Community College, but he might know something he's not even aware he knows."

"Like that Brittney thought Derek was scary?"

Detective Williamson nodded. "And some girls like guys who scare them."

He looked at her as if expecting her to agree. She did, but wasn't about to have this conversation with a guy—especially not one with a badge who reminded her of why she didn't particularly trust cops.

The detective came into the room and took

the chair Max had just vacated. "I wanted to ask you a few questions, but first, why don't you tell me about the conversation you just had with Max."

"He mostly wanted to apologize. He assumed it was his fault. Then, he talked about being responsible for Amanda and in awe of Brittney."

"Pretty much what we got out of him yesterday."

"He's worried about Amanda. She's missed school for a couple of weeks, and he's been trying to get ahold of her nonstop, but she's not answering. I didn't think I should mention that they've gone out of town. I didn't want to have to lie when he asked why."

"Amanda's a good student?"

"She's very talented in art." Carefully, Janie gathered the covers and sat up. She needed to be alert for whatever Detective Williamson threw at her. Lying down made her sleepy. Of course, sitting up made her dizzy. She paused for the wooziness to ease and then waited for Detective Williamson's next question.

"She keep an art book, too?"

"All the students did."

"Tell me what was in Amanda's."

"Why?"

"I'm curious."

"She mostly draws clothes. I think she hopes to be a fashion designer someday." Janie smiled. Amanda often was guilty of taking what the other students were wearing and drawing mix-and-match attire. She'd pair one student's cowboy boots with another student's shorts and yet another student's T-shirt.

"So, you're quite comfortable with her style? You'd be able to identify her artwork?"

"Yes, I believe so."

"Did she ever draw anything about her brother, Tommy?"

Janie almost said that Rafe had been asking questions about him, too, but she didn't.

Detective Nathan Williamson didn't inspire her trust. Not like Rafe did.

CHAPTER FIFTEEN

RAFE STARED AT the stack of papers on his desk. Some contained information he'd already memorized inside and out. Other files had joined the heap during the last few weeks, when he'd been focused on the Travis case. Now it was time to pay the piper, switch on his computer, start hobnobbing and catch up.

The benefit of being a small-town sheriff was a small paperwork-to-hands-on ratio. He'd met sheriffs who did nothing but paperwork and political posturing. Their ulcers were bigger than his.

But maybe they were slightly more sane.

Not that he could turn his back on paperwork and political posturing. It was as much a part of the job as grading was to teaching—

Speaking of teachers…

He picked up the phone to dial Janie's hospital room, thought better of it and dialed her sister, Katie, instead. "Call her yourself, Rafe," Katie ordered before he could even get the words out.

If Janie were in the Scorpion Ridge Hospital, he'd call either her doctor or one of the nurses. The hospital was small and he knew most of them. But Adobe Hills was bigger, and there'd be more red tape.

He glanced at the phone and then at his desk. Truth was, he didn't need to talk to Janie; he simply wanted to. Bigger truth was, he had to get some work done, and today was booked solid with responsibilities.

Janie should be just another item on his to-do list.

An hour later, he'd dealt with a dispute between a member of his custodial staff and one of his volunteers. Apparently, only he had the authority to appease both parties. Next, he approved the date for the next Bike Safety Day. Candy Riorden wanted a bike rodeo, but so far, Rafe had managed to rein in her exuberance. Though according to one of the memos on his desk, she'd already made the Bike Rodeo signs, so it seemed his hold on the reins was at best tentative.

Settling back, he perused a court case two of his officers served on. It had returned a guilty verdict. Good. A repeat offender had not only been caught in the act, but had resisted arrest and had actually bitten one of the arresting officers. Same thing had happened a year earlier, but thanks to a technicality the kid had been put back on the streets.

This time, the jury had found the guy guilty and Rafe sighed in relief, in triplicate. In police work, everything was in triplicate.

After sending an email to the lieutenant on a job well done, Rafe caught up on statistics—so far this week there'd been twenty-five incidents, nine arrests, twenty traffic tickets, twelve jail bookings and nineteen civil papers served.

Other than the Travis case, he'd call this a slow month.

At noon, after returning a dozen phone calls and what felt like a hundred emails about tomorrow night's awards banquet, he headed out the door for lunch.

Lunch was uneventful. Instead of the Corner Diner where the locals, especially his mother, would be hovering for information about the Travis case, he headed for home, a little two-bedroom that he'd bought from his uncle Leo.

It hadn't changed much from Leo's day. Leo, a bachelor, had been a long-distance truck driver, and hadn't needed much when it came to "home." It made for an empty look. The brightest spot in the room right now was the painting over the couch.

Crisco in all his glory.

His mother had already noticed it and remarked that he could use Janie's touch in all the rooms. Rafe was well aware she wasn't talking exclusively about paintings.

Rafe grinned as he cleaned up his sandwich and left his empty house.

His next responsibility was giving a speech at the high school. Scorpion Ridge High had just over six hundred students. He would be speaking to the graduating class, about one hundred and fifty-two students. Rafe knew about half of them.

When Rafe had sat in the audience of the high school as a graduating senior, his dad had been the speaker.

At the door, Rafe was met not by Sam Winslow, the principal, but by Sam's father, Sam Senior. He'd been Scorpion Ridge's high school principal for fifty years before retiring.

"Good to see you again," he boomed.

Rafe clasped the older man's hand. Sam had been one of his grandfather's cronies. And while Rafe had been hoping to speak to Sam Junior, find out what he thought about Amanda Skinley's connection with Brittney's case, it was like old times to talk to Sam Senior. "Good to see you, too. What are you doing here?"

"Sam's at a conference, and he's got one vice principal out because his appendix decided to burst last night, and the other vice principal—" Sam Sr. checked his watch "—is probably just now hearing the words *it's a boy*."

Rafe laughed. "I didn't realize how much I missed you."

"And it's as if I've never been gone." Sam Senior led Rafe down the hallway. "I hear that one of our students might be in a bit of trouble…."

"Just one?" Rafe chuckled.

"I'm talking about Amanda Skinley."

Rafe followed Sam Senior into the auditorium. Except for a janitor sweeping up something in a corner, it was empty. But the feeling of chaos—organized chaos—was in the air. Just as a high school should feel.

"Amanda here today?" Rafe asked. The thing about Sam Senior was that he claimed to be too old to care about student-confidentiality issues. He believed a community raised a child, and if a parent wanted to fight him because of something that happened in school, let the parent try and fight. Sam Junior was more a let's-leave-the-office-door-open-so-we-have-a-witness principal….

"No, and we've been informed that she'll not be finishing out the school year. You want to explain that? We send our brightest to that college for concurrent enrollment, and now one is missing, probably dead, and the other is about to have a nervous breakdown. She'll not even be at graduation. Did you know that?"

"No, sir, I didn't."

It was past time to call the Skinleys again. Rafe had their new cell number.

"You just have the two seniors taking classes at the college?" Rafe asked.

"Five started," Sam supplied. "Two dropped out and one moved out of state."

"How does that work, high-school seniors taking college classes?"

"It's a special program, fairly new," Sam replied. "High-school seniors can take college classes, usually the core subjects like English, math and such, and if they pass, it counts for both high-school credits and college credits."

"So mainly your college-bound students are interested in the program?"

"The top two percent, mainly those who are sure about what they want to do in the future," Sam said. "Like you were."

No one had been surprised when Rafe majored in criminal justice. He'd entered the police academy right out of college and was hired on in Scorpion Ridge at the ripe old age of twenty-two.

And his mother had cried.

Seven years later, at the tender age of twenty-nine, he'd successfully run for sheriff.

"Can the high schoolers take any class they want?"

"It's not encouraged," Sam answered. "There's a block of six classes we prefer them to take. The students pretty much go in as a unit. The five we sent were considered a cohort. They had a counselor who guided them."

Whoever that counselor was, he or she would be getting a visit from Rafe soon.

"How well do you know the Skinleys?" Rafe asked.

"Well enough to form the opinion that they're too easy on the son and too protective of the daughter."

Rafe's opinion also. "How about Brittney Travis? Are you familiar with her?"

"Lee's my insurance agent. Brittney is a bright girl, school comes easy for her. She didn't always apply herself, though. Likes the boys. Her parents kept taking her car away trying to get her on the straight and narrow."

Nothing Rafe hadn't already heard, but he was surprised by how much information Sam Senior had. The man still had his finger on the pulse of Scorpion Ridge High.

"Adobe Hills Community College is a bigger venue—more kids, more things to do—and that attracted Brittney like a moth to flame," Sam continued.

"Who would you say Brittney's friends were?"

Before Sam Senior could answer, the main auditorium door opened and a student poked his head through. He looked undecided about entering, but whoever was behind him wasn't undecided. The door opened and students careened forth.

A few minutes later, standing before the graduating class, Rafe said the words he'd said for almost a decade, but he felt as if he was in a vacuum.

Brittney should be in the audience. She should be poised to bolt into her future, make all the mistakes and have all the successes a teenager is supposed to make and have. Amanda Skinley should be in the audience, too. Something wasn't right in Scorpion Ridge, and Rafe needed to find out what. A sea of graduating seniors, now and in the future, depended on him.

Which meant he had to distance himself from Janie, stop thinking about her 24/7 and start thinking about the case 24/7.

As he reached the auditorium door, he

switched his cell phone back on. A message beeped.

"I've been trying to reach you for an hour," Nathan complained.

"Now you can appreciate how I felt on Tuesday."

Rafe wasn't sure how to read the silence that followed. Nathan was usually a straightforward, let's-not-waste-time kind of guy. At least, when he wasn't sending get-out-of-my-jurisdiction signals.

"We found something in Patricia's apartment during our investigation, and I recently finished going through it. It's Amanda Skinley's art book."

"It would have been nice to hear about this sooner," Rafe said.

"Patricia had more than two hundred student art books in that house. It took us a few days to go through them. Amanda's appears to be newer than the rest. I also want to impress you with the fact that we can find an art book and not lose it," Nathan said drily. "We've had time to look through Amanda's book, at the drawings and words. Probably with as much care as you gave Derek's art book."

Rafe recognized a dig when he heard one.

Nathan continued, "The last few pages are

the most interesting. They're a fairly detailed description of Brittney's death."

Rafe didn't believe it. He'd sat with Amanda as she drew their only investigative lead. She wouldn't have failed to mention that she'd also drawn the crime scene.

And there'd been no other female mentioned in Derek's art book.

Nathan continued, "Now we have two art books with leads. Janie should do a comparison. I stopped by her hospital room this morning. She indicated that she's familiar with Amanda's drawing style, and could say whether this is legit or a wild-goose chase."

"It's a wild-goose chase," Rafe said.

"Maybe," Nathan admitted, "but Amanda's parents are not returning my calls or emails, and Amanda's account of what happened to Brittney is nothing like Derek's."

JANIE WATCHED AS her sister, Katie, went from the stove to the fridge to the sink and then started all over again. Soon, there'd be enough ham, mashed potatoes and green beans to feed the whole neighborhood. Today she'd also cleaned the house from top to bottom.

Her brother-in-law, Luke, simply shook his head and waited. He knew Katie would break any moment and whatever was bothering her would all come spewing out.

Janie figured whatever it was, it had to do with her. Katie had been on big-sister-overload ever since they'd driven home from the hospital. Janie almost wished she hadn't spilled the details of Max and Nathan's visit.

"I really need to call Rafe," Janie finally said. "I want to find out what he thinks about Amanda's art book showing up in Patricia's apartment. Plus, I should tell him everything Max Carter said when he visited me."

"I guarantee he already knows everything there is to know about Amanda's art book." Katie stuck a rack of rolls in the oven and shut the oven door with enough force to rattle the pot of gravy simmering on top. "Including that it's just too convenient that it appears in Patricia's apartment for no good reason right after her death."

Janie rearranged the three green beans already on her plate. She covered them with a tiny shake of salt. Luke, who'd made the green beans, raised an eyebrow. Janie hated what was going on. Not only was it wrecking her life, but her sister and brother-in-law's, too. Taking the smallest piece of glazed ham, Janie tried to pretend she was hungry, but food was the last thing she wanted. What she really wanted was for Katie to calm down and for Luke to quit hovering.

It was touching, really, but a bit overwhelming.

"I'm fine, really," Janie insisted. She wasn't about to tell them how very scared she was. They'd only hover more. "Really, I'm fine," Janie repeated. "The Adobe Hills County sheriff is taking this seriously and that should deter whoever is pulling all these stunts."

"I wouldn't call murdering Patricia Reynolds a stunt," Katie snapped.

"Stunt was a bad choice of word," Janie admitted.

"Rafe's not doing enough." Katie pulled the rolls from the oven. "He'd better start doing mo—"

As if bidden, the doorbell rang. From the kitchen, there was a clear view of the front porch thanks to a large window.

"Doing more," Katie finished. Her somewhat amused look wasn't lost on Janie.

The Rafe Salazar who followed Luke into the kitchen was clearly tired. His hair badly needed trimming, and his uniform, usually spot-on, was rumpled and creased, as if he'd slept in it.

"Pull up a chair," Luke said. "Katie somehow sensed you were coming for dinner. She made plenty."

Rafe sat next to Janie. His eyes went from her bruised wrist to her black eye. He looked concerned and protective.

It was the *protective* that gave Janie goose bumps.

And for the first time in days, it wasn't the scary kind of goose bumps. What a time to start noticing—really noticing—the opposite sex.

Finally, as if convinced she wasn't going to pass out right at the dinner table, he took out a recorder and said, "Let's hear it. I want you to repeat the whole conversation you had with Max Carter."

"What about the conversation I had with Detective Williamson, and the fact that they found Amanda's art book at Patricia's?"

"Complete waste of time," Katie muttered.

"We'll talk about that later." Rafe was back to being all cop. He pulled a tiny notebook from his pocket and while Janie spoke and the recorder taped, he added notes.

Katie ate in silence, listening to every word. Every once in a while, her lips pursed together and Janie knew her older sister was just dying to add something to the account. Rafe ate his dinner with one hand, making notes with the other.

When Janie finished, he played back the recorder. "Did you leave anything out? Want to add anything?"

Janie shook her head.

Rafe silently nodded. "Something Max didn't share with you, apparently, is that he did ask Brittney out for a date. She turned him down."

"He didn't mention that."

"I think," Rafe said, "after seeing you in the hospital this morning, he realized just how serious this whole mess is. Nathan had him at the station for a second go-round of questions. He came up with a few more details."

"You did offer him counsel," Katie said, more a statement than a question.

"I'm sure Nathan did." Rafe opened the briefcase he'd carried in with him and slid over a second stack of papers and a red pen. "Here's a list of students who could have been in the area before and after you were pushed, taken from the witnesses and from class rosters. For almost every name we have, we've managed to get an accompanying picture. Nathan's already looked into who was absent and where they were. He's also got someone squirreling out who was meeting friends before and after class. The instructors are listed there, also. I want you to put a star by any name you recognize and then make a brief note of how you know them. Circle any picture that seems familiar. I've also included a few eyewitness accounts. Read them. Note any names not on the rosters."

"Eat while you go through those names," Katie ordered.

Janie glanced at her plate of cold ham and wilting green beans. Not a chance. Nothing tasted right. Rafe didn't seem to mind. He dished out a second helping while Janie examined the pictures and names.

There were more than three hundred names. Janie only recognized eleven, including two professors.

"Rebecca Townsend is a full-time English teacher. She's considered the resident complainer. CeeCee Harrington is an adjunct. She's been teaching English for a full year and wants to be full-time. I think she has money problems. She's always talking about going to different grocery stores to get the best prices, and once she said that the power company turned off her electricity. I don't recognize anyone else. Being part-time and working nights means you come, teach your class and go home."

"Did either Townsend or Harrington have a beef with your department chair?"

"No, everyone loved Patricia. Besides, Patricia wasn't in charge of their division."

Rafe didn't even blink, reminding Janie that *someone* didn't love Patricia, and maybe that same somebody didn't love Janie, either.

"How about the eyewitness accounts? Did you recognize any of those names?"

He returned to his chair, finished another piece of ham, then another, and waited. When she finished the last account, she shook her head. "No. It happened so fast."

He nodded, and scanned Janie up and down, starting with her bandaged arm and lingering on her black eye. "How are you doing?"

"Fine."

"She's not fine. She didn't eat one bite of dinner, and she's going to need pain medication to sleep because her arm is hurting so badly. And look at her face!" Katie wore her Defender of the Universe expression. Janie'd seen it often during their childhood—usually when she went one-on-one with their aunt over some injustice.

Katie could always talk her way out of trouble, using logic and maturity. She'd always been mature for her age. Little sister Janie had always tried being creative. She'd spent a good deal of her youth getting nowhere.

Right now she was too tired to care.

Rafe didn't flinch at Katie's outburst. He just stared at Janie, his brown eyes so searching that Janie felt a blush warm her cheeks. At least the bruises would hide the proof of what his scrutiny was doing to her.

He glanced away before she started to squirm.

"I'm fine. I just want to find out who really pushed me, and what has happened to Brittney." She didn't mention how scared she was.

Rafe finished his glass of milk and took some more photos from the briefcase. "I was hoping you'd feel that way. Apparently your trip down the stairs—no pun intended—caused Nathan to have second thoughts about how he's handling this case. He's even leaning on the medical examiner to take a closer look at Derek's death—the family's happy about that, by the way—and he's even cool with Scorpion Ridge having equal footing in the investigation." He laid the new photos on the table.

"Why is the family happy?" Luke asked.

"It will prove what one of our informants has been saying all along. Derek wasn't a cook. He didn't make the drugs. He didn't die because he was stupid."

No one had to say what they were all thinking—Derek Chaney had died because of what he'd written in his art book. The one that only Janie and Patricia had read.

Closing her eyes, Janie fought off the waves of dizziness that threatened to end her participation in tonight's queries. She wanted, needed, Derek's killer found so she could go back to feeling safe. She also needed to understand how the killer had found out that Derek had even submitted it, and how the killer had taken the book from the AHCC's campus security safe.

Janie had to believe that someday she'd feel safe again. Right now, the people she loved most didn't even seem to notice her fear or require her input. Katie was so busy poring over the pictures Rafe had laid on the table that she wasn't clearing the plates. Luke, too, was peering over Rafe's shoulder. Of the three, he was the most squeamish.

"Hey." Janie started to get up. It was that or pass out. She chose getting up. "Do I get to see or what?"

"Sit!" Rafe ordered. He gathered the photos and walked over to kneel beside her.

"Ahem." Katie cleared her throat.

Janie examined the pictures Rafe spread out in front of her. They were photos of Patricia Reynolds's office. The office was cluttered, but Janie barely noticed the stacks of papers and towers of books. In the middle of the room, Patricia slumped back in her chair. One pale white hand held a stack of papers in place. Her legs were lost between two towers of books. Janie could see one red heel still on her left foot, the shoe leaning against a toppled book tower. Her face—eyes open, mouth in a silent scream—was tilted upward.

She hadn't died pretty.

"Are you sure you're up to this?" Luke asked, looking more like *he* wasn't up to it.

"She's up to it," Katie said.

"I'm up to it," Janie agreed.

"Janie?" Rafe said gently. "You were her lab assistant. Do you notice anything out of place? The secretary says nothing else is missing. All the books are in place, the files were not riffled through, papers were undisturbed."

Janie peered closely at Patricia. Her blue pantsuit was not the type that wrinkled. The red blouse she wore underneath it perfectly matched the red high heels.

"The pin."

“What?” Rafe looked into Janie’s eyes.

“Patricia always wore an angel pin, on her pantsuit, right above her heart. It’s missing.”

CHAPTER SIXTEEN

RAFE HUNG UP the phone and leaned back in his chair at Katie's table. "Nathan is sending an officer to search Patricia's office again. According to the bag-and-tag records, the pin was neither on the body nor on the floor. Of course, that office was a mess, so something as small as a pin could have been misplaced."

"Sometimes on a hit, the killer takes a personal object in order to prove the hit's been made," Janie suggested. "I've seen that on television more than once." Luke nodded. Katie and Rafe both shook their heads.

"You're thinking of a mob hit," Rafe said. "Patricia's death was not a mob hit. And if it had been, it probably would have been her driver's license that would have been taken as proof."

"A pin means nothing," Katie added, removing the dishes from the table. "You can buy an angel pin just about anywhere."

"That angel pin meant a lot to Patricia. She always wore it," Janie said, pointedly ignoring the look Katie gave her about not touching her dinner.

"You know," Rafe said, "there might be something to the angel pin's disappearance. Patricia let her murderer into her office, probably welcomed them in. That somebody had the wherewithal to provide the brownies in a way that didn't arouse Patricia's suspicion and keep her from using her EpiPen in her purse. Her death wasn't a hit. It was much worse. I'm sure of that. It was most likely committed by someone she considered a friend."

"Someone who either attends the college or works there. And someone who could doctor Amanda's art book and then plant it at Patricia's," Janie added, closing her eyes and picturing her boss's office—the scores of people who traipsed in and out all day.

"Do you have any suspects?" Katie asked, settling down, no longer in housewife-cleaning-the-table mode.

Rafe shook his head. "Nathan and I agree that Adobe Hills Community College strongly figures into Brittney's disappearance. The one thing both Derek and Amanda's drawings claim, even if Amanda's are fake, is that Brittney was with other young people in a car. Derek's shows that they were on their way to kill her. Amanda's indicates that they were on their way to the middle of nowhere to party."

"On the coldest day of winter?" Katie clearly didn't buy it.

"Wouldn't matter to kids," Janie said.

"What's Amanda got to say to all this?" Katie asked.

"The family has made themselves scarce. Until we can talk with Amanda, we're focusing in on Chads and Chrises."

"Exactly what I expected, but you didn't answer my question about Amanda." Katie pointed out.

Rafe shifted in his chair.

"Hey," Katie said. "Janie's the victim here. She has a right to know what's going on in a case that involves her so much her life is threatened."

The expression on Rafe's face was so comical, Janie had to laugh.

"What's so funny?" Katie demanded, indignant.

"You two are what's so funny," Janie admitted. "You've stopped being my sister and become my lawyer. And Rafe here is about to fall out of his chair because you're asking him to share information about a case."

"I never stopped being your sister. It's just—"

Rafe held up his hand. "The only thing I

can share is that Amanda wasn't in class when Nathan took the art books from the other students." He looked at Janie. "Remember, she left the room crying."

Janie nodded. "I remember. Which means we can't verify that the one you found at Patricia's house is, in fact, Amanda's. But it seems as if..."

"Someone's gone to great lengths to throw a second trail," Rafe said softly.

"Poor Derek," Janie said. "He was afraid turning in that art book would make him the target of a killer."

"So," Luke said. "In a way, he was brave."

"No," Rafe said. "If he'd been brave, he'd have confessed to a cop, someone in authority. The way he did it, with that art book, he basically signed two more death warrants. Patricia's has been carried out."

"Rafe," Katie said, "you can't keep what Amanda allegedly wrote a secret from us. Janie's in danger. You did bring a copy with you for Janie to verify."

Rafe bent down and pulled a folder from his briefcase. In it were several pages photocopied from Amanda's art book. Katie reached for the papers, but with just a look from Janie, she withdrew her hand and Rafe handed them to Janie.

“This is my problem,” Janie said.

Katie opened her mouth and then wisely closed it as Janie began to read.

The writing looked like Amanda’s. The words were slanted and loopy, and in a few places the *i*’s were dotted with tiny hearts. Unfortunately, Janie had done no more than glance at Amanda’s handwriting before.

Her drawing, now, that was a different story. In her re-creation of the murder, Amanda had drawn the same weather as Derek, the same time of evening, but different people and events.

“Nope, not a chance. These first few pages are hers, but the last few drawings… This isn’t Amanda’s work,” she muttered.

Katie started to issue another sounds-like-a-question-but-is-really-a-statement but at the last minute her tone changed to a command. “You are having the handwriting analyzed.”

“We are,” Rafe said. “Why don’t you believe this is Amanda’s work?”

“She’s a meanderer.” Janie studied the drawings for a while, then paused to explain. “She’ll start on one part of a drawing and then leave it halfway through just to start on another section, so her lines are never fluid. Ever. It’s an interesting style, and not depicted here at all.”

“You haven’t read all the words, have you?” Rafe asked.

"No."

"Finish," he ordered.

The last sentence of Amanda's art book was a bit different from Derek's, but no less powerful. While Derek had ended with *She tried to run and stumbled. Then, Chad shot her in the back.* Amanda had finished with *All partied out. She was dead, and no longer pretty.*

"Was there any sign that Amanda was jealous of Brittney?" Rafe asked.

"If anything," Janie said, "Amanda was in awe of Brittney. And, if Amanda had been at this kind of party, she'd have fainted dead away."

"She has a brother who's an avid partier," Luke pointed out.

Katie was done being patient. She snatched the pages from Janie's hands and read quickly. Her face went red and then white. Her hands shook as she aimed her anger at Rafe. "What do you plan to do about this? You will keep Janie safe."

"She's my top priority," Rafe agreed. "I've already arranged to have officers drive by the house on the hour. Of course, that's not enough. We'll make sure she's never alone. It's a plus that she's here with you. That's round-the-clock protection, in a way."

"It also puts them in danger," Janie pointed

out. "Maybe I should do what Amanda and her family have done—just disappear. I already have my passport. Maybe I should go to South Africa alone, do what I've been dreaming of."

"You have that kind of money?" Rafe asked.

"I have it," Katie offered.

"If I head to South Africa," Janie asked, "what happens to the investigation concerning Brittney?"

Rafe and Katie shared a look. "Seventeen-year-old Amanda Skinley would become the cornerstone," Katie said.

Janie felt the walls closing in. She couldn't leave. Amanda wasn't just seventeen, she was a young seventeen.

"Or the investigation will grind to a halt," Rafe said, "unless we can find a tie between Brittney's death—"

"Alleged death," Katie interrupted. "There's still no body, and she's listed as a runaway."

"—and Patricia Reynolds's death."

"So, no matter what," Janie acknowledged, "somebody loses."

"We're not losing anybody else," Rafe said. "Running to South Africa is a short-term flight from a long-term problem. Everybody would have to move, otherwise, you would never get to visit your new niece or nephew, or—"

For a moment, Janie thought he might say, "me." Instead, he continued. "We're beefing up security around Janie. I'm putting my best man on it."

"Every officer you have already believes I'm their personal drive-by," Janie said. "I can't turn around without seeing Candy or Jeff—"

"You're on a first-name basis with them now?"

"Have been for weeks."

"Until we find out who pushed you, you'll only be dealing with me."

"And me," Luke added.

Rafe didn't look convinced her brother-in-law was up for the task.

"Hey," Luke protested, "if I can shoot a hippopotamus in the ass to sedate him, I can shoot an intruder if one tries to get near my favorite sister-in-law."

"Only sister-in-law," Janie reminded him.

Katie stared at her husband in awe. "I like it when you go all macho."

"What do you have planned tomorrow?" Rafe asked. "Where should I focus my efforts?"

"I'll be here all day, painting, probably. I can't teach injured like this."

The four of them huddled around the table

going over the schedule for the coming week and making sure that at no time was Janie left unguarded and alone.

"You got plans Saturday night?" Rafe asked.

"No."

"You do now. We're going to the Police Officers' Awards Banquet. Almost all of the law-enforcement officers in the area will be there, including the ones who should be driving by here every hour. You'll go with me. There's no safer place for you."

Janie wasn't sure she would describe a night with Rafe as *safe*.

JANIE COULDN'T REMEMBER ever feeling this nervous before a date. But, then, this wasn't a date. This was a bodyguard getting stuck with an assignment on a Saturday night.

She'd feel even more nervous if she'd had a spare minute to worry. As it was, after last Tuesday's question-and-answer session, she'd gotten used to having Rafe around, practically 24/7. The only time she was sure he wasn't around was at night, when Luke took over. Jasper, who'd worked for her father and now was a keeper for Luke, took to spending the night in the living room, even though Janie had insisted he should be with his new bride, Ruth.

Janie had spent the last four days feeling

bruised and scared, but determined to go on with her life, including going on nondates. Plus, Janie had never been one to stay home.

Still, she wasn't sure what to wear to a police officers' awards banquet. She settled on a gauzy dark green skirt and white cotton blouse with a silky green sweater. But Katie took one look at her and turned white. If not for the bruised arm and accompanying pain meds, Janie never would have allowed Katie to be included in any how-should-I-dress dilemma. But Katie knew when she had a pliable client, and managed to convince Janie to wear something more "dateworthy."

Instead of his Jeep, Rafe showed up in a pale blue rebuilt Mustang. And instead of his everyday uniform, at least the one she'd always seen him in, he was in dress blues, complete with spit-shined shoes, a gold name tag and numerous badges.

Judging by his reaction to her appearance, Janie was glad she'd listened to her sister.

In Scorpion Ridge, almost everything was ten minutes away. From Katie's house, the Scorpion Ridge Community Hall was a mere nine minutes away. No place had never looked so safe to Janie. Every fifth vehicle was a squad car. Tonight's event involved all of Rafe's counties, from Scorpion Ridge to Adobe Hills to

Gesippi. A police officer, acting as a valet, directed Rafe to a prime parking spot.

"One of the perks," Rafe said.

Janie smiled. She'd always liked dressing up, but her version of dressing up meant a gauzy skirt and simple white blouse. Not appropriate, apparently, for the twentieth annual Police Officers' Awards Banquet.

Instead, she was adorned in a fire-engine-red, midcalf silk dress, complete with a cute little white clutch purse and sensible white flats—women on pain meds should not wear heels. Janie definitely felt like a somewhat broken but extremely happy princess.

Rafe was definitely prince material.

He came around the car and opened the door. Janie stepped out to a chorus of wolf whistles and "Hey, boss, where you been hiding her?"

"I guess they don't care about the black eye," Janie whispered.

"You have a black eye?" Rafe teased, leaning in and planting a gentle kiss on the evidence of her fall. "I didn't notice."

She reached up, touched where he'd just kissed, and started to lean toward him, wanting another kiss—and not on her eye! But he was already walking toward the entrance, his whole demeanor purposeful.

Rafael Salazar was on duty.

Whoever sponsored the event had gone all out. Instead of arrows pointing the way to the event, nightsticks did. At the entrance, each door was made to resemble a giant police badge. In the middle of the white tablecloths were target practice sheets. The centerpieces were gorgeous flowers with yellow cordon-tape bows.

It was grander than the art exhibit they'd gone to together just over a week ago. "I take it you weren't in charge of decor?" Janie said as Rafe guided her to a table up front and center.

"No, that would be the wife of the sheriff who held office before my father. She also happens to be the mayor's twin sister. Not someone you want to mess with. This is her baby. She started the banquet back in the 1990s when Darryl was just starting to think about retiring and every year it's the highlight of her life. Last year we even had a theme." He pulled out a chair. "What can I get you to drink?"

"Whatever you get is fine with me."

Rafe disappeared into a sea of boisterous men and women. Some were in dress uniform, some in street uniform, some in dress-up and others in dress-down. All greeted Rafe as if he were the most important person in the room.

The guys looked back at Janie with open admiration, despite the bruises. The women couldn't conceal their curiosity.

Before Janie could decide which bothered her more, an older gentleman appeared at the table, pulling out a chair for his companion. Displaying graying temples and a military stance, he wore a top-brass uniform and still managed to seem underdressed. There was nothing gray about his wife. With shock-white, upswept hair and a regal pose, she would have fit in better on a magazine cover instead of at a small-town policemen's banquet. Before introductions could be made, the gentleman did the "What can I get you to drink?" bit and disappeared.

Lipstick the exact color of Janie's dress and sparkling blue eyes turned to peruse Janie. "About time Rafe brought somebody interesting to these outings."

Janie laughed.

"I'm Mitzy Webber. That was my husband Darryl. He was sheriff long before Rafe or Rafe's father. And you are…?"

"I'm Janie Vincent."

"Ah, Katie's sister." Mitzy glanced around, spotted Katie, and waved. "We love, love, love your sister. I've never seen a woman who can walk among lions so effortlessly. Oh, and what she's done for the Rittenhouse boy."

Janie nodded, almost afraid of what Mitzy might say next, especially if she was willing to call Luke a boy.

"The Rittenhouse men have always been attractive. Why, if I were thirty years younger…"

Janie let loose the breath she was holding.

Mitzy didn't seem to need any help carrying on a conversation. She continued, "Rafe's a confirmed bachelor, but I've always said *confirmed* is just *confused.* So, tell me, did Rafe's mother fix you up? She's been dying for—"

"No," Rafe said, setting a drink in front of Janie. "My mother did not set us up. Janie's part of an investigation, and since we were working on the case today and might even get a few things done tonight after the banquet, it made sense to combine business with pleasure."

That made her pause for a second, but one thing Mitzy Webber couldn't seem to stand was white space. After a moment, she launched into the story of how she and Darryl met. Janie could tell by the expression on Rafe's face that he'd already heard the tale. Since he was politely listening, though, he couldn't see how conflicted she was.

Was she more business? Or more pleasure?

It bothered her that it bothered her.

And, if she was completely honest, she was hoping he put her more in the "pleasure" category.

"And," Mitzy finished, "we've been married for fifty-three years!"

Before Mitzy could continue, Rafe interrupted. "You have a sister over in Adobe Hills, don't you?"

"I do." Mitzy practically glowed. "I'm surprised you remember."

"There's a family there," Rafe said, "who could really use a friend. The Chaneys. The memorial for their son Derek is this Monday."

Janie glanced up. "Really? You didn't tell me that."

"Yes, I'm familiar with the story," Mitzy said. "I've heard of Derek." Looking at Janie, Mitzy's expression changed. "That's who you are. You're the teacher who turned in Derek's journal."

"Art book," Janie corrected. Then, to Rafe, she asked, "Are we going to the funeral?"

"Yes."

Mitzy nodded, "I'll call my sister tomorrow morning. I'm sure her Thursday-morning Bible-study group will take Derek's mother under their wing. She'll get her husband to work on Derek's father."

"There's another son, too."

Mitzy was already opening her purse, taking out a small calendar and writing in it. Before Rafe could say anything else, a few officers stopped by the table to talk shop. They all gave Janie the once-over, but apparently being with Rafe gave her hands-off status.

Then someone blew a whistle and the evening officially commenced. The meet-and-greet segment of the evening was over. One last couple joined their table. The gentleman settled his wife and headed for the stage. Scorpion Ridge's mayor, who looked quite a bit like his sister except for the glitter and lipstick, took the mic and welcomed everyone. After a short speech, he finished with a big thank-you to his sister for starting this honored tradition.

Then Rafe took the stage.

He didn't do the "thanks" song and dance. He addressed his speech to the citizens of Laramie County, emphasizing the importance of building positive relationships—more than one cop glanced her way when Rafe said that—and upholding positive values. He managed to make what should have been a "same old, same old" speech not only interesting, but also humorous.

His task done, the buffet line opened, and

after a moment Janie was left alone with Mitzy as the whole table went to fill their plates.

Janie'd fully intended to get her own plate filled, but Rafe just looked at her and shook his head. She was still stiff, yes, but she wasn't helpless.

"Oh, let him take care of you," Mitzy said. "He's the sheriff. Filling your plate is definitely a step in his building-a-positive-relationship theory."

"Is that why your husband is filling yours?" Janie asked.

"No, he's filling mine so I can find out all the gossip about you and then fill him in about it when we get home."

"No gossip about me," Janie said. "I'm the boring Vincent sister."

Mitzy laughed. "That's not what I heard. So, you're the one who helped little Amanda Skinley draw a suspect, too?"

Janie scanned the room for Rafe. Just how freely could she discuss the case?

"My husband still knows everything that goes on in Adobe Hills when it comes to criminal activity," Mitzy explained.

After three or four futile searches for Rafe in the buffet line, Janie gave up her hope that he would rescue her and changed the subject from Brittney's case to herself.

Janie Vincent: the sister who hadn't found her niche yet.

She was interrupted, but not by Rafe.

"Janie? I'm surprised to run into you here."

Nathan Williamson was dressed much like Rafe, right down to the spit-shined shoes and gold name tag. It was the first time Janie had seen him all dressed up. He was the same height as Rafe and had the same thick hair. But the similarity ended there. Nathan's chin wasn't nearly as strong and his eyes weren't the same deep shade of brown-bordering-on-black.

Mitzy grinned. "Nathan? I wasn't aware you'd met Janie." She reached over to pat Janie on the hand. "My, my, you do know all the single men."

Janie, rarely at a loss for words, could only stammer. "We're…"

"Working a case together," Nathan finished.

Mitzy didn't look convinced.

Janie smiled weakly.

"You're here with Rafe?" By his tone, Nathan was surprised.

"Yes, he's making sure I stay out of trouble."

"Hmm."

Janie tried to interpret his *hmm,* but the attempt only took her mind back to wondering if she was business or pleasure. She wasn't feeling much like business at the moment, but she wasn't sure if her psyche could take the idea of becoming involved with a cop. Yet, so far, this evening had been one more reminder of why Janie *should* give officers more of a chance: it had been a night of camaraderie and fun.

Someone shouted from the back of the room. Nathan excused himself and ambled toward the commotion.

"He's a good cop," Mitzy said.

High praise, but Janie was still wary of the detective. There was just something about the way Nathan had acted early on in the investigation.

"My sister lives in Adobe Hills," Mitzy continued, "and her husband is a detective on the force. Sometimes his cases cross over to the DEA or into Nathan's authority. We go to my sister's for dinner about every other week. Nathan often joins us. Apparently their issues with the drug trade have escalated in the last five years, especially meth."

Janie searched again for Rafe. He should be hearing this. But maybe he already knew.

"Nathan's responsible for keeping more dealers off the streets than anyone else," Mitzy continued.

More likely Justin was responsible, but Justin couldn't take the credit, because he was undercover.

Mitzy wasn't finished. "I just wish Nathan would find somebody. He's never gotten over his divorce. Foolish woman. Imagine being loved that much and throwing it away."

Janie looked over at Nathan. He was standing at the rear of the buffet line, alone, the only Robinson Crusoe in the room. It was hard to imagine this man cozying up to a relationship.

Mitzy followed Janie's gaze. "He worshipped her. I remember thinking how lucky she was. How lucky I am." As if proving her point, her husband arrived and handed her a full plate and kissed the top of her head before taking off again. A server stopped at their table to refill their iced tea.

"Was it a nasty divorce?" Janie asked.

"I don't know all the details, but his young wife got addicted to drugs and wasn't willing to stop using. I guess Nathan tried interventions, sent her to rehab, everything. One day, she just packed up and left. He was devastated."

The buffet line moved forward, Nathan with it. Maybe, Janie wondered, his uptight stance and the rigid set of his shoulders had more to do with pain than with misplaced pride.

She pitied him, though he probably wouldn't appreciate the emotion.

Like Rafe, he appeared to be a man who garnered respect from everyone he met.

Not that respect, or rank, was helping either Nathan or Rafe earn front-of-the-line privileges at this event. Parking was one thing, food another. Grinning like the cat who ate the canary, Rafe returned, setting a serving of lasagna, garlic bread and salad in front of her and then scanning the crowd to find what had her attention.

It didn't take him long to figure it out. "Nathan? What's Nathan doing here?"

As if sensing he was being scrutinized, Nathan turned and looked first at Janie and finally at Rafe.

"He was surprised to see me here," Janie said.

"I'm surprised to see *him* here." Rafe didn't sound pleased. "He's received more than one outreach award from us, but he's never bothered to—"

Mitzy cleared her throat, loudly.

"Not that he's receiving one tonight," Rafe supplied smoothly.

"Maybe," Mitzy said, "it's not the prospect of an award that got him out of Adobe Hills." She smiled pointedly in Janie's direction.

Now, instead of a canary, Rafe looked like he'd swallowed a lemon.

Janie's appetite returned. Nathan was not her type, but watching Rafe's hackles rise was the best thing that had happened all night.

"This lasagna's great," she said after four bites.

"It's from a restaurant in town," Rafe said, "called Yano's. I'll take you there some night."

Mitzy shot her a sly glance. Definitely pleasure, not business.

And then Rafe added quietly so no one else could hear, "Brittney worked as a hostess there during the summer. She made it clear to another employee that she was single—which means she and Derek were definitely not a couple."

CHAPTER SEVENTEEN

WHILE JANIE'S MOUTH opened to a silent, lingering "Oooh," Rafe downed three bites of lasagna quickly. He'd learned, at these functions, not to attempt leisure. Other officers seemed to feel that they had to stop by, shake hands with the sheriff, make small talk. And that meant too often he'd either eaten cold food, or simply pushed the plate away and didn't get to eat at all.

Neither put him in a good mood.

"You're kidding." Janie smiled as Candy Riorden and, yes, a boyfriend, came up, introduced themselves, smiled covertly at her and then disappeared into the crowd.

"I'm not. See the boy at the end of the buffet line?" He waited while Janie located a young man busily switching a full pan of steaming vegetables in for an empty one.

"That's Samuel Pynchon," Janie whispered. "The preacher's oldest boy. What did you do to him? He looks ready to throw up."

"I didn't do anything to him, he did it to

himself. And I'm aware that he's the preacher's kid," Rafe whispered back. "I've known him since he was a baby. Maybe that's why he felt comfortable asking me when I'd started dating you—"

Someone else interrupted them. This time, a dispatcher and her husband.

"You did tell him we *weren't* dating, right?" Janie asked in a low voice after the dispatcher and her husband had walked away.

"No, I didn't. It's none of his business. Plus, I didn't want to explain why we're here together. Let him think what he wants. But then he mentioned that Brittney worked for Yano's, which we—"

"Had already discovered," Janie finished.

Jeff Summerside came up. He was one of Rafe's newest hires, just three years on the force and rising through the ranks quickly, already chief of police. He kissed Janie's hand, the one that didn't hurt. It only took the tiniest narrowing of Rafe's eyes to send Summerside to another table.

"Of course we knew Brittney had worked at Yano's, but what we weren't aware of until just two minutes ago, was that the preacher's son had a thing for Brittney and he says she returned it."

Janie took a good long look at Samuel. "He

told you that, just now? That makes sense. Amanda said that Derek and Brittney weren't a couple. I think we—or I, at least—kept lumping them together because he wrote about her."

Before Rafe could comment, another officer stopped by to say hello. Rafe tried to smile, but he almost felt like he was at a Dean Martin roast, and that at any moment someone would get behind the mic and admit that the whole force had gotten together and determined that neither fine dining nor uninterrupted conversation was on the agenda for Rafe tonight.

Rafe carried on what he hoped was an intelligent conversation with the officer from Gesippi while he kept one eye on Janie, who was chatting up a guard from the jail division in Florence, Arizona. This particular man could down a polar bear with one arm but usually lost his tongue when faced with a female. Janie had him blushing but made him comfortable enough around her to remain coherent.

Hmm.

Rafe could stand on his chair and shout to the room that they weren't a couple, but people believed what they wanted to believe. And for some reason, just about every soul on the Scorpion Ridge police force wanted Rafe and Janie to be a couple.

Before Rafe had a chance to whisper to

Janie the rest of what he'd heard or even finish his first piece of garlic bread, the conversation at the table turned to a debate over the use of the M26 Advanced Taser.

Mitzy rolled her eyes and pretended to shoot her husband. He put a hand over his heart, winked and continued talking. Janie said that she wanted an M26 Advanced Taser to help keep her safe, and Rafe felt a lump in his throat that he couldn't blame on the garlic bread. But just then Mitzy's husband threw down his napkin and headed for the stage.

One thing for sure, tonight wasn't going as planned. It would sure help if Janie Vincent was boring. Then maybe when his crew accused him of having more than a professional interest, he could at least pretend they were wrong.

Not that she was making it easy. In the last twenty minutes alone she'd managed to touch his hot buttons.

Rafe was territorial, and he was starting to consider Janie his territory, not just his responsibility. In his profession, he rubbed elbows with plenty of charming, attractive women. None came close to making him feel the way Janie made him feel.

He shouldn't have invited her tonight. She

would have been safer with her sister and brother-in-law.

He motioned for Chief Jeff Summerside and said, "I've got some things to do tonight. I'd like you to see Janie home and stick around until you're sure she's secure."

Jeff seemed a bit confused but immediately said, "Yes, sir."

Someone on stage called his name, and suddenly Rafe had two plaques in his hand: one an outstanding achievement award and the other a President's award. He tried to act nonchalant, but winning an award felt different when somebody in the audience was clapping not for the sheriff, but for Rafe Salazar, the man.

GIVEN THE OPPORTUNITY, Rafe could sleep for twelve hours straight. As sheriff, those opportunities were rare. Sunday morning the alarm sounded at just after six, and with ease born of practice—after only six hours of sleep—Rafe rolled out of bed.

Before working out, something he'd not been doing faithfully for the last month, or even eating breakfast, he called Jeff for a status report. He reported that while Scorpion Ridge didn't have a clean bill of health for last night, the wounds were all superficial.

Except for Rafe's.

He headed for the spare bedroom and started his regimen. Push-ups came first. With each crunch, he felt pain. Not from the hard floor under his mat or from the pull of his gut. He was suffering from an acute case of regret.

Had he put the brakes on a bit too hastily with Janie? She'd been the perfect date, especially for one who attended the function not as a guest but pretty much as a prisoner. For the entire evening, she'd charmed his men.

Charmed Rafe.

Then, at the end of the evening, when he'd handed her over to Jeff Summerside, she'd not only acted as if she understood but as if she didn't care.

Rafe grabbed his jump rope and headed to the backyard.

So Rafe Salazar apparently was attracted to a woman who was not attracted to him. That was a first. He'd never had any trouble with women. It was discouraging them that often proved difficult.

Somebody should tell Janie.

After hitting a hundred jumps, Rafe went back inside and switched to some resistance weights. Up, down. Up, down. Of course, when Rafe reassigned Jeff and reinstated himself as the lead on the case, there'd be talk. Down.

He could take it.

Just before he hit the shower, he realized he'd broken out in a sweat, and somehow didn't think the workout was to blame.

He hadn't minded Janie's I'm-not-interested act back when her sister and his mother were doing the matchmaking. He minded now, and agonizing over Janie almost made him late for church.

Great, not only was she distracting him at work but now she was affecting his faith.

After dressing, eating breakfast and taking a quick drive through his town, Rafe pulled into the church's parking lot, choosing a spot that would allow him to exit quickly if he had to, and headed for the door.

He was blessed with three families: his mother, the police force and the church.

Based on the looks that followed the "good mornings" he received, most of the congregation were interested in his date last night. They considered it their right to pry into his personal business—small-town justice.

Miles Pynchon, the minister, stood by the door. He somberly clasped Rafe's hand. "I hear my son gave you some new information last night."

Rafe was somewhat surprised. Miles knew better than to bring up an ongoing investigation during church. Still, Samuel was Miles's oldest boy, and this might be the first time one of his sons—he had four—was in a bit over his head.

"Were you aware that Samuel and Brittney were interested in each other?" Rafe asked.

"It didn't occur to me to mention it," Miles said. "All the young men were enamored with her."

Rafe nodded. He'd figured the same thing, but hadn't realized that Samuel and Brittney had actually gone out together.

"Speaking of enamored," Miles said. "I hear you had a date last night with Janie Vincent."

"How'd you hear that?" Rafe asked.

Miles grinned. It didn't reach his eyes, but then, he was probably thinking of his son. "You might want to help her out." Miles glanced toward the foyer. "She's not a veteran like you, and a few of our more curious members seem to have her cornered."

Cornered might not be a strong enough word. Usually when the ladies of the church did a mass huddle, it meant someone was dying, a soon-to-be bride or a new baby.

He'd seen Janie at church only a few times with Katie and Luke. He guessed she was here today because Katie and Luke weren't letting her out of their sight. As Rafe neared the huddle of women, two things happened. One, the ladies parted like the Red Sea to let him pass.

Fringe benefit of being the sheriff.

Two, the woman standing next to Janie stepped away from her. The woman was Angela Talbot. Two years ago, she'd been Rafe's date to the awards dinner and a few other events. By the expression on her face, she'd realized why she hadn't been invited to last night's event.

He recognized pain when he saw it.

He hadn't meant to hurt Angela, and truthfully, they both knew that if there truly had been a spark, it would have ignited years ago.

Not sure what to say, he just cupped his hand around Janie's elbow and quickly guided her away.

"Thanks," Janie whispered as they went into the main auditorium. "They've always welcomed me when I came, but not quite like that."

The church's old guard greeted newcomers, took food to the sick, organized going-away parties and all kinds of showers: baby, new home and wedding. Rafe knew exactly what they were thinking.

He just had no idea what Janie was thinking. He could, however, tell how she was feeling: broken and tired. Without realizing it, she was hugging one of her arms—the one that had borne the brunt of the fall. The bruising around her eyes testified that just six days ago someone had pushed her down the stairs.

Rafe didn't bother to head for his customary spot in the church. He plunked Janie down in the nearest pew—center, next-to-last row—sat beside her and asked, "How are you feeling?"

"Fine. I kept insisting to those ladies that I was fine, but they seemed to want more."

Rafe wasn't about to say that what they were really hoping she'd answer was a question they hadn't really asked, the question of how she and Rafe were doing…relationship-wise?

The old guard wanted to throw a wedding shower.

Right now, Rafe just wanted to keep Janie alive.

"They mean well," he finally said.

"I can see that."

It was a good thing that was all she could see. He'd hate to think she already saw into his heart.

RAFE, THE MOST eligible bachelor at the Main Street Church, had just kidnapped Janie from the grip of the church ladies. Her cheeks hurt from smiling, and she was sure the whole congregation was whispering, "That's the young

Vincent girl. Seems she's finally made up her mind."

Her sister certainly believed so.

Walking into the auditorium, Luke at her side, Katie wore a Cheshire smile. Unfortunately, the smile didn't reach her eyes. Katie was scared. She wanted Janie to stay at home, in a locked room, until they figured out who had killed Patricia and who had pushed Janie down the stairs.

"Hey, Rafe." Katie sidled in beside him. "We wondered if you'd ever get here." Meaning, *Luke and I left Janie alone on purpose so you'd have to rescue her. What took you so long?* Katie followed that with, "Any news?"

At least Katie did recall that someone had more or less put a hit out on Janie.

"No," Rafe said. "So far, it's been a quiet morning."

Katie nodded. "You back on guard duty for the rest of the day?"

Janie waited. Jeff certainly had smooth ways about him. He opened car doors, offered coffee, and even listened to country music, but he didn't make Janie feel completely safe, not like Rafe did.

"I never left."

But he had. Something she'd done last night had spooked Rafe, something that had nothing to do with cop and civilian and everything to do with male and female. Enough so he'd turned her over to Jeff and found other things to do at the banquet. Jeff had done some muttering about priorities. Mainly he'd wanted to be with the girl he'd brought.

Before Janie could ask Rafe what the game plan for today was, a man stepped behind the podium, cleared his throat and announced a song number.

A minute later, Janie realized she might never listen to country music again. Rafe didn't sing with gusto. No, like everything else, his approach to music was purposeful. He had a deep, rich bass. Deep enough to awe Janie; rich enough to make her close her eyes and enjoy.

The man certainly had plenty of hidden talents.

Of course, when one's life was in danger, it was never a good idea to close one's eyes for too long. Janie's eyes were still closed when Rafe suddenly stopped singing. She opened them when the rest of the congregation's singing staggered to a halt, too, even though the song wasn't over. On the screen, the words still waited. The song leader's mouth was open in a silent *O*.

Rafe quickly turned to Luke. "Don't lose

sight of Janie." Then, with an ease most big men couldn't quite master, he slid out into the aisle and faced the back of the auditorium.

Tommy Skinley probably didn't see whose arms were reaching out for him. His tears were that thick. He also probably couldn't hear the words of the congregation. He was too busy cursing. He had one hand in the pocket of his jacket and the other pointed at Janie.

Unfortunately, neither words nor sobs stopped him from lunging at her.

CHAPTER EIGHTEEN

RAFE DIDN'T DOUBT for a moment that Janie was in danger. But the people of the congregation were in more danger as they stood between her and Tommy. The boy was in the middle of a meltdown and Rafe suspected some kind of stimulant was fueling the kid's actions.

Worse, Rafe couldn't tell if the kid had a gun or not.

His gut warned him that any loud noise would spook Tommy. So Rafe turned sideways, moved slowly and kept his eyes on Tommy. He motioned downward with his hand and then to the side. Most of the people in the church's left and right sections got the crouch-and-go message and headed for the side doors.

Good.

It was the center section that was in trouble.

Janie's section.

And she was in the back, quickly becoming a clear shot.

Come on, Luke, get her out of here.

But hindering Luke were the hundred people exiting the auditorium. The fact that most were glancing over their shoulders while pressing forward didn't make things go faster.

Then, too, not everyone had moved out of the church. Some were frozen, unable to move, caught in the crux of their own fear. Others, especially the men, were unsure of the best action: should they go or stay and help? Rafe quickly gestured for them to go.

Luke finally got Janie headed for the exit.

Rafe focused then on the boy. "You don't want to do this, Tommy," Rafe said softly.

"It's my fault. All of it. My fault."

"And shooting Janie will change that?"

"I'm not going to shoot her. I..." Tommy looked confused. "You think I have a gun? Man, if she hadn't read the stupid art book maybe this would have all gone away."

"She read the art book after Brittney disappeared."

"No one needed to know."

"Were you one of the men in the car?" Rafe asked, wishing he'd taken the time to check Tommy's middle name. Suddenly Thomas Christopher Skinley seemed like a possibility.

"No!"

"Then, exactly what is your fault?"

Tommy answered at the exact moment Rafe got to him, bumping his legs apart and pulling his arms behind him. Quickly Rafe ascertained that the only thing in Tommy's pocket was a bag of meth. Even as Rafe lamented his lack of handcuffs, Tommy confessed.

"I'm guilty of introducing Derek to my sister."

TOMMY SKINLEY WENT to the hospital first. Rafe drove; Jeff Summerside sat in the backseat keeping Tommy under control. Which was difficult since Tommy was under the impression that he had superhuman strength. He even managed to give Summerside a bloody nose.

Great.

Luke, meanwhile, had promised to dog Janie's every move. While Tommy appeared frightening, Rafe didn't for a minute think he was Janie's biggest enemy. For one thing, someone with serious intent would not have made his move in a full church and with no weapon. Tommy's misstep had more to do with drugs than with forethought. Maybe they'd made Tommy brave for a minute, but they'd made him weak everywhere else. Compared to a year ago, Tommy was now underweight, his face somewhat pockmarked, his teeth starting to blacken, and he kept scratching at something invisible on his elbow.

The Scorpion Ridge hospital was just twenty

rooms. Two elderly women from church called out to Rafe as he walked down the corridor to ICU. There was only one other person in ICU, an elderly man that Rafe didn't recognize because of all the things hooked up to him.

He was fighting for his life.

Tommy was throwing his away.

Sitting up in the hospital bed, Tommy appeared closer to thirty than his true age of twenty-one. And he acted sixteen. He sneered at Rafe and turned his head when the nurse offered him a cup of something. Speaking to the wall, he attempted to tell her all the reasons he, personally, did not need to be in this hospital.

"You have to drink it," she said. "It will draw the poison out of your body." It was only after the nurse threatened to call the doctor and hook Tommy up to a tube that he drank the charcoal.

There were too many people in and out of the room for Rafe to make questioning Tommy his first priority. Tommy was then stripped of his belongings and the curtain of his room was left open so that anyone passing by might be able to hear. The passersby heard plenty, as Tommy had plenty to say, mostly about the travesty of justice that had brought him to the hospital.

Rafe ignored him and checked his phone.

Janie had texted to say she was fine and busy at the zoo. His mother had also sent him a message to say how brave he'd been at the church. Summerside, who'd left Rafe and Tommy at the hospital to return to the station, radioed to check if Rafe needed anything.

All Rafe wanted was some time alone with Tommy and to get back to Janie.

Just after two, Tommy's mom called Rafe and asked if he'd seen her son.

"You want to talk to him?" Rafe asked Helen. "We're here at the Scorpion Ridge hospital. Tommy's had a drug-related episode."

"Man," Tommy mumbled.

He took the phone and Rafe heard him say, "No, it was an accident. No, I'm not going to do it again. I'm all right. You know how cops are. I'm fine." Tommy's face scrunched up sourly before he handed Rafe back his phone. "She wants to talk to you."

Helen took in the news of her son's attack in the church, followed by his visit and stay in the hospital, without crying.

Maybe she was all cried out.

"Rafe," she said, "I've got a pregnant seventeen-year-old daughter and a son in the hospital because of drugs. Everything, all my dreams and prayers, have died this day. Just say what I have to do to make this right."

Pregnant? Little Amanda?

"What size shoe does Amanda wear?"

"What?" Helen sounded incredulous.

"And does she have a pair of green high-top tennis shoes?"

"She did," Helen said hesitantly. "She lost one a few months back."

"Who's the father of Amanda's baby?" Rafe asked. He couldn't afford to waste precious minutes tiptoeing around the question.

"She hasn't said yet, but I've got my suspicions."

"When did you find out Amanda was pregnant?"

"I found out last night. Amanda apparently figured it out a few weeks ago."

"How long has Tommy known she was pregnant?"

"He found out yesterday at the same time as me."

Rafe glanced at Tommy, who was now sitting straight up in the bed, moaning and drinking the charcoal as if it was the most interesting concoction in the world.

He said to him, "I guess now the question is who do I question? You?" He looked Tommy full in the face. "Or, do I question a seventeen-year-old girl who's dealing with the death of her baby's father, among other things? Who's the bigger person?"

"Let me talk to my son," Helen demanded.

Rafe handed the boy his phone.

Tommy didn't say a word, just listened. After a full two minutes of nodding, he said, "Yes, Mom," and returned the phone to Rafe. Helen had already disconnected.

"I guess I'm talking to you," Rafe said.

"I should have come to see you the minute Brittney went missing," Tommy muttered. "But I was afraid for Derek."

"*For* Derek or *of* Derek?"

"For Derek. He wanted to be a good guy, but it's not that easy to walk away from the drugs. Sometimes…" Tommy gazed down at the almost empty cup of charcoal and then touched his mouth and winced. "Sometimes, it's fun."

Rafe didn't agree. "Who are Chad and Chris?"

A nurse came back in, took Tommy's blood pressure and checked his eyes. Then she handed him a towel. Rafe hadn't even noticed how much the boy was sweating.

"I don't know who Chris is. I've only heard the name once or twice, and that was by accident. Derek didn't talk about him. Chad is Chad Ruskey. He used to work at the pizza place over on Main. That's how Derek met him. He delivered a pizza to some party Derek was at, and they started hanging around. This was before I was friends with Derek."

"Is Chad the man that Amanda drew for Janie?"

"Probably."

"Yes or no."

"I didn't see the drawing. And, honestly, I only met him once or twice."

Okay, now that Rafe had a name, he could find out this information on his own. "When did Derek meet Chad?"

"A couple of months ago. I got the idea that Chad didn't stay places long."

"Places in Arizona, or are you talking about state to state?"

"State to state. He wants to travel the world. He headed to South Carolina sometime after Christmas for basic training. He wanted to go to school but couldn't afford it. I think he's going to try for veteran's assistance when he gets out."

"He's a soldier?" Rafe said, more to himself than to Tommy. After a few more questions, Rafe quickly pulled out his phone and called Summerside with the new last name.

"So," Rafe continued, "is Chad capable of murder?"

Tommy considered that for a moment. "It sure didn't surprise me that he joined the service. But it's hard to picture him killing someone. I mean, I partied with the guy once."

"He does meth, too?"

Tommy eyed the room as if afraid someone would overhear. "Yes, but he worried he was using too much. He's hoping the military will come between him and the drugs."

Tommy looked like he was starting to relax. Rafe wasn't sure if that had to do with the meth still in his system or because he'd been given something by the medical staff to counter the meth.

"So, why didn't you come forward a month ago when the names Chad and Chris were released to the public as possible witnesses to Brittney Travis's disappearance?"

"I, uh, I wanted to," Tommy mumbled.

"Why didn't you?" Rafe tried to remain patient.

"Because the same time I heard about Chad, I heard about Derek. I'd been at that farm earlier, before it blew. It could have been me."

"And having a friend die because of meth isn't enough to get you off of it?"

"You don't understand," Tommy practically shrieked. "The meth got me through Derek's death."

"And will lead you to your own," Rafe said, standing. Before he left, he had one more question. "How did a journal with Amanda's name on it get into Patricia Reynolds's house? Did you put it there?"

"I didn't put it there."

"Did you know that the book showed Brittney's murder?"

Tommy sat up. "Not possible. Amanda couldn't have been there."

"How can you be sure, Tommy? Do you know when Brittney was taken, where, how?"

Tommy slumped. "If Amanda had been there, she'd have been a nervous wreck. She cries over TV movies and commercials. She only started crying when she started worrying about not seeing Derek."

"Anything else you want to tell me?"

"Chad's not really a bad guy, but his girlfriend changed him, and she pretty much calls the shots. If he really did shoot Brittney, it was on her orders."

"Her name?"

"He just called her 'the girlfriend.' I got the sense she was older, a cougar, you know, and didn't want her name bantered around."

"Why?"

"She's the one who controls the meth. She has power and friends. Chad called her a 'subcontractor' once. I have no idea what that really means. If I actually met her, I'd pee my pants."

That was quite possibly the wisest thing Tommy had said yet this day.

"Why would she want Brittney dead?" Rafe asked.

"No idea," Tommy admitted, suddenly looking his age again, vulnerable and scared. "But it's why I didn't come to you before. If Brittney had been killed because of what she'd seen, maybe Amanda would be next. I didn't want Amanda's name anywhere."

Rafe understood. He felt the same way about Janie. And, unlike Tommy, Rafe had a very good idea of what a subcontractor was and how closely they were aligned with the cartels in Mexico.

Rafe couldn't remember the last time he'd felt the type of fear that could take him to his knees. He felt it now.

Because Janie's name had already been etched on a virtual tombstone by someone very dangerous.

CHAPTER NINETEEN

RAFE NOTED THAT looking unkempt seemed to be a condition experienced by many these days: the old, the young, the innocent, the guilty. Along with Rafe, Justin Robbins and Nathan Williamson had both lost weight during the last month.

Sitting across from Nathan, Rafe—wearing gloves—flipped through Amanda's art book. "We have to figure out who could plant this book as well as who would know what to put in it."

Nathan nodded. "I spoke to Chad's drill sergeant and sent him Janie's drawing. They're one and the same. Man said he was surprised Chad had made it to the white phase where recruits get to shoot guns. He said Chad's whole demeanor changed the moment they put a gun in his hand. They gave him a psych evaluation and discharged him."

"I've put out feelers," Justin said. "No one even admits to knowing him."

Nathan hit a key on his computer and a page

appeared on the screen. “He’s lived in sixteen states under five different names, and although he’s wanted in connection to a dozen crimes—none of them murder, by the way—he’s never been physically brought in for questioning.”

“He’s good,” Justin said, and it wasn’t a compliment.

It had been more than a month since Janie’d redrawn Derek’s art book, and Rafe wasn’t sure he could make it through any more days of waiting. He wanted Chad here now.

Taking out his cell phone, Rafe redialed Helen Skinley. He really didn’t want to disturb Amanda; he agreed with Tommy that Amanda was fragile. Well, she needed to toughen up. She was about to be a mother.

“How’s Tommy?” Helen answered the phone.

“They say he’s going to be okay. His heart is fine, there’s no kidney damage and he’s breathing regularly.”

“That’s a relief.”

“He was quite a help. We’re finally closing in on whoever’s behind the drug situation at Adobe Hills Community College. We’ve got to stop the operation.”

Helen didn’t say anything.

“I have to ask Amanda a few questions.”

“I’d rather you didn’t. Everything’s a mess. We’ve been in this hotel room for days. She doesn't want to leave. It's all I can do to get her to eat properly. She's sleeping right now."

"I wouldn't call if there were any other way."

"I—"

In the background, Rafe could hear someone talking. Then, Helen said, "Amanda has things she wants to say. She's glad Tommy's all right. Thanks for getting him to the hospital. He was pretty upset about the baby."

"Tell her Tommy cares about her."

Helen jiggled the phone before saying, "Amanda knows. What do you want to ask her?"

"Her art book got into Patricia Reynolds's house, and the last few pages were changed."

Again, moments passed while Helen interpreted Rafe's questions.

"She says that the only thing in her book would be drawings of clothes. She wanted to draw her and Derek, but wasn't ready for anyone to realize they were a couple."

"Where did she see her art book last?"

"That day when Detective Williamson came to the school. She had to leave the class, but Max Carter came out and said that you were picking up all our art books. She gave it to him and he handed it in. At least she assumed that's what he'd done."

"She says Max Carter turned it in for her," Rafe said to Nathan, "the day you picked them up."

Nathan shook his head, shuffled through some papers on his desk, and then dialed his own phone.

"Thanks, Amanda. That's all I wanted."

Rafe waited a moment while Nathan asked for Max Carter. After a moment, they discovered Max had handed it to one of the campus police officers: Barry Dime.

Next, Nathan called the college and spoke to the officer in charge. Barry Dime was off today. Quickly, Nathan sent one of his men to Dime's place to bring him in for interrogation.

"Hopefully we'll get some answers from Dime. I've talked to him twice already. He's an ex-cop, hurt in the line of duty. There is nothing in his past to suggest he's the type to work both sides of the law."

"I'm glad we have a name. It's starting to come together. We'll solve this."

"Amanda didn't tell me she'd given the journal to Max." Nathan shook his head. "I hate drugs. I hate watching people destroy lives—their own and others'—with drugs. Look at what drugs did to Derek. They not only took his life, but they robbed him of watching and nurturing a new life. And then there's that poor girl's brother." Nathan shook his head. "Nothing destroys a family quicker than drugs."

Rafe agreed, remembering how drugs had destroyed Nathan's young marriage. But they didn't have time to dwell on the past.

"Remind me," Rafe said. "Has Max ever been in trouble?"

"Just small stuff like skateboarding after curfew."

"Try their Facebook pages again," Justin suggested. "It's been a while, and we're deeper into the case. Maybe we'll see something we missed."

"I still don't get," Nathan said to the undercover officer, "how you hadn't heard of either Chad or his girlfriend?"

"Chad was only in our area a couple of months. I can't be everywhere. The only girl I know who hung around with Tommy and Derek, and who also admits to being friends with Chad, is Ramona Turk. She's only scary when she's jonesing for a fix. I've chatted her up a dozen times since all this went down. She wasn't involved."

Nathan started typing into his computer. After a moment, he had a photo of Tommy Skinley's Facebook page on his screen. He looked like a typical angry kid.

Kind of like Justin, who—still undercover

and camouflaged as a teenager—was shaking his head as he studied the screen. "He's around a lot."

Rafe watched as Nathan played with the computer some more. Chad didn't have a page, apparently, if that was his real name.

Amanda's photo was there. Her list of friends wasn't long, but her blog and accomplishments were. Both Justin and Rafe moved around Nathan's desk to get a better look.

"I've never seen her," Justin said.

"I hope you never do," Rafe said. "At least, while you're undercover."

"What do we do next?" Justin said.

"We need to act as if we're taking Amanda's art book seriously. Let's put out a public bulletin that says we're searching for the type of vehicle she supposedly drew and the type of people she drew. We'll also put out feelers for the first two numbers on that license plate."

"Giving our real perp a sense of security," Nathan said.

"A false sense of security," Rafe agreed.

Anything to keep Janie safe.

SUNDAY WAS A quiet day at the zoo. Janie sat behind the counter of the gift shop and rang up sales. Katie wouldn't let her do anything else. "You've already hurt your arm—your painting arm. We need to make sure it's healed when you win the visiting-artist slot in South Africa."

This was the first time Katie'd spoken of the opportunity as if she were all for it. For the last year, ever since Janie'd started planning for it, all Katie could say was, "Africa's so far away. You're young."

Rafe showed up just after five, about an hour before the zoo closed. He pitched in, straightening up the gift shop and even helping customers. But Janie could sense he was distracted. She felt the same way. Tommy Skinley had scared her this morning. She finally understood why Rafe was so opposed to her returning to teaching, but really, this morning's attack had been at church!

When the last visitor left and the computer receipts were tallied and saved, Rafe held the door open for Janie.

"You want to go to the diner and get something to eat?"

"No, I don't want to answer all the questions people will have."

He nodded. "I can go get something and bring it back. I'll get enough for Katie and—"

"They're going out tonight. It can just be us. I'll cook."

Instead, they both cooked. Janie made the

noodles and sauce; Rafe assembled the meatballs and garlic bread. In the kitchen, they worked like a well-oiled machine. Even the few times they bumped into each other only garnered smiles.

"You going to tell me what's new in the case?" Janie asked.

"Amanda's pregnant."

"What!"

"And the baby most likely belongs to Derek. The green shoe you found is hers."

"I think I should sit down."

Rafe took over setting the table and getting their drinks. He continued, "We've got a last name for Chad, but unfortunately he was discharged from the military and has disappeared. We're not even sure what alias he's using."

"Wow and double wow. You keep talking, and I'm going to need to lie down."

"The drawing you and Amanda came up with seems to be Chad. We'll confirm as soon as we find him."

"And why did he kill Brittney?"

"All we have now is speculation, but it seems he was under orders from his girlfriend."

"Who is...?"

"We're not sure. But we're hoping when

we figure that out, all the pieces will fall into place."

"Why was Brittney killed? Have you figured that out yet?"

"I think it has to do with drugs. She saw something or someone she wasn't supposed to, but until we find her killers, we can't say what." He sat the last plate on the table and bowed. "Dinner is served."

As she took her seat, she wondered out loud, "Can we make it through a meal without talking blood and gore and death?"

He reached over and took her hand, aiming the palm toward him, and gently traced her fingers with his own. Heat started to pool in her heart.

"I'm willing to try," he said.

So they talked art and animals and favorite movies.

When the meal was over, they loaded a movie into the DVD player and sat on the couch. He carefully put his arm around her. For the next two hours, all he did was hold her, the warmth of his body mingling with hers until she didn't think she could ever be cold again.

The DVD ended and the TV automatically switched to the news. Janie reached for the remote. What she was feeling didn't call for background noise.

He was tightening his fingers around her shoulder, drawing her closer.

But before she could hit the off button, the news anchor said, "New developments in the Brittney Travis case."

Both she and Rafe turned around, the mood broken, and settled back to watch.

The picture from Amanda's art book was displayed, plus the two numbers from the license plate she'd drawn, as well as the type of vehicle she'd identified.

"This time we utilized the press. Which means you can relax a little," Rafe said. "Not completely, not until we find Chad. But we hope we've given the girlfriend and Chris, the ones we haven't identified, a false sense of security."

"This doesn't give *me* a sense of security," Janie muttered.

"Then let me give it to you," he offered. This time, he reached for the remote, aimed it at the TV and clicked it off.

That's when her phone rang.

Janie bit her lip. But the caller ID announced Katie's name. Katie knew that she and Rafe were alone; she wouldn't call if it weren't important. Janie shrugged and answered the phone.

"Tonight you just might be an aunt!" Katie sang. "We're on our way to the hospital."

THEY SPENT HOURS at the hospital. The nurse who'd worked on Tommy was still there. She merely raised an eyebrow at Rafe's presence and tried to make Katie comfortable.

Rafe paced in the hallway with Luke and stopped by to check on Tommy until fatigue drove him home.

Janie promised to stay at the hospital and sleep.

Monday dawned cold, gray and dreary. Fitting for the funeral of a young man who should have had more time to enjoy life. Rafe wondered if becoming a father would have turned Derek around.

He'd already been trying to change.

Now, they'd never know.

He met Janie at the hospital. Somehow she'd managed to get home and change into something that was somber, especially for her. Black silk pants hugged her long, lithe legs. A black-and-gray-striped shirt with a black jacket over it completed the outfit. She wore sensible shoes. As she walked beside him to the SUV, he realized that at no moment had he imagined going to Derek's funeral alone. He'd always believed she'd be beside him.

Unlike Patricia's funeral where he'd tried to keep track of everyone, this time, his job was Janie because he wanted it to be.

"Do you really think the killer might show up?" she asked.

"It's happened before. I'm counting on you to tell me the minute you recognize someone connected with Derek from Adobe Hills Community College."

"Believe me, I won't leave your side. The fact that Chad is AWOL is enough incentive for me."

The Adobe Hills Funeral Home was a red-brick house that dated back to the late 1800s. Rafe couldn't remember when it had not been a funeral home. His grandfather had had his service here.

Rafe didn't like funerals; he'd been to far too many.

Nathan was outside, parked on the street. Rafe nodded for Janie to stay put and headed for him. "What did you get from Dime?"

"Just finished questioning him thirty minutes ago. The man's addicted to prescription drugs. He'd been getting them from Derek. The night the art book went into the safe, Barry got a call from Chad. He threatened to reveal to the college president a few indiscretions that Barry had hoped to keep buried forever. Until today, Barry's wife didn't realize he had a problem. He's hoping his kids will never find out."

"So all along this campus police officer could have pointed us to Chad."

"Yep, but drug addiction is a powerful vice." Nathan spoke low, his voice sad, his eyes even sadder. "It brings the strongest man to his knees and makes him do things he never thought he'd do."

Rafe could only nod and return to Janie who was fidgeting with her purse. He now knew she only fidgeted when she had to go somewhere she didn't want to go. He agreed. Funerals were nerve-wracking, especially for a life cut too short.

A news van was parked to the side of the funeral home. Nathan was already walking over to the reporter. No doubt asking her to respect the parents' privacy.

He took Janie's arm and ushered her inside before they were noticed.

"It's weird being here," Janie admitted. "In reality, I only knew him from class. Since reading his art book, however, I feel like I know him quite well."

"His parents will appreciate you being here."

She nodded as they entered the foyer where a man stood by a podium and suggested they sign in.

Janie's signature was big, flowing and artistic—no surprise. His was tiny and in print. Years of filling out reports and trying to get in every detail did that to a cop. He studied the guest book, scrutinizing every name, recognizing a few. After they signed in, they walked down a hallway and into a room filled with pews, six on each side. Janie stopped so suddenly, he almost ran into her.

"Been to many funerals?" he asked.

She didn't answer, just shook her head.

He realized that right now, she needed him.

Rafe wasn't sure what to make of how protective he was feeling. It wasn't typical. Usually, he was the master of keeping a respectable distance. At the moment, though, he wasn't the master of anything. Last night at her place had certainly proved that. He'd been planning the whole let's-get-to-know-each-other scenario.

"This is my second funeral," she said. "I'm told I went to my mother's. I've always felt guilty because I didn't go to my dad's."

It occurred to Rafe that he'd never really heard either of the Vincent sisters talk about their dad except that he'd abandoned them.

They talked about their mother, who'd died when Janie was very young, and about each other, and growing up in Texas.

"Why didn't you?"

"Katie was adamant that she wasn't going. Quite honestly, back then, I was content to follow her lead. Given the chance again, I'd make up my own mind. Katie's had a hard time forgiving my dad for sending us to live with Aunt Betsy."

Rafe's dad had been the cornerstone of the Salazar home. Every morning his mother made sure his dad's uniform was pressed and his lunch packed. Rafe had grown up watching his mother kiss his father right before Dad headed out the door. During the day, she took care of the house and planned a meal Dad would appreciate. After he died, she'd bought the Corner Diner and turned it into something special.

When Rafe was a kid, every afternoon, minutes before his father was due home, he'd be at the screen door, waiting.

"A watched pot never boils," his mother would say.

Yet, until his father came through the door, the day would somehow be incomplete.

Rafe had been in his late twenties when his father had died. Jerry Salazar's funeral had been standing room only, too, but it had been held at the church. In the Main Street Church, there'd been friends, family, policemen from Scorpion Ridge, from Adobe Hills, from more than five other counties.

The church was where his father had lived and died.

"And you've forgiven him?" Rafe asked.

"Sad to say, I was never angry. I never considered him much of a parent. My only goal was to be with Katie. The first funeral I remember, you were with me. It was Patricia's. It didn't feel like this one."

Rafe agreed. "Patricia's was more of a celebration. She'd lived a good life, and—"

Before he could continue, Derek's mother stepped up. "Thank you so much for coming."

Beside him, Janie's hand tightened on his elbow. Rafe faced Derek's mother. He couldn't say, *I'm hoping your son's killer shows up today and that's mainly why I'm here.* Instead, speaking for both himself and Janie, he said, "We wanted to pay our respects."

Rafe thought back to the names in the guest book. His name was number twelve, hers thirteen. Nathan hadn't signed in; Rafe didn't blame him.

"A few of Derek's teachers are here," Janie whispered to Rafe as Mrs. Chaney moved away.

"From the college?"

"Yes, I'm not familiar with his high-school teachers."

"Make sure to introduce me. Any students?"

She nodded and then stepped aside to lean against the wall.

Rafe headed for Mr. Chaney. Like Janie, he seemed miserable. Except while Janie had her arms crossed, as if shielding herself from pain, Mr. Chaney's hands were buried deep in his pockets. He leaned against the wall looking like he wanted to disappear. Rafe was searching for the right words to say when Mr. Chaney beat him to the punch. "You find any new information?"

"We're not sure yet," Rafe responded easily.

"Last month, about this time," Derek's dad said, "I was sitting at my desk thinking maybe over the summer we'd rent a cabin, maybe up in Orchard, the whole family. Over some trout fishing, maybe I'd get Derek to open up."

"And if Dad couldn't, I would try." Another man came to stand beside Mr. Chaney. The similarity was enough to give Rafe pause. "This is my oldest boy, Jimmy."

Mr. Chaney would soon stop saying "oldest boy" because the phrase would remind him that at one time he'd had a youngest boy.

"You expecting any of Derek's friends to stop by?" Rafe asked Jimmy.

"I think one or two will, with their parents. They'll be the kids he was close to in junior high and the start of high school."

"No one from recently?"

"We don't know any of his current friends," Mr. Chaney reminded him.

"None of his current friends," Jimmy said. "They have better sense than to show their faces."

"We appreciated you stopping by the station and going over mug shots."

"I only recognized two," Jimmy said. "Tommy Skinley, who hasn't been around in a while, and Joshua Beardsley."

The media hadn't caught on that Tommy was involved and in the hospital. They would soon, though, since a whole church had witnessed his meltdown.

And as for Joshua Beardsley… When he gazed into the mirror, Justin Robbins gazed back.

"Dad," Jimmy said suddenly, "go take care of Mom."

Mrs. Chaney was standing next to a woman and boy. The boy was poised to bolt. The woman was shaking her head.

"Who's the boy?" Rafe inquired.

"He used to be our next-door neighbor. From the time Derek was eight until about two years ago, they hung around a lot together. Then the family moved. Mom says they left because his dad got a better job and they could afford a better house. But, in reality, they moved so Billy would be away from my little brother."

"Would Billy know any of Derek's current friends?"

"No, if anything, Billy was probably secretly relieved to move."

Before Rafe could ask anything else, a tall man in a black suit started herding people into a small room set up with folding chairs. As he went to fetch Janie, he glanced at the guest book. It was up to twenty names.

Billy was the only teenager, and he stayed glued to his mother's side during the entire service. The minister conducting the eulogy obviously hadn't met Derek. After twenty minutes of generalizations, followed by a few funeral-specific scriptures, the service was over.

Mrs. Chaney just stared ahead, shell-shocked.

Her husband had no expression at all.

It was Jimmy who was holding it together. He helped his mother to her feet and led the way out the door.

"I hate funerals," Janie muttered.

Rafe could only shake his head. The minister who'd performed his dad's funeral had been a family friend. He'd cried during the service, and Rafe overheard his mother comfort the man with "It'll be all right. Now, now."

Of the twenty at the funeral today, only eight attendees made it to the burial. Nathan missed it. Rafe had seen the other officer take a call and leave soon after.

In the end, Rafe even acted as a pallbearer.

CHAPTER TWENTY

IT SEEMED TO Janie that being by Rafe's side was becoming a way of life. Yet, after Derek's funeral, she couldn't imagine anyone she'd rather be with. Only he could understand the sense of loss she felt.

"I'm surprised Justin wasn't there."

Rafe's phone beeped. Keeping his eyes on the road and one hand firmly on the steering wheel, he answered, "Salazar."

Janie got to listen to another one-sided conversation.

"Yes, he was at the funeral. No, he left early and didn't attend the burial."

She guessed he was talking about Nathan.

"No, I've not tried to call him. If he's not answering, then he's obviously busy. If I hear from him, I'll give you a call."

"Nathan missing?" Janie asked.

"Apparently he's not answering his phone. He was due at court thirty minutes ago. I gather there's one unhappy judge who's threatening to suspend Nathan."

"Sounds serious."

"It is. As for Justin, he didn't dare show at the funeral. If he'd come undercover, alone, it would have raised questions. And if he'd come as himself, well, there'd be even more questions."

Janie shook her head. "It's not easy being a cop."

"No, but when you're doing a job that makes the world a better place, a safer place for our children, then the hardship is worth it."

"Children mean a lot to you."

Rafe was silent for a moment. "I've never told you about my brother, have I?"

"No. Gloria at the zoo mentioned something about you losing a brother, but you said it wasn't her story to tell."

"It's been a long time since I've shared the story with anyone. It's one of the reasons why solving Brittney's case means so much to me. I couldn't help but think, as we said goodbye to Derek, that he was the last thread to Brittney. That we buried her whereabouts with him."

"We'll find her. We know a whole lot more than when we started." It didn't escape Janie's notice that she was saying "we," speaking almost as if she was his partner.

She sure didn't want to be a cop.

So what did she want?

She hurried to speak again before an answer she wasn't ready for occurred to her.

"You mentioned that missing-persons cases are your specialty."

"I don't remember saying that, but they are the ones that keep me up at night. And, funny, it doesn't matter the age of the missing person. About a year ago, we had a ninety-year-old woman wander off. She was missing for two days before we found her."

"I remember. She'd gotten on a bus and somehow made her way to New Mexico before someone realized she really had no destination and no more money."

"For two days, I didn't sleep. I did for her exactly what I did for Brittney. I interviewed all her friends. I walked the streets near where she lived. I visited her doctors. When the police in Albuquerque called, I'm the one who drove to get her."

"I had no idea you did all of that."

He was silent for a moment, then blurted, "Somewhere I may have an older brother."

"I thought you were an only child." She recalled the pictures in his office. There was one baby photo, dead center on a shelf. She'd assumed it was Rafe. In some of the photos, he'd been standing by other men, but if he had a brother, he'd have mentioned the man, or Katie would have. She didn't go a day without sharing something about Rafe with Katie.

"No, my older brother is missing."

Janie had no idea what to say to that. It made sense, though. She remembered that first day in his office, when he'd pulled a stack of missing person fliers from his top desk drawer. There'd been something poignant in the way he'd held them.

"My mom had trouble conceiving. She'd about given up. Then she got pregnant at age forty. This made her high risk, so she was supposed to go into Phoenix to have a C-section. Her blood pressure had shot up."

"You seem to know the story well."

"I've heard it a million times."

"So, what happened?"

"They, my dad and her, only made it to Gesippi. If anything, their hospital is even smaller than the one in Scorpion Ridge. It would have been better to go to Adobe Hills."

Janie wasn't sure if he was comparing the quality of the hospitals, or commenting on what happened next.

"They had a record number of babies born that day. Three. They usually average three a year. It's that small a town. Plus, many there prefer to go to the big city. In one Scottsdale hospital, they even have a spa for new mothers."

"They probably didn't back then," Janie pointed out.

"No, and thirty-six years ago we didn't have safeguards in place like we do today. When my brother was two days old, someone dressed as a nurse came into my mother's room, took Ramon, and left. All we have is a picture taken a few hours after his birth. We've done age progression, but the FBI closed the case years ago."

"And that's why your dad changed professions and became a cop and then a sheriff."

"It was a way," Rafe agreed, "to be on top of my brother's case and also to help others the way we had been helped. All three towns—Scorpion Ridge, Gesippi, and Adobe Hills—rallied together to search for my big brother."

"And then your mom had you."

"At age forty-four."

"I'm so sorry. I can't imagine losing a child. I was heartbroken when I lost my sister just for a year, and I knew where she was."

"The good news is we've always believed he's still alive. Most people who kidnap children do it because they want a baby. Someday I'll meet him. I've always had faith."

Janie wished she'd had more faith during

that year she'd tried to get away from Aunt Betsy. Katie had always fought for her. Until today, this minute, she hadn't realized how much harder she, Janie, had made the whole process by continually running away. How much grief she'd caused Katie.

"Oh, speaking of babies, I should call Katie."

A moment later, Janie found out she still wasn't an aunt. "They've sent Katie home. Seems she was having something called Braxton Hicks contractions. She's supposed to rest and drink lots of water."

"Well, at least you didn't miss the important event."

Janie nodded and asked, "Is it a lot harder to kidnap a baby today?"

"Near impossible thanks to special security bands that set off an alarm if anyone tries to remove the baby from the floor. So, what are your plans today?"

"I'll work at the zoo. With Katie on bed rest, they'll need me."

"Luke will be there," Rafe seemed to say to himself. "And, I'll tell Candy to do some drive-bys. You'll be okay."

"You said yourself that this Chris person is probably convinced of his safety. Let's hope that's true."

Rafe pulled into the front drive of Katie and

Luke's house and then walked Janie inside. She changed into a pair of khaki pants and a BAA shirt. Together they walked back outside and stood awkwardly next to their cars. Janie almost felt bereft at the idea of heading to her car alone.

"You'll be fine," Rafe said, as if reading her mind.

"What are you going to do?"

"I have a jail visit and need to work on the budget."

"Exciting."

"I'll tell you what's exciting..."

Before Janie had a clue of his intentions, he'd drawn her close and dipped his head for a kiss. It wasn't demanding, it wasn't chaste. It was in the middle, making promises about forever.

When he let her go, she wished she had something to lean against. Instead, he simply touched her cheek, and then watched as she got into her car.

She liked knowing he watched over her.

But what she pondered was that he hadn't said, *I'll come by later.*

Mondays at BAA weren't the busiest, and right now there were no baby animals to advertise, no students doing documentaries or even a field trip scheduled. Janie parked her car and then headed for Luke's office. She plugged her phone into the wall to charge before checking BAA's phone for messages.

"I've already done it." Meredith Stone, who was head keeper, stood in the doorway.

"Anything important?"

"No."

"What do you want me to do, since you're short-handed."

Meredith, always a taskmaster, easily answered, "If you could do the cleanup checklist, that would be awesome. Then, Jasper could use some help at his three-o'clock show. He's done a show already today with the orangutan. He's not got the strength that he used to."

"But—" As a rule, Janie didn't get up close and comfortable with the animals. She loved them, painted them, championed them, but her gift wasn't working with them. They sensed her hesitancy, her fear.

"Just act as a barker while he does the show with George and Crisco."

That Janie could do. She'd known George forever. He'd been her dad's favorite trained bear. He was a personal favorite of Katie's, too. As for Crisco, Janie had been there when Crisco was found, tied to a fence by a remote farm that fell in the no-man's-land between Scorpion Ridge and Gesippi. She'd held Crisco when he was a baby, helped nurse him and was now creating the wall mural that showed his path from rags to riches.

Jasper didn't go into the bear enclosure any longer, as George was getting old and crotchety and Crisco was Katie and Ruth's baby. He responded well to them. Jasper hadn't put in the hours with the bear.

Grabbing a bottle of water from the fridge in Luke's office, Janie first checked her mail slot. A wrinkled manila envelope was the only offering. Her breath caught. She seldom got mail, but when she did, it usually had to do with art.

Fingers shaking, she opened it and pulled out a letter.

Dear Miss Vincent,

We are pleased to invite you to be one of our artists in residence for this coming summer.

She sat, squealed, and then stood to jump up and down. She'd be leaving. In just six weeks. She sat back down. This would open doors for her. She could see the world, apply for other opportunities.

Who should she call first?

The joy slipped away as quickly as it arrived.

For the first time, getting the residency in South Africa wasn't her top priority, the *only dream* she had. She put the letter back in the envelope and stuffed it in her mail slot. She needed to think. Her longing for adventure had changed. Her focus and love of drawing animals wasn't her only calling.

All those years, drawing animals had been an escape for her; it was a place she could go, a world she could create, that represented safety.

But now, for the first time, it was people that made her feel safe and needed. She was about to be an aunt. And there was Rafe. Who'd kissed her just thirty minutes ago.

Whom she wanted to kiss her again.

She made her way outside, wishing she'd worn her other BAA shirt, the summer one. It was unusually hot for April.

The checklist took longer than usual because a few tasks weren't complete. On the smaller animals, like the birds or Luke's favorite iguana, Janie willingly picked up the slack and cleaned the cages or supplied the food. For the big cats, though, she simply made a mark in her notebook and would tell Meredith later.

Heading for the bear's enclosure, she decided to first call and check on Katie. That's when she remembered her phone was still charging in the office.

By the time she picked it up, she had just one minute to get to the three-o'clock show. Hurrying to the bears' enclosure, Janie watched the families as they gathered. During the school semester, small children in strollers dominated the pathways. There were also a few older couples out enjoying the day. They all had stories.

She wanted to draw them, to focus on the lines on their faces, the gleam in their eyes, the way they looked at the world.

Animals were awesome, but people were, too.

Jasper had just left the kitchen and had food for George and Crisco.

"Good, you're my helper," he said, drawing near.

"Long time since I've done this."

"All you have to do is talk to the crowd, describe what's going on, and give them both George and Crisco's stories. You're as familiar with the details as I am."

Jasper used to be able to do both work with the bears and talk with the crowd. As he aged, though, his voice wasn't as strong.

He still seemed strong to Janie. He was a remnant of her childhood, the days before Aunt Betsy. Jasper had pushed her in a wagon, she remembered that. He'd been the one to put her on the back of a camel for the first time. He'd sat beside her and colored right along with her. Neither of her parents, or Katie for that matter, had liked to draw or color.

Janie wondered if Rafe liked to draw.

She'd have to ask.

Fewer than a dozen people showed up for the show. One was a family of six, four of them too young to appreciate what they were seeing and hearing. Then there were two couples. Plus, she recognized CeeCee Harrington from the Adobe Hills Community College. She was taking pictures of Crisco while Janie spoke.

She smiled weakly at Janie.

After the show, Janie went over and sat beside her on the bench.

"I couldn't go to work today," CeeCee said. "It's never easy losing a student. But Derek's funeral… What a show."

"I didn't realize you were close to Derek."

"He took two of my English classes. I remember when he walked into my class, I thought, 'This kid with his attitude will never make it.'"

"But he did."

"He earned a C the first time. He moved up to a B on his second go-around."

"I regret that I didn't know him better."

"Me, too." CeeCee stood and walked toward the bear enclosure. "I remember Crisco's story. The place where they found him is out near where I live. I knew the couple who lived on that farm. Not well and not socially, but when you live outside the city limits you become familiar with the people who live around you."

"Rafe says most of the people who have homes out there just want to be left alone."

"It's true. I moved out there after a divorce. I guess I needed time to lick my wounds and move on. It took me a few years. I was becoming a recluse. That's when I applied to become an adjunct at the college. Best thing I could have done."

"Your students do like you. I hear them talk."

"That's the reason I teach. I want to influence the generation of our future." CeeCee checked her watch. "You got someplace to be next, or are you free to get something to eat? I don't want to go home. I don't want to be alone."

CeeCee must not have a Katie or a Rafe in her life.

"I'm free. We could eat here. Or there's the Corner Diner. Rafe's mom works there."

"Rafe?"

"Sheriff Rafe Salazar, he's—"

CeeCee laughed. "I know who he is. I'm just not used to hearing him called by his first name. Are you two an item?"

"No."

"I'm not sure I'm convinced. You want to tell me the story while we eat?"

Janie almost said no. But she'd not eaten lunch yet, not even a snack. "Really, I can't unless we eat here or the Corner Diner. I should stick close by. My sister's about to have a baby. That's why I wound up helping Jasper with the bear show."

"The Corner Diner it is," CeeCee agreed.

Janie hurried into one of the public bathrooms and washed her hands. Then she followed CeeCee out to the parking lot. At Adobe Hills Community College, they'd been little more than two teachers passing in the hallways or sitting in the student union after classes.

At least now Janie understood why CeeCee preferred to grade her papers in the cafeteria. No one to go home to.

CeeCee had dressed somberly for Derek's funeral, too. Usually, CeeCee was flamboyant, preferring loud colors and flowing jackets.

She was someone Janie could draw!

Funny that Janie never used to look at people as her muse.

Today she wore only brown. Her hair, very thick, was drawn back in a ponytail.

"I'll drive. When we come back, I think I'll walk around the zoo some more. Take more pictures."

Janie followed her to a blue sedan, an older car. It had seen a lot of years. The inside was a mess.

"Yeah, the car's ancient. After the divorce," CeeCee said, "I had a few money problems. Things are much better now. I'll probably get a new car soon. Sorry about the mess. I lose things in here constantly. Supper, by the way, is my treat."

CeeCee started the car and pulled out of BAA's parking lot. Janie noted that she made no move to turn on the air conditioner even though it was hot. Janie took hold of the window handle and started to crank as CeeCee said, "Crisco sure is big. I wish I'd made it by when he was still little. Do you have any pictures?"

The window didn't roll down easily, that was for sure. Janie stopped trying for a minute, pulled out her phone and brought a photo of the bear up. At the first stop sign, she handed CeeCee the phone.

"I'm glad there's no traffic," CeeCee said.

"Cute bear. Did you know a bear's gallbladder can sell for as high as thirty thousand dollars?"

Janie didn't have a chance to respond. From behind her, someone rose and grabbed her around the throat and dragged her into the backseat.

She fought for a moment, but the man was much stronger. One slap from him had her ears ringing. That was the least of her problems, though.

She recognized him.

From the drawing she and Amanda had created.

It was Chad Ruskey.

RAFE CHECKED HIS cell phone for the fifth time. Ten after six. He punched the key that dialed Janie's number and waited. It rang twice and then her voice mail came on. Unavailable. She'd been unavailable since he'd dropped her off. According to Katie, whom he'd called after he'd left his third message on Janie's phone, Janie was helping around BAA and might have her phone off. The ringing sometimes disturbed the animals. It was a viable reason, but Rafe still felt a vague uneasiness in his gut.

His chief of police had been to BAA just after three and saw Janie helping with the bear show. But, no one, at least that Rafe had spoken with, had seen Janie since then.

Detective Nathan Williamson was still missing in action, too, which worried Rafe. Rafe had sensed something was off about Nathan and this case since Janie had read the art book. Maybe Rafe should have probed deeper into why.

But Nathan was someone he'd worked with often, someone he trusted and had never before had a single issue with.

Rafe pulled up in front of the police station and hurried in. Candy shook her head. She'd had no contact with Janie.

"Her sister's starting to worry, too," Candy said.

Rafe sat at his desk and pulled his notebook from his pocket. He'd spent most of the afternoon talking to a burglary suspect who Rafe suspected was guilty of more than stealing copper from the nearby elementary school. Then, he'd met with another officer over a civil matter. Used to be, Rafe had his finger in every pie and knew everything that was going on. This last month, though, he'd had to delegate a lot more, and he was quite impressed with how his officers—especially Jeff Summerside—had stepped up to the plate.

After typing in his notes, which took all of

twenty minutes, he quit trying to catch up on his work. He needed to get to BAA and find Janie.

BAA was only ten minutes away. It was already closed. Which meant Janie had no excuse for not contacting him when she knew he'd be worried.

He'd made it about one mile when his cell rang. Justin, sounding a bit frantic, said, "I'm out looking for Nathan. One of the kids I pal around with said they noticed his car out near Mailbox Mesa."

"Why is that important?"

"Because he blew off at least three appointments, atypical, and that location is near the same farm where Crisco was found."

Rafe frowned. The land between Scorpion Ridge and Adobe Hill was unincorporated and fell under Rafe's jurisdiction. At the very least, Rafe deserved a courtesy call if something was going down.

"I'm heading up there now," Justin said. "It's fairly close to where Derek died."

Another coincidence?

"You want to meet me since it's your jurisdiction?"

Rafe was four minutes from BAA. It would take him at least a half hour to search the zoo and find Janie if she wasn't responding to her cell.

"I'll be there as soon as I can," Rafe said.

Should he continue to the zoo or head for the deserted farm? Zoo or farm? His every instinct screamed farm.

Rafe spun his SUV around. He headed down the back roads of Scorpion Ridge and toward the rural areas that housed a few survivalist types, a lot of hippies, a growing number of homesteaders, and, yes, too many drug growers and dealers. He quickly called Candy Riorden.

"I want you to track Janie's cell phone. Use Locaid, it should only take a minute."

"That will invade her privacy. And it's illegal. It could cost you—"

"I'll take full responsibility. And there are some things more important than my job."

It had been a long while since he'd felt that way.

He called the zoo. No one answered. All he got was a recording about the zoo's hours, fees and upcoming events. He really didn't want to bother Katie, so he called Luke.

"We're on our way to the hospital again," Luke said instead of a hello. "This time it's for real."

"Make one phone call for me. Call someone

and have them search every nook and cranny of BAA. No one's heard from or seen Janie in over an hour."

Luke was silent for a moment. Then he said, "I'll call Jasper. He loves the girls like they're his own children. He'll know where to look."

In the background he heard Katie's voice, sounding a little frantic. "What's happening with Janie?"

Luke had barely disconnected when Candy called him. "She's out past Mailbox Mesa. She's moving, though, in a northeast direction. The next marker is Picture Rock."

The name was beautiful; the area was not, not anymore. If there'd ever been a rock worth naming the area for, it was long gone. This wasn't farmland; it was dilapidated mobile-home land. Most of the people who lived here kept big dogs because they wanted to be left alone. Most didn't combine the words *sheriff* and *helpful* in the same sentence. Rafe had been out there more times than he could count. He took a shortcut.

"I want the name of every resident in a ten-mile radius. Cross-reference the names with any having to do with Derek Chaney's case."

"I'm on it."

Justin called. "I'm following a blue Chevrolet," he reported. "I can only see two people in it. A male and female."

"Are they doing anything suspicious? Any chance the female's Janie?"

"The female's driving. Nothing suspicious, but they're the only ones out here."

"They make you?"

"I just spotted them. I probably have a mile or two before—wait, they just turned off. Mile marker 182. I'm gonna pass it and find a spot off the road to check if they just didn't want someone behind them."

"I'll call Candy and find out who we have living near mile marker 182," Rafe said.

"I was just about to phone you," Candy said when he got her on the line. "We've three parcels listed in that area. One name is connected to Derek Chaney. CeeCee Harrington."

"The teacher?"

"Yes, and do you want to know what her name was when she was married?" Candy asked.

"Yes."

"It's Williamson. She's Nathan Williamson's ex-wife."

CHAPTER TWENTY-ONE

JANIE'S HANDS WERE tied behind her back. "They did that to me once," Chad said. "Handcuffed me. My drill sergeant said the troublesome ones get treated harsher."

Janie guessed she was troublesome.

A rag was stuffed in her mouth. It smelled like mildew and tasted like bad wine. When she tried to spit it out, it only choked her more. The sound made Chad glance at her. He'd wedged her into the floorboards of the backseat amidst textbooks, an old sweater, fast food sacks and even a backpack.

"Stupid kid. Stupid art book," CeeCee said. "We had a good thing here. Eventually, given time, we could have made money, lots of it."

"We should have just moved," Chad said. "Started over somewhere else, changed our names."

"I was hoping we wouldn't have to."

Chad shook his head. "After this, we will have to. Too many people have died. And this one, unless I miss my guess, has the sheriff's eye. Bad move, messing with someone who belongs to a cop."

Janie didn't belong to a cop. Did she?

In that moment, trussed and terrified, she recognized the truth. For the last month and a half, Rafael Salazar had occupied her every moment. Had meant more to her than her art. She woke up thinking about him, spent her days either with him or wondering where he was, and when she went to sleep, she dreamed about him.

Yes, she belonged to a cop, and the biggest mistake of her life was that she hadn't told him so. Oh, how she wanted to have that conversation now. She didn't need to go to South Africa for adventure. She'd had more adventure in the last month than she'd had her whole life.

And she didn't want to have any adventure alone.

"I still say doing this in the same place is a bad idea," said Chad.

Same place?

"It's the perfect place. No one's even come close to it looking for Brittney."

Janie closed her eyes. She didn't need to see. She knew right where they were taking her. She'd drawn it.

"That other car turned off a ways back. It worried me," CeeCee said.

"Probably going to the Stewart place. If they were following us, they'd have reappeared by now."

Rafe? Could it have been Rafe?

Janie tried to move, but they had her face-down and in such a position that she couldn't twist right or left without getting an elbow caught on the backseat or on the bottom of the front seat. Something sharp dug into her arm. She squirmed, but movement was not really an option. Still, she managed to shift a tiny bit, and that's when she noticed it.

A tiny pin, an angel. Patricia's missing pin. It was stuck on the bottom of the backpack on the floorboard of CeeCee's car.

Patricia had trusted CeeCee, and she'd died as a result. CeeCee had been so uncaring that she'd taken the one thing that Patricia cared about.

Janie moved her tongue. The gag seemed to have a mind of its own and grew, filling her mouth even more. Quietly, she blew out, pushing with her tongue, not minding as saliva ran down her chin.

When she finally managed to spit out the rag, she took a breath. It was enough to draw Chad's attention. He said a bad word, hunched over the seat and thrust the rag right back in her mouth.

She felt nausea rise. Because of the rag, she couldn't retch, and she gagged instead.

"She'd better not throw up in my car!" CeeCee spat.

"She's going to."

The car came to a shuttering halt. CeeCee was out of the front seat in no time, dragging Janie by the legs. Janie fell to the hard gravel road, landing on her knees, feeling the ground bite into her skin. Janie tried to crawl, wanting to get away from the car, but her strength was gone. Instead, she lost all control and threw up. The rag flew out, almost hitting CeeCee's shoe.

CeeCee backed up.

Right into the grip of Nathan Williamson.

NEVER BEFORE HAD Rafe used cell-phone tracking to prevent a kidnapping. Or a murder?

Jasper had searched all of BAA. Janie wasn't there. One of the maintenance men had seen her go off with a woman, possibly mid-thirties. He said they appeared to know each other.

Janie knew CeeCee.

Candy kept a running dialogue as to what Janie's cell phone was doing. The best news was that he was very close to her now. Meanwhile, Candy gave him the scoop on Nathan's divorce.

"His wife was a decade younger, quickly got bored with being home alone a lot, and got into drugs. He tried everything. He even took a leave of absence. Apparently, he really loved her, was devastated when she left him."

"I wonder when he figured out it was her?" Rafe said.

"Maybe he didn't. Maybe something else happened."

"No, he's figured it out," Rafe said.

"She's stopped moving," Candy announced. "You're just two miles away."

CeeCee would hear his vehicle, but Rafe wasn't sure how to prevent that. Maybe she'd have second thoughts about hurting Janie if a car approached.

It wasn't safe to go any faster. Rafe wanted to, but he'd be of no help if he overturned in some ditch. The road weaved to the left and then made a sharp right.

Rafe almost slammed on the brakes as he noted the scenery: tall trees, deserted road.

Janie's drawing.

Brittney's murder.

He gripped the steering wheel hard. Derek had claimed in his art book that Chad had managed to park the car off the road, so if they were at the same place, he should be looking both right and left, not just on the road.

Too soon the scenery changed, and Rafe hadn't found anything. He slowed, searching for a place to turn around. He found a place where the trees weren't right next to the road. It would give him enough space to turn. He had his SUV perpendicular when, through the trees, he saw them.

Nathan Williamson tightly held his ex-wife with one arm and in his other hand, he held a gun, pointed at another man.

Rafe blinked.

Chad Ruskey?

Chad Ruskey had Janie. He, too, had a gun.

It was aimed at Janie.

Chad didn't notice Justin Robbins, moving in a crouch between the trees, coming toward them. CeeCee saw him and struggled to escape Nathan's grasp, get his hand away from her mouth.

Rafe drove his SUV off the road, over a berm and scraping against trees. The vehicle bounced up once, twice, before stopping right behind Nathan. He practically fell out the door, trying to get to Janie. He grabbed at his sidearm, wanting to do something, anything, to get Chad's gun away from Janie.

And get him to aim at him instead.

It worked.

Chad let go of Janie and pointed his gun at Rafe, pulling the trigger. Rafe had the driver's-side door to thank for stopping the bullet. Nathan wasn't so lucky as the second bullet hit him, knocking him off balance. But he didn't release his hold on CeeCee.

Janie scrambled away from Chad, but he turned his gun back onto her.

Rafe took him out with one bullet.

CeeCee went to her knees, keening, and Nathan went down with her, holding her, rocking her back and forth. Only one word came from him, over and over, choked out through his tears. "Why? Why? Why?"

Justin was already talking on his radio, giving their location, although surely Candy already had backup on the way.

It took Rafe three steps to make it to Janie's side and to pull her up, brushing the grass and twigs from her shirt and gently using his fingers to unclench hers.

"You're all right," he whispered. "You're all right."

"I knew you'd come."

Rafe couldn't remember the last time he'd cried. Maybe his dad's funeral. No. Maybe as a young boy listening to his mom cry every

December 3rd—the date Ramon had disappeared.

But he cried now and wrapped his arms around Janie, drawing her close and promising himself that he'd never let her go. His habit of making all cases—especially missing persons—his life wasn't making him a better sheriff. It kept him from understanding that he needed other people, emotionally as well as physically. He couldn't solve every crime, couldn't change what had happened with his brother, but he could move forward and change the future.

His future.

Janie had never looked more beautiful. Her eyes were red and bloodshot. A deep scratch was at the edge of her mouth. It complemented the black eye that was just starting to fade. Her BAA shirt had dirt and something else on it.

"It's all right." Janie gave his words back to him as she touched his face.

It was Justin who handcuffed CeeCee. In the distance, the sirens sounded—help was on the way.

Nathan still held on to CeeCee, ignoring the blood pouring from his wound. "When Derek died at that farm, I worried. I knew Chris had a place nearby. But she seemed to be doing so well. She was working and hoping for a full-time position. But suspiciously, she was working at the very college where everything was going wrong. It was the angel pin, the one that went missing, that made me face the truth. Chris loved expensive jewelry. She could pawn it for top dollar. Still, I was hoping I was wrong. I mean, could I really have loved a killer? But the reporter this morning mentioned the pin, what it was worth, and I knew. I knew."

He seemed to collapse, his voice growing softer. "I was waiting to speak with Chris. Then I heard the vehicle, heard it stop, and came to see what was going on. They had Janie. I'd figured it out, acted on it, too late."

Rafe took one step in Nathan's direction. The man was lying to himself; he'd figured it out before today.

Janie put a hand on his elbow.

"I'm all right." She took his chin in her hands and turned him until he was looking her in the eyes. "Even more, we're all right."

"Forever," he agreed.

CHAPTER TWENTY-TWO

"BUT I REALLY don't want to draw animals anymore," Janie protested.

"We're talking three months. This South Africa gig is the chance of a lifetime. You beat out five hundred applicants. That's something."

Janie shook her head. Just two weeks into a committed relationship and already Rafe assumed he knew what was best for her.

She gazed at the tablet in front of her. Then, she glanced over at Tabitha Jane Rittenhouse.

"I like drawing people. I'm good at it. I nailed Chad, didn't I?"

Rafe frowned.

"I did," she protested. "Amanda and I were spot-on. And the place where Brittney was buried, I had that, too."

"And it's given you nightmares ever since."

Now it was her turn to frown. Her sister, Katie, was telling tales without Janie's permission.

"I've never taken a vacation," Rafe said.

"I've got leave coming, and my chief of police has never been more capable."

"Jeff will love that."

Rafe walked over and set his chin on the top of her hair. Her pencil stilled.

"So," Rafe continued, "I was thinking. I could go to South Africa, too. I've got the money. Maybe we could combine your residency with my vacation, get to know each other even more."

The pencil fell from her grasp. Just her and Rafe, together, as a couple? Her and a cop!

She opened her mouth, but before she got her response out, Rafe's phone rang. He rolled his eyes and answered it.

"Yes, doc," he said.

It only took Janie a moment of listening to yet another one-sided conversation of copspeak to figure out Rafe was talking to the police counselor from Phoenix. Rafe had already been put on administrative leave until the investigation into Chad's death was concluded.

The Brittney Travis murder had captured the public's heart. Even Nathan, who'd lost everything—his career, his reputation—had the public's sympathy. After all, he'd given up everything for love.

CeeCee proved to be a piece of work. She'd

been dealing to kids to support her own habit and line her pockets. She'd confessed to the three murders, as well as to stealing Derek's book out of the campus safe, and to doctoring Amanda's art book and planting it at Patricia's.

"Yes, I donated blood," Rafe was saying. "Why..."

He paused, uncertainty crossing his face.

"I didn't realize I had donated blood for Nathan Williamson. But it makes no difference to me."

Janie picked up her pencil and looked at her drawing of Tabitha Jane Rittenhouse. Already she could see the similarities between Tabitha and Katie: the curve of the cheeks, a certain smile.

"I have the same rare blood type as Nathan? You're kidding," Rafe was saying. "I... How old is Williamson? Thirty-six. Really?"

His voice slowed. "Four years older than me. No, no, I don't need to come in and see you. I'm fine. Shocked. Is this solid enough that I can tell my mother?"

For a minute longer, Rafe remained on the phone. He nodded, grunted, and occasionally said yes. Finally, he hung up and Janie stepped into his arms.

"Nathan is Ramon?"

Slowly, he answered, "Appears so."

"Are you okay with this?"

"It will take some getting used to," Rafe admitted.

"Yes," Janie agreed. Already in his arms, it took no time for her to nestle close, look into his eyes and move her lips close to his.

Almost kissing, not quite, she whispered huskily, "Imagine, you've gotten a brother and me on the same day."

He didn't wait for her to kiss him. He brought her forward, strong, ambitious, questing, needing.

"I'm the luckiest man alive," he said. "I'm in love, with you."

She kissed him a "Me, too."

Possibly the longest kiss in history.

* * * * *